Praise for Stephanie Tyler
and the Shadow Force series

LIE WITH ME

"Crafty plot twists and cleverly intertwined relationships dominate book one of master storyteller Tyler's Shadow Force series . . . The fun, thrills, and romance never let up, and Tyler delivers on all her promises."
—*Publishers Weekly*

"The first book in Tyler's Shadow Force series, *Lie with Me* hits the mark. Tyler constructs seemingly flawless romantic suspense plots rife with danger, intrigue, complicated heroes and strong heroines. It's the perfect weekend getaway read."
—*RT Book Reviews* (four stars)

"Get ready for a high-octane ride. *Lie with Me* is fast, furious, and sexy. I couldn't put it down."
—*New York Times* bestselling author
BRENDA NOVAK

"Red-hot romance. White-knuckle suspense. True-blue military heroes who will leave you breathless. Stephanie Tyler writes with a rare blend of grace and power that will keep you coming back for more. Absolutely fantastic, and not to be missed."
—*New York Times* bestselling author
LARA ADRIAN

PROMISES IN THE DARK

"Red-hot sparks [ignite] copious and satisfying fireworks."
—*Publishers Weekly*

"Tyler is a master of suspense. Book two in the Shadow Force series has the same intense level of steamy passion and gut-clenching suspense as its predecessor, *Lie with Me*. A gripping and complex plot mingles well with complicated and emotional characters."
—*RT Book Reviews* (four stars)

"Fans of action-adventure romantic suspense will thoroughly enjoy *Promises in the Dark*. Ms. Tyler has written an action-packed story filled with complex emotions and deep passions. Olivia and Zane, both wounded in their own ways, make an intriguing couple. Unresolved secondary plot lines will leave you eagerly anticipating the next book in the series, *In the Air Tonight*."
—Fresh Fiction

NIGHT MOVES

BOOKS BY STEPHANIE TYLER

NIGHT MOVES

IN THE AIR TONIGHT

PROMISES IN THE DARK

LIE WITH ME

HOLD ON TIGHT

TOO HOT TO HOLD

HARD TO HOLD

BOOKS BY STEPHANIE TYLER
CO-WRITING WITH LARISSA IONE
AS SYDNEY CROFT

TAKEN BY FIRE

TEMPTING THE FIRE

TAMING THE FIRE

SEDUCED BY THE STORM

UNLEASHING THE STORM

RIDING THE STORM

ANTHOLOGIES

HOT NIGHTS, DARK DESIRES
*(including stories by Stephanie Tyler
and Sydney Croft)*

NIGHT MOVES

A SHADOW FORCE NOVEL

STEPHANIE TYLER

DELL

NEW YORK

A Dell Mass Market Original

Copyright © 2011 by Stephanie Tyler

Published in the United States by Dell, an imprint of The Random House Publishing Group, a division of Random House, Inc., New York.

DELL is a registered trademark of Random House, Inc., and the colophon is a trademark of Random House, Inc.

ISBN 978-0-440-42305-8
eBook ISBN 978-0-440-42306-5

Cover design: Lynn Andreozzi
Cover illustration: Blake Morrow

Printed in the United States of America

www.bantamdell.com

9 8 7 6 5 4 3 2 1

Dell mass market edition: October 2011

For TJ and DP—they know why.

PROLOGUE

Kell Roberts had been at the foster home in Dillingham, Alaska, for three months, four days and sixteen hours and had managed to lie his way through every damned minute when the blond kid arrived with a deep Southern drawl, a bag Kell would later discover contained barely anything and an attitude as big as the hills, all to share Kell's room. He barely acknowledged Kell's existence, got into bed and didn't get up for twenty-four hours straight.

Kell didn't think enough of it to ask anyone his name. Roommates came and went here and he'd always found it better to not get involved.

On the second day, Kell's wallet went missing, along with various and sundry other items, and although Kell had no proof other than his gut that it was the work of the blond kid, it left him alternately pissed and impressed.

On the third day, the blond kid registered for school and never made it to his first class because the counselor who met with him recommended homeschooling, deeming the kid *unfit for a school environment due to the undue negative influence he had over other students in previous environments.*

On the fourth night, Kell woke up to find his new roommate climbing out of the third-floor window. He followed the Louisiana-born boy with the deep drawl to their foster mom's four-wheel-drive truck and wondered how he thought he could take it for a ride during an icy storm. And then he decided he needed to see how much of a death wish Blond Kid had.

He'd always had a pretty big one himself.

Blond Kid, who he'd soon find out was named Reid, had the truck hot-wired by the time Kell pushed into the passenger's side. "You're going to kill yourself."

Reid glanced at him coolly. "And you're coming along for the ride?"

Kell answered by shutting the door and securing his seatbelt. Reid didn't bother to follow suit.

"I want my fucking wallet back," Kell said finally, and Reid laughed as the car skidded down the long driveway, leaving Kell feeling as out of control as he'd ever been and strangely liberated at the same time. "Where are we going?"

"There's got to be a bar around here somewhere."

"They all card." Both boys were tall for their age but no way were they passing for twenty-one. What the hell was this kid thinking?

"I borrowed some ID," Reid said with a calm

drawl, like he didn't have a care in the world. Kell knew that was complete bullshit and was quick to learn that in Reid's vocabulary, *borrow* meant *steal*.

Kell had grown up with that type of vocabulary as well.

Reid drove for about ten minutes with surprising skill, and then the car skidded and Kell saw his life flashing before his eyes, just like everyone said it did. The sad part was, beyond remembering all the cons he'd learned to pull over the years, there wasn't really much else. He heard Reid cursing throughout the slide and then he came to and they were in the ditch.

Reid was unconscious and the police would no doubt be called by passing motorists, so Kell got out of the car and he started walking back to the house, covering his footprints behind him because he wasn't taking the blame for anyone else.

Everyone in this world is out for themselves—that's the way you have to live, son—look out for yourself and screw everyone else.

He remembered, in that brief moment, that his parents had included him in that sentiment. It was the reason he'd turned them in and ended up in a foster home in Alaska instead of with them.

He returned to the car and hauled Reid out, knowing nothing about spinal injuries and not moving unconscious people. All he knew was that he wouldn't leave Reid behind to shoulder the blame alone, even though the damned kid had stolen his wallet. He still hadn't known the blond kid's name until he'd opened his eyes and mumbled it, because Kell had finally asked.

"This state sucks," Reid mumbled then and closed his eyes to stop the tears. Kell pretended not to notice and then, a few minutes later, Reid was up, leaning on him as they walked the frigid mile back to the foster home.

Kell's parents would be so damned disappointed in him yet again—he'd saved Reid's ass so he'd definitely been born with the conscience they lacked.

Well, shit, you did learn something new every day.

They caught hell, of course. The foster mom was not stupid, although she did protect them from the police. It took Reid and him the better part of six months to work off the damage to the car, piecing it back together with the local mechanic and honing their skills in the process.

It was Reid's fourth foster home in the space of a year, and Kell's first and only. They lasted out another full year before emancipating and heading out to work along the docks of the Bering Sea, punishing, cruel work.

It was nowhere near as bad as the work that would follow, but being young and strong with a death wish would always work in their favor.

CHAPTER

1

The stolen Jeep, courtesy of Reid, was parked away from the road while Kell and Reid lay, belly-down, twenty feet apart in the middle of the long stretch of desert road west of Ciudad Juarez in Chihuahua, Mexico.

The pitch-black road the drug kingpin they were after traveled weekly.

The night smelled like smoke and danger. Kell could taste both on his tongue; the familiar tingle began in his spine and Reid murmured in his miked ear, "Any minute now and the little chicken's going to cross the road."

Not much had changed in fourteen years. These days, Reid's accent had mellowed; only when he was tired or angry did the deep drawl emerge, although Reid himself hadn't mellowed at all.

These days, Kell was still trying to balance the genes of his grifter parents by not caring for too many damned people while still using those skills to their fullest. He used to work jobs for Delta Force so highly classified that they didn't exist on paper and their existence would be denied to anyone outside of the men performing the task. Now he was out of the Army and doing black ops missions that were still as highly deniable—and just as deadly.

This one was no exception. Six days in the hot Mexican sun and cool nights reconning for the perfect opportunity was neither fun nor safe, but it was necessary.

Juarez was a city of heaven and hell, depending on what you were looking for. The land surrounding it was a target-rich environment for illegals, slave traders, drug runners and the like—their last chance before they had to try to cross the official border.

The man they were after had no need to cross—his empire was a million-dollar enterprise and he worked out of Juarez and lived in a mansion in the hills.

That man was their payoff and he was finally here, about six klicks away, driving at a normal rate of speed so as not to catch the attention of cops or robbers. But Kell knew this was no simple nightly joyride.

His belly tightened, as it always did at the height of the chase. "Two in the cab—Rivera riding shotgun, his bodyguard at the wheel," he confirmed, and why was Rivera sitting up front?

Kell shifted, waited until they closed the distance and focused in on the backseat.

No way—they couldn't be this damned lucky today. "It's Cruz." Which was a jackpot . . . except for the tall blonde in ripped cargo pants and a tank top showing underneath a loosely buttoned denim shirt running along the side of the road at top speed toward Cruz's car, trying to stay out of sight and not exactly succeeding.

Kell would have to be the one to tell her that her time might've just run out.

Hi, couldja run in the other direction because you're about to blow a carefully planned op out of the fucking water with your sweet swinging hips, and yeah, he needed a woman, and soon.

Just not this soon.

"Problem," he muttered.

"Take care of it," Reid growled through the earpiece from his position down the small embankment, the way he'd been growling this entire trip.

Yeah, sure, *take care of it.* "Who the hell runs around Mexico all by themselves at night like this?"

"Idiots. And operatives," Reid answered.

She was no operative and Kell would soon find out about the idiot part, but he suspected whatever or whomever she was running from wasn't what this op needed.

"It's a woman."

"We are dealing with the Mexican Cartel, Kell, not trying to get laid."

"Speak for yourself," Kell muttered, and Reid cursed at him and the next thing he knew Reid was coming toward him and it was easier not to argue.

Kell was usually the control freak in these situations, always had been, and since Reid was typically out of control, it all worked out.

But since Reid had nearly died on the last official op he was on, the roles had reversed. Kell had gone off looking for revenge like a one-man killing machine and it had taken a long while to reel himself back in.

Some days, he felt as if he'd never left the jungle, wore his knife on his arm both in the shower and while he slept, refused to let his guard down and generally felt as though he'd come unhinged and couldn't be put back together properly. What's more, he didn't want to be. Running wild suited him, suited the missions he would be part of the foreseeable future.

It also made Reid nervous as hell—but then, Reid had been doing that to him for years, and payback truly was a bitch.

"I can take the shot," Reid said, and the car was just the right distance for either man to do it . . . except the woman running directly at them had blown that.

If nothing else, they didn't want any witnesses, and she'd sped up when she'd heard the sound of the car. But if he was honest with himself, the frightened woman seemed to bring out a chivalry in him he no longer wanted.

"Abort," Kell said sharply and Reid cursed again as he hustled toward him in the dark. They'd been waiting for hours in position, sanctioned by two governments to take out Rivera.

But Cruz . . . that would've been a hell of a get.

A pipe dream now, since the woman was on target to run directly into him in less than five seconds.

Shit. He scrambled up just in time for her not to trip over him. He caught her against him, instead, and she started fighting him, clawing and kicking, and he nearly lost his balance and rolled down the small embankment.

Fortunately, Reid steadied them both, and she stopped fighting for a second, enough for Kell to get a hold on her.

"Who the fuck are you?" Kell snarled in her ear, using cruelty to suss out whether or not she was a plant . . . and that made the woman struggle harder. He smelled the fear on her and decided that she was simply in the wrong place at the wrong time, and his grip loosened a little.

Whoever she was, she might as well be wearing a Kidnap Me sign and so what to do with her now wasn't even a question—they co13uldn't leave her here. She was prey for just about anyone in this country, including himself.

"Car. Down," Reid said, and dropped. Kell did the same, had the woman on the ground in seconds, a hand covering her mouth as the car with Cruz flew by, spilling light over where they'd stood seconds before.

She was pushing against him and trying to bite his hand as Reid was telling him, "We've got to follow—catch them around the hill."

It was risky . . . just the kind of mission Kell liked, but not with the add-along of a freaked-out woman. One who'd ruined their perfect shot simply by running in front of their target.

One who was someone else's target, and Kell couldn't risk her getting hurt if she was innocent.

To that end, he directed his next words to her. "Who are you running from?"

He took his hand from her mouth so she could answer, but she didn't. He rolled off her and helped her to her feet. It was pitch black and she didn't have NVs, so she was lost. She was breathing hard, her bag was on the ground somewhere by Reid's feet and when she didn't answer, he grabbed it and started to rifle through it, looking for ID.

Nothing. No wallet or passport or money. Just a change of clothing, a key to a motel room and a brush. And a loaded, illegal handgun—a quick swipe with his thumb had found the roughness where the serial number had been ground off and Kell swiftly unloaded the chamber and pocketed the bullets without her noticing, since she was now staring at Reid, who was muttering and cursing to himself while he checked maps on his phone. He handed her the bag and she focused her attention back on him.

She took it, wound it around her shoulder and, finally, she managed to speak. "Please—I need help. A ride . . ." She stopped talking, put her palms on her thighs and leaned over, trying to catch her breath.

"Do we look like a taxi service?" he asked. "What the hell are you doing out here alone?"

She ignored the question. "I need to get to the border now." Fear kept her voice tremulous and no doubt her body shook from both it and the exertion.

"Not happening."

Her breathing wasn't getting any easier. "Please," she said again. "I . . . need to know . . ."

"Honey, we have no time for manners—spit it out," Kell told her.

"Are you . . . the good guys?"

He looked at Reid and then back at her. "That depends on whose side you're on."

She didn't ask any more questions, and seconds later he heard the low rumble of an oncoming vehicle. "More company."

"Ours? Or for her?" Reid asked even as he scanned with the NVs, and it really didn't matter at this point because Kell hated this shit, did not want some girl—woman, whatever—needing his help when he was in the middle of an op.

Worst timing ever. And it took a lot to be able to say that.

"For . . . me." She sat herself on the ground, drawing in harsh breaths and close to hyperventilating—and he and Reid hit the floor too. He pushed her down, lay over her for camouflage as the old truck rumbled by slowly, surveying the side of the road. Kell caught a glimpse of NVs before he put his head down and let them pass.

When the truck was far enough down the road, he moved so he was crouching over her and that's when he noticed the bloodstain on the shoulder of her shirt. He tried to rouse her, but she'd passed out sometime after hitting the ground.

"She's in shock," he told Reid. He carried her over to the Jeep and put her in the backseat, checking under the denim shirt she wore and finding a flesh wound—a nick from a flying bullet. Reid was next to him, passing him a gauze pad to stop the bleeding until they could get to safer ground.

She remained curled up on the seat—her breathing was calmer now, but she was pale.

Kell turned to Reid. "We have a major problem—those guys were mercs." He could recognize them better than most, being one himself.

"Beyond the fucked-up op and this woman?" Reid glanced between Kell and the woman currently passed out in the Jeep. "And it seems like they want her badly—so what the hell did she do?"

"That's what we need to figure out."

"First, we need to get the fuck out of here," Reid said calmly. Too calmly, which meant . . . "Incoming."

As bullets flew overhead, they dove into the Jeep, Reid in the driver's seat and Kell in the back, giving the woman cover with his body and his rifle as Reid skidded along the rocky sand back road toward safety.

Kell turned to try to get a glimpse of who the hell was shooting, managed to fire off a couple of warning shots from his own rifle but didn't bother trying to do more damage—because why waste ammo when you were firing into the dark—but even with the NVs, he could barely make out anything in front of his face.

"Could've just been kidnappers or drug dealers . . ." Or men trying to cross the border. Or any number of random occurrences that were oh so popular in this part of the world.

"We're clear," Reid said, but he didn't slow down, nor did he head right to the safe house.

Kell stared down at the sleeping woman cradled in his lap and wondered what they'd gotten themselves into this time.

It only took a few moments for the men to decide they would finish the op tonight. There was only one second chance, and it would be at Rivera's mansion, making the job infinitely harder—and in some ways, more appealing.

First, they needed to make sure the mercs weren't circling back to tail them—and after half an hour, both were satisfied.

Reid spun the Jeep over the open back road as Kell readied himself for what their next steps would entail. Because this was their plan B and they'd prepped for this eventuality with the keen eye they'd been taught in the Army.

Rivera's mansion was high on a hill, with more security than one man would ever need unless he was paranoid as hell. That paranoia was his weapon against other men like him—or gang members, all looking to take his place. The guards around Rivera's property were always on the lookout for blitz attacks, well trained for displays of shock and awe, but Kell and Reid would give them something unexpected.

He closed his eyes and pictured the map they'd pored over earlier. Courtesy of Dylan, it had the most up-to-date approach possibilities.

Dylan Scott was former Delta Force and the man they currently worked with—and for. Dylan had been recruited by the CIA at one point and refused their offer, contending that he worked better alone. These days, he utilized the men he considered friends, like Kell and Reid, wanted them to stick together and keep one another safe in this business of private-contracting black ops, off-the-book missions.

Reid stopped the Jeep at the bottom of the hill, outside the range of security cameras and in a circle of foliage that would do nicely to camouflage the vehicle and the woman inside it.

Kell stepped out of the car after handcuffing the woman's wrists together and to the inside door handle. She didn't move, although her chest rose and fell and her color was good when he flashed a penlight on her face.

Exhaustion, mixed with stress. Or maybe she had a concussion or something worse, because he didn't know a goddamned thing about her beyond the fact that she was a major liability.

He turned away from her to concentrate. The wind rustled. A thin sheen of sweat covered his body and he flexed his hands inside the fingerless gloves he'd pulled on.

Wetwork was his speciality. He could do more with a ballpoint pen than most men could do with an AK-47. Close-quarters battle, silence, stealth. He'd spent the first half of his life being invisible in a crowd. He'd perfected that ability during his time in Delta Force, knew that the line between life and death was a fine one, and he readied himself now.

There was always the possibility of things going wrong. He and Reid had dealt with every contingency but Kell knew they'd be hanging the unconscious woman out to dry with no one to help her.

"If you uncuff her, she'll run—no doubt straight into this op," Reid said when he saw Kell look back at her for the millionth time. "She's safest here."

"Which isn't safe at all."

His friend shrugged. "We don't even know why those mercs are after her. She could be worse than Rivera and Cruz."

Reid was right, Kell knew that. But still, his protective instincts were all fired up, and no one was safe from them. "Why don't you stay here?"

"To protect her?"

Kell didn't answer that, because that wasn't the only reason he wanted Reid out of danger. "I've got this."

"You're fucking kidding me, right?" Reid basically gave Kell the equivalent of the middle finger with his expression and took off up the hill, leaving Kell no choice but to follow.

He gave a final, backwards glance to the well-hidden Jeep and then moved forward, finding two dead guards along the way whom Reid had taken out soundlessly.

The guards had gotten cocky and it would be their downfall tonight.

Kell discovered that Reid had saved a couple of guards for him. They were watching the perimeter of the house from the west, but they were tired, and only focusing on what was in front of them, had not been properly trained—Kell could spot that lack easily.

Kell took down the first man quietly, so as not to alert the second. When the man slid to the ground with his neck snapped, his partner turned to Kell, who took him out efficiently with a pen to the carotid artery, all the while thinking of the destruction this gang of drug dealers and thugs had caused over the past months for the city's residents. And now nothing else mattered but getting this job done. He moved silently to the mansion, which was lit up like a Christmas tree. If there were guards on the roof, they hadn't spotted him or Reid.

It was time to put the drug lords to bed for good.

This was his element—had been for a long time. As he left thinking behind, everything became easier. This was instinctive—the prowl, the hunt . . . even the kill had become as much a part of him as breathing.

He wove around to the back of the house—saw the basement windows half buried behind thick bars.

The glass wasn't bulletproof, hence the crisscross of metal Rivera thought would keep him safe in the fire-and bombproof bunker.

Assholes should've gotten rid of the windows completely. It allowed Kell to see the targets sitting on a couch, drinking and talking. If he looked directly across the room from his position on his belly, he could see Reid, a mirror image to him.

Cruz and Rivera in one place—something big must be going down, because this was incredibly stupid on their part.

Almost as stupid as he and Reid leaving a woman handcuffed in their Jeep, unprotected.

Head in the game, Kell.

Both he and Reid had a perfect shot of their targets. "I'll take Rivera," he whispered into the mic around his neck, the words barely voiced, and still Reid heard them clearly.

"Affirmative. From five—my count," Reid said. Kell steadied his rifle, adjusted the scope and waited for Reid to begin the countdown. They'd have to take the shot at the same time or they'd lose one of the men in the ensuing confusion, for sure.

Kell's hands remained steady on the trigger. Although he wasn't a sniper by trade, he'd been trained by the best and he could do this dance when necessary. And when Reid uttered the word *one,* he and Kell fired simultaneously, Kell's bullet catching Rivera in the heart and Reid getting Cruz between the eyes.

"Show-off," Kell muttered, but there was pride in that statement.

"Let's move out," Reid said in his ear. "Drop the cards and let's go."

The government wanted to send a message to the gangs and the drug lords—*we can get to you, and we will.* So Kell dropped the calling cards he'd been given, with the name of some of the higher-ups in the Mexican government who'd promised to clean up the streets of Juarez, even if it killed them—which it might—and then backed down the hill toward the Jeep.

Time to get the hell out of Dodge. Both men were in the Jeep in record time, finding the woman had shifted a little but was basically in the same position as when they'd left. Kell climbed in next to her to stop her from falling out of the vehicle when Reid gunned it as the house alarms finally sounded.

Too late to do any good, but it would bring the calvary. They needed to be as far away as possible, which Reid managed with ease. Within twenty minutes they were on the deserted road that had led to their destination, the wind whistling against Kell's skin calming the adrenaline-fueled rush he'd come to associate with these missions.

"And the night's saved," Reid muttered as they pulled up to the safe house they'd been using for the past few days. "I'll let Dylan know it's done."

God, tonight could've been the biggest fuckup imaginable. Still could be, with this woman next to him, but at least their main goal of taking out Rivera was done. Cruz was the icing on the cake—unexpected, and that would be appreciated by the two governments who'd commissioned this job.

Yes, more men would take Rivera's and Cruz's place, but not immediately. There would be too much strife and distrust for the gangs to recover completely, and in that time the local *policia* and other agencies would have a field day ripping Rivera's place apart and gaining new intel.

The gang had been holding the surrounding towns and cities hostage for too long. This quick shot of violence would put an end to much more—and that's why Dylan had agreed to take on the job in the first place.

Save the innocents. It was their main goal now and the only thing that comforted Kell as he prepared to bring the woman inside for questioning.

The files were still highly classified. So much so that they were thin as anything and sparse on any real intel, and he put them aside and let the frustration ball inside his chest the way it had for the past four years every time he thought about how Dylan Scott had screwed him.

He'd thought about it a hell of a lot. There'd been nothing else to do while in hiding. And now that he'd paid his debts, it was time to resurface and give his old friend a what's-up.

He hadn't needed anyone to fill him in on some of the more pertinent details.

Like the fact that Dylan Scott had been mercing for years. He'd trained the bastard.

That he'd turned the CIA down, the same way Kell Roberts continued to do.

"Kell Roberts is currently running wild. Last known location—Jakarta. Sri Lanka. The Congo. Key Largo."

Unless stopped, the agent sitting across from him would continue to list all the places Kell Roberts had supposedly been spotted within the past week. "So basically, no one knows where the hell he is, or where he's been."

"The guy's good. They all are."

He meant the rest of Dylan's group of merry men. Roberts was rumored to travel with Reid Cormier, a Delta operative who was still active duty but ran black ops missions on the side. A man who'd told his CO he would not re-up next year, when the time came. "If they're that good, then we have to be better."

CHAPTER
2

Teddie came to when gunshots shattered the quiet and she jerked up in the darkness. Out of sorts, she struggled to move and realized after a long moment that her wrists were handcuffed together and to the door of the open-topped Jeep she was in.

That's when the night's events came rushing back to her like a tsunami and she struggled to breathe.

Shots. Blood. Running . . .

Don't be stupid, Teddie . . . put the gun down.

A rustle of air, and the men appeared seemingly out of nowhere and the Jeep began to move again at a frantic pace.

She closed her eyes to block it all out, played dead because it was easier than screaming, not wanting to think about what she'd gotten herself into . . . and how it might even be worse than what she'd been running from.

Her shoulder throbbed along with her head, no doubt from running and screaming for so long.

Finally, mercifully, the Jeep came to a jolting halt and the man who'd been holding her in place got out, undid the handcuffs and picked her up.

He set her down on her feet and she opened her eyes, surprised, and steadied herself with her arms on his shoulders, all too aware of his too close proximity. Under these lights, she could see the outline of a ruthlessly chiseled face, narrowed eyes and dark hair . . . lips that were full, almost sensuous, made to make a woman scream.

"I knew you were faking it," he said gruffly.

"Not the whole time."

"No. You've been shot."

She nodded, felt the bandage he must've taped over the wound when she'd fainted. Her mouth was dry as sand and her skin felt tight and hot. She was feverish for sure, hadn't thought an infection could set in so quickly.

Then again, she'd been wrong about so many things.

"What's your name?" he demanded.

She used her real name for the first time in three hundred and sixty days. "It's Teddie."

"That's a boy's name. You want to be a boy?"

"What? No, it's . . . I didn't name myself," she sputtered, and his eyes met and held hers . . . rimmed silver with blue and brown striations, intense and unsmiling and it still sent a thrill through her, a hard jolt that surprised the hell out of her.

You're not as jaded as you thought.

She definitely did not want to be a boy. "Theodora."

He cocked an eyebrow.

"My name is Theodora. Italian on my mom's side. It was my grandmother's name—everyone called her Teddie too." She paused. "What's yours?"

"It's Kell. The other guy's Reid. Those men who are after you—the mercs—what do they want with you?"

So much for the introduction portion of the evening. No more small talk, and she supposed that was smart. The mercenaries could come back, and she had to know what Kell planned on doing with her. "Are you going to turn me over to them?"

"Should I?" Her heart beat so loudly with terror, she was sure he'd hear it, and she could only shake her head no. "Then I won't. Tell me how you know them."

There was no way really to lie—she'd been caught running in the dead of night through Mexico with mercenaries on her tail. Nothing but the truth would do . . . and she wasn't even sure if that would suffice to make this man believe her story.

"I'm not supposed to tell anyone."

"Not even the guy who saved your ass?"

He didn't mention the man he'd called Reid, and she hadn't seen him since she first came to in the Jeep. She looked toward the house and saw a light, supposed he was in there.

Reid appeared to be the nicer of the two, but that wasn't saying much since he'd barely spoken to her. She knew what they were. Night vision goggles. Rifles. Men dressed in all black, hiding by the side of the road, ready to take out a drug smuggler or something like that.

More American mercenaries. Talk about out of the frying pan . . .

Her bag was wound around her and she pushed her hand inside it, searching out what she needed, as stealthily as she could. Kell's eyes were on her face anyway as she started to speak. "A year ago, those men killed my father—he was a U.S. diplomat living in Khartoum—they also killed my stepmom and my half sisters. I was there—upstairs. They didn't see me, but I saw them."

He stared at her for a long moment, as if weighing the truthfulness of her story. "You're sure that the men who came after you tonight are the same ones who killed your family?"

"Yes."

"How do you know?"

"Because I'll never forget their faces," she whispered fiercely. The night air was as heavy as a blanket around them and a thin trickle of sweat ran down her back, between her breasts. Everything was sticky, including the way she played this.

He had to help her. Otherwise . . .

Don't think about it.

"How did they find you?" Kell asked.

She bit her bottom lip for a second and then told him, "I came to Mexico to meet with someone who had information for me—a man named Samuel Chambers. They found me with him and I shot one of the mercenaries and escaped." Barely.

"Did he die?"

"I didn't stick around to admire my handiwork. I knew I couldn't take all of them down."

And she was as dangerous as she looked, all five-foot-ten, honey blond–haired, innocent-looking inch of her. She'd shot a merc, was on the run from his cohorts and probably the U.S. Marshals too. And now she was here with him.

Yep, business as usual when he and Reid were together. At least Teddie was telling the truth—as a practiced liar himself, Kell could spot a lie the way most people could spot the sun when it was shining. "What happened to Samuel Chambers?"

"I don't know. I think he ran too. It was chaos."

"You have to come with us."

He waited for her to refuse, but she didn't. Rather, she pulled her gun out of her bag and leveled it calmly at his chest and said, "I'll take the Jeep instead."

Kell bit back a laugh but only because she was so deadly serious and he had to give her some credit for that. She backed away a couple of steps toward the Jeep, held out her free hand and said, "Toss me the keys."

"You're going to have to shoot me if you want them," he told her, and goddamn it all if she didn't aim and pull the trigger without hesitation. Of course, the fact that he'd taken the ammo out of the gun earlier made it far less intense than it could've been, but she hadn't known she'd be firing empty.

She'd been aiming to kill him—and she would have. For a long moment, they stared at each other, while the enormity of what could've just happened hit her. She'd held a look of confidence, even with the fear behind it.

Now she simply looked terrified . . . of him. And she damned well should be, so why the hell did it bother him so much?

He closed the distance between them with two long strides and took the gun from her hand. "Sorry, darling, you didn't get your wish tonight." The Jeep and his life remained intact and she took a step back, away from him. He grabbed her, pulling her body close to his. "Are you in witness protection?"

She didn't respond—wasn't supposed to, he knew, and he loosened his grip on her just a little. "I'm going to assume you are, especially because of the nature of the shooting. You should call your handler."

She didn't answer that either, her big brown eyes boring into his, like she was trying to read his mind and figure out what he'd do to her now.

"Is there any other family you need to contact?" he asked, and she shook her head slowly without breaking their gaze.

"No family left," she said quietly.

He tore his eyes from hers, glanced toward Reid, whom he knew was standing in the doorway of the house.

Kell had asked the same question of Reid many years earlier, when Reid was recovering from his concussion after the car accident and Kell stayed up with him.

Where's your family?

Reid had just shaken his head in a decidedly *I don't want to talk about it* fashion, but that didn't mean Kell gave up. No, he'd gone through the foster mother's cabinet, gleaned what information he could and then did his research at the local library.

Some days Kell wished he hadn't, because discovering Reid had lost his entire family in a house fire caused by a careless cigarette his mother had fallen asleep with—and that it had been a happy family—was heartbreaking. But it was better that he knew, because his friend's tendency to self-destruct was then something Kell could pull him back from most of the time.

Self-destruction had given way to survivor's guilt. What happened last year with four of their Delta team getting captured—Reid included—had nearly sent all of them over the edge. But Reid, who had missed being massacred for the second time in his life because he was unconscious . . . well, you could look at it as irony, or wonder if Reid had his very own guardian angel.

"If I do, that guardian angel is one sick motherfucker," Reid would mutter when Kell talked about his theories.

Kell had been on another mission, but still had to live with the fact that it had ultimately been his fault the team had gotten captured—the captors had been looking to take their revenge on him, and when they couldn't, they did the next best thing.

Maybe Reid was right about the sick motherfucker of a guardian angel.

"Why tell me all this?" he asked her finally.

She swallowed, hard, looked like she wanted to pull away from his grip, but she didn't. "You're an American mercenary too—I figure, if you were going to kill me, you already would have. The worst you can do is turn me over to the other men . . . and I'll find a way to kill you or myself before I let that happen."

Teddie listened to the low voices, unable to make out more than a few words here and there. Frustrated, she stared at the fan overhead that pushed the air lazily around the room in warm swirls that brushed the hair lightly from her face.

Kell had led her into the small house—clean, sparsely furnished—and into the sole bedroom. He'd handcuffed her to the bed with a long enough chain so she could move from side to side, sit up even, but she couldn't go farther than that. The bed was old, low to the ground, little more than a mattress attached to a wood board that would no doubt crack if she applied the right pressure. That would bring the men in the other room running, so no point in that.

Her stomach rumbled, and she wondered what they'd do to her. Turn her in to the marshals, maybe, if they believed the marshals weren't compromised.

Did they believe anything she'd said?

She turned on her side and curled up in the fetal position, stared at the wall, which was a faded lime color. Heard Kell's voice raise a little and then lower again.

Kell.

She was unable to shake the feeling of his body against hers. The fact that she could feel, that her belly actually tightened in a good way in response to his cock, hard against her, thrilled her in a way she never thought possible.

Whether he was turned on by the fact that she

would've killed him had the gun been loaded or that he remained very much alive, she didn't know or care.

She rubbed her palms together, could still feel the weight of the gun in them, could hear the click as she pulled the trigger like she'd been taught to—shoot to kill and don't hesitate—her second shot of the night.

You would've killed him. And that realization made the tears form although she refused to let them fall. What she'd been forced to become . . . she didn't recognize herself when she looked in the mirror and that scared her.

But she'd shot at those men who'd taken her family, and for that, there was no guilt at all.

Kell and Reid had stopped talking—apart from the whoosh of the fan, there was only silence.

She would always remember the silence. It shouldn't have been so silent . . . because silence meant peace, and this was a long stretch of nothing but pure black despair. If she closed her eyes, she would see the images from that night playing out before her like a movie. She saw *them,* knives on their belts. Stealth and danger, sent to murder the diplomat and his family, and she'd been the lucky one, hidden away in the loft, reading, as she liked to do late at night, the light from outside enough for her to see without turning on lights and disturbing anyone.

The massacre that happened below her would never be fully erased from her mind. When she'd come out of hiding, pulled from the loft by the local police, she'd seen her family, their throats slit, lifeless eyes. They were all gone . . . and she was alone.

She'd been told that mercenaries killed her family, dogs of war who killed for cash, working for the highest bidder. American mercs killing American diplomats for reasons yet unknown, although she'd known the reasons. She'd just kept them to herself, because to reveal what she knew then would've put her in even more danger.

Her father had always taken the jobs in high-risk areas. Even after he married and had her, he hadn't seen a reason to stop, felt she needed to grow up knowing what a life of service was.

Her mother died of breast cancer when Teddie was seventeen; she'd stayed with her father for a month, then left to start college in the States. When she reluctantly returned to Jakarta for summer break, she discovered her father had met someone . . . and that she made him happy.

Teddie had been glad she had three more years of school left, and after that, she didn't move back in with her father, just returned for vacations every now and again when she could grab some time away from work.

Her work as a photographer and videographer, capturing images of children in poverty in order to draw attention to their plight and working with UN goodwill ambassadors tied closely into her father's idea of service, which was deeply ingrained in her.

Her work that was now over for the foreseeable future.

For the past year, there was nothing but sadness and fear, although she preferred that to the numbness that overtook her in the beginning. That all-pervasive feeling of nothingness was like falling into a deep pit with no way out except to crawl upward through the dark, clawing and scratching.

She'd put her cameras away, but still, she packed them up and took them with her every time she moved. She hadn't brought herself to use the equipment again, for fear of capturing something bad on film that would ultimately end her life.

As scared as she was of living, she was far more scared of dying.

You couldn't have known.

But she had. She hadn't snapped photos of those men in the marketplace for any other reason except she'd had a feeling about them, nestled deep in her gut. And she'd ignored it.

The afternoon of the murders, her father had told her he suspected he was being set up, and that night the men from the market had broken into their home and killed her father, her stepmother and her two young half sisters.

The local police figured the staff was in on it. They almost didn't believe her when she insisted that Americans had committed the crime. After she showed them the photos she'd taken, the investigation—and her life—came to a standstill.

The marshals wouldn't answer her questions. They offered her sanctuary, which she accepted after a car bomb exploded at the funeral, another attempt on her life.

She hadn't seen the mercenaries again until last night, when they'd come into the restaurant where she was meeting Samuel, who'd been her father's best friend, a man retired from the diplomatic community who claimed he had some answers. She'd knowingly put her life at risk for the meeting, had been the one to set it up, not telling her handler and sneaking out of Texas and across the border.

What she hadn't told Kell earlier was that she'd shot two men tonight. After the mercenaries tried to corner her, she knew she'd been set up by Samuel and so she'd grabbed him and held her gun to his neck, ignoring the screams of the restaurant patrons. She'd tried to back out of the place, got close to an exit, pushed Samuel forward and shot at his arm for a distraction. Then she'd fired a round at a man she recognized from the marketplace, the murders, and he'd gone down. During the ensuing chaos, she ran out the door and into an alley, leaving behind the sounds of yelling and the sirens.

She could've waited for the police, except she still didn't know whom to trust. She just needed to get to the border, and then maybe she could look into contacting some of her father's old contacts, the ones the marshals had cut her off from, for her safety and theirs.

She'd run for miles and miles. Had grabbed an old bicycle for part of the journey but she'd blown out a tire and had to abandon it.

"Teddie."

Kell's voice. She hadn't heard footsteps or even the door open, but when she turned he was standing in the doorway, holding a first-aid kit, a soda and what looked like a sandwich.

She sat up and he came forward and put everything down on the bed. Took one of her wrists and released it from its cuff so she had more freedom. He'd showered recently—his hair was damp and he smelled like soap. The black T-shirt he wore stretched across his chest, and although he wasn't broad, he was in shape—she'd known as much when he carried her like she weighed nothing.

At least he was staring back at her, so she didn't feel like such a damned fool. "What is it?"

"I need to clean that wound better. Then you can eat and get some sleep."

She didn't say anything, just turned her back to him and tugged the denim shirt off her shoulder and Kell pushed aside the tank top strap gently.

"This will burn some."

"Good, let it." Because it couldn't be any worse than the pain of constantly being alone in witness protection.

He put the cold cotton soaked in peroxide on the wound and she grit her teeth and let him do what he needed to. She hadn't even felt the shot at first—it wasn't until the sticky blood ran hot down her back that she realized the men had grazed her with one of their many shots.

She'd been lucky—and fast.

"It could've been a lot worse," he told her now, his breath warm against the back of her neck, his hands skilled as they worked.

After about five minutes, he put a bandage on the wound, pulled the tank top strap back up and she tugged her shirt over her shoulder.

"That should hold for now. I'll give you a shot of antibiotics later. I don't think you'll need stitches."

She turned to face him where he sat on the bed behind her. "You're a doctor now?"

"No." His dark eyes bore into hers. "You would've killed me without a second thought."

"Yes."

"Who taught you to do that?"

"To shoot—or to have no feelings?"

"Both."

How could she answer that when she didn't know herself? "I just need to get to the border." She sounded like a broken record and she didn't care.

"I know."

"Why won't you take me?"

"Because the men who are after you will be looking for you at the border. When they don't find you there, they'll backtrack until they do."

"And then what?"

"I'll take care of them."

"And that makes you a good man?"

"I never said I was a good man, Teddie."

No, he hadn't. But the look in his eyes when he spoke, she noted regret there . . . and something else she couldn't quite place. And since she didn't know what to say, she didn't say anything at all.

At some point while Kell had been in the other room with Teddie, Reid had gone through her bag more thoroughly and if Kell hadn't been a hundred percent sure about the men in the truck being mercs, he was now.

The picture Reid handed him had been taken in a crowded marketplace—*Khartoum* was written on the back of the photo—and he recognized the man who'd been driving the truck and looking for Teddie, although he wasn't facing the camera straight-on, plus two other men who were clearly trying to blend into the crowd and not doing so successfully enough to fool the photographer.

"She's good," Kell noted.

Reid nodded in agreement, because it took a lot to finger operatives in a crowd. "They were watching her. Seems odd that they'd follow her back to the diplomat's house and kill everyone but her. Where was she hiding?"

"I didn't get that far with her."

Normally, that would be an easy opening for Reid, but he didn't take the bait. Instead, he told Kell, "I called Vivi—she's running intel on Teddie's family," his own voice tight and Kell didn't have time to ask if he was all right because that sixth sense that had saved his ass more times than he cared to count was screaming at him.

At Reid too, because when Kell said, "Hit the lights," Reid was already in the process of doing so, even in Teddie's room, telling her to sit tight and not make a sound.

Kell swore he heard a low whimper from her and made a note to get the remaining cuff off her fast. Nothing worse than being scared and in the dark and tied down.

No reason for her to feel that helpless ever again.

Even if she had tried to kill him.

He stood by the window, Reid on the other side of the room, checking the back—the road ran both ways. No one was there. Not yet anyway, but their instincts were both sharp and never to be ignored.

Delta didn't need to teach either man disguises, deception and diversions, but they sure helped to hone the skills.

While Kell had never grown more than an appreciation for running cons himself, he could spot them a mile away. Remaining silent was the most important part of any con, because listening and watching told you everything you needed to know about any target. And Reid had bounced around the foster care system enough to pick up his own tricks of pickpocketing, safecracking and more.

"It's not Cruz's or Rivera's men—they're not that organized," Reid said. "Which can only mean one thing."

"If it's the guys who are after Teddie, they could've tailed us to Rivera's. And seen what we did."

"I didn't feel anyone watching," Kell said.

"We weren't exactly focused on that."

"I'll send the picture to Vivi—maybe she can do some face recognition and see if these guys are former military. I'd bet my life at least one of them is."

And if that was true, they'd also been trained in the art of stealth and tracking. Kell and Reid had been covert in their comings and goings, but that didn't mean neighbors didn't spot them—and turn them in for cash or drugs. "Reid, we've got to get the fuck out of here," he said as the hairs on the back of his neck began to stand on edge.

"I was thinking the same thing," Reid muttered, and he'd been gathering their things even as Kell had been looking at the photo, which he now pocketed. "I'll get us a better car once we disappear into the city."

Going back into the heart of Juarez was their best bet for the moment—crowded as hell, it would be hard for the mercs to pull their shit there without causing a major ruckus. Hard, but not impossible—for right now, those were the best odds they could get.

He went back into Teddie's room and didn't need to feel the breeze from the easily opened and somehow goddamned noiseless window to know she'd gotten out. He'd left one of Teddie's wrists cuffed so she could eat, and at first he thought she'd escaped by working it down from the headboard and taking the entire chain with her.

Then he saw the chain and the cuffs on the floor. "She's gone."

"How'd she get the key?" Reid asked even as Kell checked his cargoes.

"She pickpocketed me," he said in disbelief.

"I knew I liked her. But man, she is throwing you off your game."

"And what, you're not a part of this?"

"Not the way you two look at each other. Come on." Reid had both their bags and they headed out the back to the Jeep, Kell stopping by the outside of the open window.

He saw her footsteps—they led toward the back road and she couldn't have gotten all that far. With their bags thrown into the rear seat, rifles across their laps, Reid moved the car in near silence, lights off, he and Kell both using NVs to search for both her and any unwanted followers.

Half a mile down the road, he saw her. She was running at top speed and he suspected she'd do so for as long as she needed to. Part of him wanted to let her go—she wasn't truly his problem and she brought so fucking many with her.

But if mercs were really after her to finish what

they'd started with her family . . . fuck, he couldn't let that happen.

"Slow down—I'll grab her." Kell was out of the Jeep before Reid stopped completely, his feet moving silently along the dirt as he tailed her without the aid of his NVs, just smelling for her shampoo and listening for the slap of her sneakers and the heaviness of her breathing.

On the hunt.

Most of the time, he felt like this—feral, as if he'd been living among wolves for too long and wasn't ready to come back in from the wild. Even when he went to Mace's house in the Catskills to meet up with the rest of his Delta team, he still felt the pull to get back out there, to keep searching . . . fighting . . .

For what, sometimes even he wasn't sure, but that didn't make the burning need go away.

"Just stop, Teddie—we can do this the easy way or the hard way," he called quietly, knew she'd heard him because she tripped a little and then she ran faster.

Okay, hard way it was. He took a few more strides and grabbed for her and she stumbled. He pulled her back to her feet and she rewarded him by lashing out, arms and legs flailing, but he quickly brought her under control. As her body heaved against his, she brought her face close to his neck, her warm breath fanned his skin and if he were alone, he might think about winding his hand in her hair and kissing her, deep and hard enough to satisfy the urges that had him all riled up.

"Let's roll," Reid said from the safety of the Jeep, ruining that little fantasy.

"Where . . . are . . . we going?" she managed.

"You're on a need-to-know basis."

She muttered something, a curse, maybe, but he was too busy getting her ass into the back of the Jeep to worry about it. "Go," he told Reid when they were secured, and the Jeep moved slowly down the road, lights off, making as little noise as possible.

After a few long minutes, Kell said, "We're being stalked."

"I know," Reid said. No bullets had flown and Kell didn't bother with the NVs again. "No tracking devices on her, are there?"

He hadn't exactly stripped her down. "Did they touch you? Did they go through your things?" he asked her.

For once, Teddie was forthcoming. "No. I was in the motel for a few hours, and then I went to a restaurant across the street."

And they'd been lying in wait there for her, had no doubt watched her go inside before making their move.

Yeah, he had a lot more questions for Teddie, and this time, he would make sure she answered them, whether she wanted to or not.

CHAPTER
3

Even getting thrown over the hood of a parked car couldn't ruin Grier's night, because that was so much better than just sitting around waiting. Her breath came out in a hard *oof* when she hit the old Mazda, the heels of her boots denting the rusted-out grill as she kicked off and went after her jump at a dead run.

The bounty hunter who'd been after the fugitive for the past month was also running with her now, having recovered from being smashed in the jaw with the butt of an illegal hand gun.

He could have the bond—Grier just wanted her hands on the asshole first. As her feet flew over the dusty pavement, her hands fisted and she let the anger surge through her body as she gained on the big man running from her like a big ole baby.

She weaved through the people on the street like

they were pylons—she was seasoned, trained and always ready for this kind of fight.

Just a few more feet and she'd have him. Head down, arms swinging, and she reached out for the back of the man's shirt at the same time the bounty hunter named Wes did. And although Grier really didn't like to share, together they managed to yank the man to the ground, ending the chase.

"You gonna let me take him in?" Wes asked.

"I won't steal your glory, but you owe me one." Grier knew that keeping on the good side of the bounty hunters in the area could only help the marshals. It wasn't a sentiment always agreed on in her office, but Grier was in charge and she ran things the way she felt they worked best.

It had been a fight to get to her position, and she planned on keeping it as long as she could. So far, it had been a hell of a ride.

Grier Catherine-Grace Vanderhall came from old money in Washington, DC, and wasn't expected to become a U.S. Marshal. No, she'd been a deb and had been as well versed in the art of politics as etiquette . . . and had barely been talked out of enlisting in the Navy when she was eighteen. She went the college route and realized that the life she'd been expected to live was looking wholly unsatisfactory.

She liked to run, to hunt . . . she liked the chase, as many an ex-boyfriend had complained with traces of both bitterness and envy. And all of that had translated into becoming a U.S. Marshal, aided by the fortuitousness of meeting a retired marshal who regaled her with stories that retained just enough truth and a lot of myth to make her believe the job was tailor-made for her.

Seven years later, she was firmly enmeshed in Texas, with regular trips across the Mexican border. She worked with other law enforcement, bounty hunters, all to bring men and women to justice.

She had a firm sense of justice. Right was right and wrong was wrong in the world she functioned in and days off were meant for having as good a time as possible without breaking the law.

Discovering she'd been adopted hadn't been a surprise—dark to her family's light, she'd always felt different, although loved and accepted.

She was well adjusted. Smart.

She would be single forever.

She chewed on that along with a sip of the caramel-flavored coffee she'd gotten mere moments before the call from Wes came in. Now that he had taken the fugitive into custody and her adrenaline rush from the chase was fueled with the semi-warm coffee, she knew sleep was not on her agenda tonight. And even though it was close to midnight, she headed to the office to finish her paperwork.

And she figured it would be all quiet for now.

But the second she stepped out of the truck, something in the way the wind skittered across the short grass, kicking up dust, made her uneasy. The fact that Bobby's truck was parked across the lot added to that.

"Got a job," Bobby called to her two minutes later as she walked through the door.

"When were you going to tell me about it?" She tried to look annoyed and failed.

"Figured you'd head in after your chase with Wes."

Yes, news did travel fast around here. She planted herself in her chair, finished off the coffee and took the folder Bobby handed her. She flipped through, found herself looking at a picture of a gorgeous woman.

"She's one of Al's charges. He's actively searching but he needs our help—bad." Al was a handler—technically, he worked under Grier and dealt with the witnesses who needed protection, while Grier's focus, for the most part, was on capturing the fugitives. "What did she do?"

"Gave Al the slip and killed a man in front of a restaurant full of witnesses."

The woman was everything Grier wasn't—tall, blond, but that didn't bother her as much as the total guilessness of the woman's face. "She was set up."

Bobby snorted and she ignored him. She always ignored skepticism in favor of her gut.

Today would be no exception.

On the outskirts of Ciudad Juarez, Reid found them a half-constructed high-rise to shore up in. Since it was Saturday, they wouldn't have to worry about construction crews coming in the morning. By tomorrow night, they would be long gone, although to where, Kell had no clue.

The upper floor was perfect—the lights from the other buildings shone in, giving them enough light to function but not enough to give away their position.

It was chilly, but both men had blankets in their bags, along with ammo and comms, and while Reid went out to ditch the Jeep and get them a new car, Kell set Teddie up on the floor on a blanket.

"I know it's not comfortable."

"Is it safe?"

"For now." He stood, propped against the window jam so he could look outside. "Your shoulder okay?"

"The bandage held." She paused. "It's throbbing a little."

He nodded, went for the first-aid kit. "Turn around so I can give you this shot," he told her, motioned to her ass, and she reluctantly pulled down her pants, just low enough for him to get to the muscle. When that was done, he shook out some Motrin and handed them to her with water. "This should help. You need to get some sleep. In case we have to run again. You know, together, not you escaping and running alone, which might've been the stupidest thing you've ever done."

"Better than trusting you."

"All I did was save your life. In turn, you tried to fucking kill me. I think you owe me your last name, at least."

"Why? So you can check on my story?"

"I don't need your last name for that, but it would be nice if you gave a little bit more."

She obviously didn't think so. She curled up in his blanket and watched him carefully. "So you were in the Army."

"Yes."

"But not anymore."

"No." He paused. "I'm sorry about your family. About everything that's happened to you. You're not a victim—don't want to be treated like one. I get all of that. You're right not to trust anyone, but at the same time, you have to trust us. We have no stake in this. We don't work for the government. And we're not being paid to take care of you."

"You're just helping me out of the goodness of your heart, right?"

"One of the perks of the job—I get to help whoever I want." Kell shifted, reached into his pocket and took out the picture at the marketplace. "Tell me about the day you took this."

She stared at it, didn't bother to ask why they'd been through her things. "It was the day before Thanksgiving, last year. I'd flown into Khartoum the night before to spend time with my father and his new wife and the girls."

"You got along with them."

She shrugged. "I didn't know them very well. My father met my stepmother while I was away in the States. After college, I went right to work, so I didn't spend a lot of time with them. I was staying through that Saturday, then flying out to India. I went to the market for the cook—I was going to help prepare some of my mom's old favorite Thanksgiving dishes, the way she and I always did before she died."

She looked so fucking sad and he wanted to hug her. Except she'd probably stab him and run or something, so he stayed put and listened.

"I'd been taking pictures in the market that day— I saw those men . . . I knew what they were. Or I suspected."

"What exactly did you suspect?"

"I thought they were special ops or mercenaries," she said. "You look surprised. But I'd been living with a diplomat in dangerous places since I was born. I was taught to recognize those types of men . . . and to stay far away from them."

She eyed him warily and she damned well should've taken that advice to heart. "So you took pictures of them."

"It's not like I asked them to pose. I was just taking photos of the open market. They thought they were blending in." She gave a small smile and then it faded. "Later, after they came into the house and I saw them, I realized they'd been following me at the market, that it wasn't a coincidence. I should've said something."

"Do the marshals have the pictures?"

"Yes."

"All of them?"

"Yes—I only kept the one. It's a copy . . . so I never forget."

He gave her a questioning look.

"So I never forget the men I want to kill." She paused. "I wasn't hunting them or anything. But I knew they'd come after me eventually, and I knew I had to be ready."

That, he understood completely. "Let me call your handler."

"I can't go back to that life—I won't. But I don't know who to trust."

"If you don't trust us, you're not getting out of this alive," Kell told her bluntly, and she looked at him with big, dark eyes, nibbled a full bottom lip for just a second.

"Okay," she said finally.

"You'll trust us?"

"I'll pretend. I've gotten really good at that," she said, and he wondered how someone with eyes that soft could hold that much steel.

Teddie had been dreaming about her mother. They were in the kitchen, and Teddie was peeling potatoes, a job she hated. And they were laughing, the radio behind them playing her mother's favorite songs from when she and Teddie's dad were first dating.

"Teddie, watch your back," her mom was saying, and it was such an odd thing for her to say that Teddie laughed . . . and when she turned around her mother was gone. She was calling for her, but she was all alone and she felt the sticky heat making her knees buckle.

"Teddie, hey, come on."

It was Kell, standing over her. She realized that she was sweating, despite the cooler air wafting through the unfinished floor of the building, and she threw the blanket off her. "What's wrong?"

He had both bags wound around his body, a picture perfectly framed of a warrior primed for battle. A warrior on her side and she wondered if she'd been crying out in her sleep, because of the way he was looking at her, his eyes lighting his face . . . seeing right through her.

"We need to go," he said gruffly.

She got to her feet, searching for her sneakers in the dim light. "Where's Reid?"

"He never came back."

"How long's he been gone?"

"Two hours. He's not answering his phone. Something's wrong." Kell wound up the blanket and stuffed it into his bag as he spoke. "Look, I've got to find him. And I can't leave you here—"

"I won't let you turn me in to the marshals. Either take me with you or let me go."

"You're not my prisoner."

She started at that—not because she thought she was, but because he didn't seem to have a problem letting her go on her own. For all her big talk, she'd realized sometime over the past hours that she needed Kell and Reid if she had any chance of surviving. "I'll go with you."

"Suit yourself." He led her to the window. "You're not going to like our exit, but it'll be effective. And you'll be alive."

"Is going out the window really necessary?"

He pointed to the far window and she left him to go look and she saw a truck that looked suspiciously like the one that had been following her earlier. She wasn't planning on getting close enough to be sure.

She was back by his side in seconds.

"It might not be the same men," he said.

"If it is, how would they keep finding us?"

"I was going to ask you the same question."

"You think I'm leading them to me?"

"I don't know—are you? Because if you're screwing with me, you're playing a more dangerous game than you know." He had her by the shoulders, shook her a little, and he looked fierce, like an untamed predator.

And that's exactly what he was. Danger radiated off him in waves and she should be running in any direction but his.

Instead, she asked, "What do you want me to do to prove it?"

"Strip."

"Are you kidding me?"

"No. I need to see if you've got a tracking device planted in your clothing."

"And that's the only way I'll convince you?"

"Yes. Or else I'm leaving you here."

"You bastard."

"I've been called a lot worse."

Furiously, she stripped the tank off, exposing her tiny, lacy bra, a leftover from her former life when fun lingerie was a luxury she'd indulged in just because she could. Her underwear matched and as she stood there, his eyes took her in, head to toe. "I need it all off. I have to inspect it."

"You can do it while it's on me," she said, and then realized her mistake, but it was too late. She would've been less exposed standing naked in front of him than she would be as if he actually touched her.

"Suit yourself." He moved close, ran a hand along the bottom of her bra, starting at the back and moving toward the front, feeling the underwire, his warm fingertips brushing the undersides of her breasts.

Her nipples puckered. "Is there anything there?" she asked, and he looked at her with a gleam in his eye.

"There's something . . . but not what I'm looking for."

She went to push him away but he looked down and she relented. Because there wasn't much time. Because she wanted to prove to him that he could trust her, and she wondered when and how those roles had gotten reversed.

His hand went around her waistband and she tried not to shiver, but failed. He was so damned close and her body was responding in a way it hadn't in forever. For the past year, she'd felt alone; sex had been the last thing on her mind.

Now it was in the forefront, despite the danger.

His hand dipped between her legs and she bit her bottom lip and tried to look anywhere but at him. He, in turn, was looking directly at her.

"Find what you were looking for?" It was all she could think of to say, to stop herself from asking him not to stop.

His voice was rough when he spoke. "No. I just wanted to keep touching you."

Before she could respond, his phone was ringing and he moved away from her, leaving her to dress while he spoke.

"Where the hell have you been? Okay, yeah, we'll meet you." He hung up. "Reid's got new wheels for us. Let's roll."

She wasn't sure who she hated more at this moment—herself or Kell. But there wasn't time to dwell because the window was open and he was tying a rope around himself and hooking it to a girder while she finished putting her clothes back on, and when he motioned for her to come to him, she did.

There was no other way for her to do this but wrap her arms around his shoulders, her legs around his waist, and bury her face against his neck as he dropped them down from the roof, the rope tied pulley-style, the metal gutter creaking as it struggled to hold both their weight.

When they got to the bottom, he let her go and she took a stumbled step back. And then she came forward and punched him, a left hook that caught his lip. He wiped the blood away with the back of his hand, grinned, and she knew she'd miscalculated. Badly.

In a flash, he pinned her to the wall, leaned in close. "I'll give you a place to put your hands, Teddie."

Despite her fear, a thrill uncurled in her belly, heat flooding between her legs at the thought of his big hands on her.

And he knew it. Bent down, capturing her mouth with his, kissing her until she was dizzy.

When he pulled back, she still tasted him—the metallic taste of blood, mixed with mint and man. Her body had definitely responded; it wanted more and he knew it. He laughed a little—a hoarse sound—and backed away.

"Let's go. We're still not out of danger."

We never will be. The thought made her shiver.

The men after her were very dangerous. The man in front of her, more so . . . and she hoped she was on the right side of danger.

She had a feeling she wouldn't know for sure for a very long time.

CHAPTER
4

Kell hadn't been lying to Teddie about the danger. Although he hadn't seen who was in the truck waiting outside their hideout, he knew that a building like this was a perfect spot for criminal activity. Plus, it gave him the perfect excuse to search her.

Someone—or several someones—were stalking them. Going out the window was the best move. They were still boxed in but he'd rather fight out here, where there were two openings for escape, than inside.

But the fact that they were still running from an unseen enemy had Kell on edge. Teddie had nothing on her that they could track. If the men after her were trained mercs, they would be good at their job, but this was ridiculous, and he and Reid weren't exactly slouches.

He licked his lips again, tasting her now. The bleeding

had stopped, but the sting was still there, and hell yeah, he'd deserved it.

He was nearly beyond the point of no return—the kiss, the slap, Teddie in her underwear had his blood boiling in a way it hadn't in months—years, if he was honest with himself—and despite the fact that this was neither the time nor the place, his dick didn't care.

But the rest of his body had better sense, because something in the air made him stop cold. He paused for a long moment, looked down one end of the alley and then the other.

Nothing.

But he still didn't move.

"Shouldn't we run?" Teddie asked softly but he placed a gentle finger over her mouth to stop her from making another sound.

They wouldn't get far. He'd been hoping by waiting it out here, they'd escape. But there was no such luck.

There was also no place for Kell to hide Teddie. "Don't move. No matter what happens, don't move away from the wall," he told her.

The danger whipped around the corner seconds later, in the form of a man wearing a blue shirt and jeans, carrying a baseball bat. Kell went for him, noting out of the corner of his eye that Teddie instinctively moved away from both of them.

Shit.

"Against the wall," he barked, but she was too busy staring at the approaching man.

Dammit. He turned his attention to the guy with the baseball bat—Kell had no doubt he was more heavily armed than he appeared to be. He also wasn't one of the mercs from the picture Teddie had taken at the market in Khartoum. His gut clenched as he realized this had nothing to do with Teddie and everything to do with him. DMH? Or something else?

Before he had time to think further, Blue Shirt made his move, coming toward him with the bat raised.

It was time for Kell to make his, to let loose the adrenaline that soared through his body at full speed.

Teddie wanted to listen to Kell, but the fear made her dizzy. It was all she could do not to scream as Kell threw himself at the danger like he could extinguish it with his body. She stepped back as if pushed by the sheer brute force of the action, right into another man's chest. Arms wrapped around her and she screamed before a hand clamped over her mouth.

It was only then that she understood Kell's directive and she promised herself to never again ignore it if she could just get out of this safely. If she'd remained with her back against the wall, she would've seen the second man coming at her, the one now attempting to drag her back down the alley and away from Kell.

She would not let this happen. If she died tonight, she'd go down fighting, and so she concentrated on escaping the man's grasp. She flailed her legs, twisted and turned and then went limp, so that her captor nearly dropped her. He didn't, though.

Instead, together they pitched forward, Teddie narrowly avoiding landing on her face with the big man on her back. But although she'd saved herself by rolling at the last second, she still wasn't free.

She caught sight of Kell, moving like a blur of action

against Blue Shirt and another guy in a yellow shirt, who'd come out of nowhere. She heard grunts and fast breathing—but oddly, nothing else. A fight to the death that was eerily silent and she fought again as her assailant pressed her body closer to his.

She jammed an elbow back, heard a satisfying crunch and a howl and suddenly she could move. Her panic rose when the man attempted to grab her tighter, but she twisted away, tried to keep her eye on Kell as he continued fighting his attackers.

Hers called her a stupid bitch, ruthlessly twisting her arm behind her back and she cried out in pain.

It was then she felt the cold barrel of a gun press to her temple, and that stilled her. She heard her breath coming fast, willed herself not to hyperventilate, if such a thing could be done.

And then her captor called out, "Kell Roberts, you need to come with us."

He knew Kell's name—his first and last? It was *Kell* they wanted?

She hadn't seen the face of either Blue Shirt or Yellow Shirt—or the one holding her—didn't know if they were responsible for killing her family. But she'd thought they were.

She'd wondered how they kept finding her, had almost wanted Kell to discover something hidden in her clothing that would explain it. But now she knew this attack at least wasn't about her at all.

That thought was confirmed when the fighting slowed as Kell glanced over at her and moved away from Blue Shirt with his hands in the air. Yellow Shirt, whom he'd kicked to the ground, stumbled to his feet now and moved forward, and his face was illuminated by one of the two dim lights in the alleyway.

It definitely wasn't one of the mercenaries who'd killed her family.

"She doesn't need to be involved in any of this. She can go, forget she ever saw you and write it off as an unfortunate one-night stand," the man who held her continued.

What would happen to her? Suppose the killers who were after her were lurking?

It seemed an impossible choice and yet she knew in her heart Kell wouldn't let her get hurt.

"Who the hell are you?" Kell demanded of the man who held her tightly. There was a bruise already forming on Kell's cheek and blood on his forehead and running down his left arm.

Her captor laughed at Kell's question, which jostled her. Her shoulder ached and she stayed as still as possible out of fear that if she moved, her arm would break.

"You'll find that out soon enough," he said.

"Who do you work for?" Kell persisted.

"We know who you've worked for. How many assassinations you carried out for Delta Force. How many more you did independently, with no record of them in any government files. Who knows what other intel I have on you, how many innocents you slaughtered on your quests . . . let me give you some examples, in case you think I'm lying."

He went on to list about ten places—countries and cities—and dates. And numbers, which no doubt meant something to Kell.

She closed her eyes as if that would stop her from

hearing things she didn't want to know—never wanted to know about anyone.

When she opened them, Kell was staring straight at her, his expression pained. "Let her go," he said slowly. "I'll go with you."

She wasn't sure what panicked her more—the thought that she would be without Kell, or that she'd be with him.

"Let her go right now."

Blue Shirt snorted and tossed handcuffs his way. "Put these on first and then walk to me."

Kell locked his wrists behind him, but he didn't move. "Let her go down the alley. Now."

Slowly, the man behind her released her arm and she winced at the jolt of pain. She turned swiftly as he brushed by her—she was no longer of interest to him, but Kell was. His face wasn't familiar either.

And she turned to Kell, not sure what to do. Leaving him behind did not seem right.

"Run," he told her as he whipped around so he and the man who'd first grabbed her circled each other and it was then she saw the look in Kell's eyes. The man she'd been literally attached at the hip to was in fact as dangerous as the men who were after her—maybe even more so.

Kell's blood ran cold. The fact that these men knew his name was bad enough, but coupled with his dubious list of accomplishments, most of which should've been completely classified since they were Delta missions . . . Damn, this was not good.

When Teddie turned tail, all three men moved in on him, treating Kell with caution, as they should.

"Start walking," the one with the gun told him and Kell turned the opposite way from where Teddie had run—and where Reid was parked—and followed the directive.

He hoped Teddie would run directly into Reid. And when he didn't hear her footsteps anymore, he made a forced stumble forward. The one in yellow grabbed for his biceps to right him. Kell took that opportunity to throw all his weight against him, smashing him against the building hard enough to knock him out.

Out of the corner of his eye he saw Blue Shirt swing his bat, tried and failed to move completely out of the goddamned way, so the bat caught him on the side of his neck and back of his head, taking him to the ground. He landed on his shoulder and when he rolled, the one who'd grabbed Teddie earlier was standing close, holding Kell at gunpoint.

Fuck.

"Don't be stupid," he said.

"Stupid would be going with you," Kell snarled.

"Dead or alive—those are my orders. I know which one I'd rather."

Just then, the blue-shirted one came up from behind him, reached out to grab Kell around the neck, holding a gun directly to his temple.

"Dead sounds good to me," he said, and Kell shifted to elbow him in the throat—a risky move, but he was not getting taken. His head throbbing, he reached blindly for the gun with his hands still shackled behind his back as he heard a sharp crack and saw the man with the other gun pitch forward toward him, gun clattering away across the alleyway.

Teddie stood behind him, still half in shock, the bat held tight with both hands—and goddammit, to his right, Blue Shirt was regrouping again.

"Go," Kell told her harshly, ignoring the fact that she'd just saved his life. "Get out of here, now!"

Finally, she moved, but only to drop the bat. It fell with a dull clatter and he cursed and forced himself to his feet.

As the man in yellow got up too, Kell swung around with a vicious kick. He heard the satisfying crack of Yellow's jaw, saw the man Teddie hit was still nice and unconscious, but having all three only temporarily disabled wouldn't be enough in this situation.

No, he needed them dead and then investigated, in that order.

As she watched, Kell rooted in Blue Shirt's pockets awkwardly, pulled out keys and managed to get his cuffs off.

The man with the gun—the one she'd hit—stirred and she shifted to move away, wondered what the hell she'd been thinking coming back here, trying to help.

You saved him.

Kell was up, moving closer to her, pushed her out of the way roughly as he neared the stirring danger, as if daring the downed man to rise.

She caught the glint of metal in the dark as Kell's

hand whizzed through the air. Only when she looked down again at her original captor did she realize the metal was the barrel of a pen. Now it stuck out of his neck.

Kell's eyes glittered in the dim light as he looked down the alleyway.

"I told you to run," he said, and in the next instant she did, refused to look back for him no matter how badly she wanted to. Instead, she concentrated on keeping her footing, on trying to anticipate what might lay ahead of her.

It couldn't be worse than what she'd left behind, could it?

Her footsteps echoed in the near-silent night, too loudly, her heart banged in her ears and she wanted to scream for help, but that would be stupid.

She was done being stupid.

A black truck screeched to a stop across the alley, and she nearly ran into it. She moved to try to go around it but then heard her name.

Reid was coming toward her. "What the hell?"

"Kell . . . a fight . . ." She could barely breathe again and she cursed her weakness.

"It's okay," Reid told her. But it wasn't. None of this was okay. She pushed against his chest in an attempt to move past him.

"Whoa." Reid grabbed her before she could escape.

She flailed again, felt the panic overtake her, and he cursed.

God, she knew these men had saved her ass, but they were also just as capable of ending her life in a second if things got too complicated.

Things had just gotten *too complicated*.

"Teddie, come on, get into the truck," Reid was saying, and she jerked when she heard the sharp echo of footsteps heading in their direction. She went still, as did Reid, and it seemed like forever before either of them moved, although if she had to guess, only mere seconds had passed.

Reid pulled his gun, trained it on the dark alley, and she struggled again as she heard Kell call out, "Get her in the truck—we've got to get out of here."

Reid shoved his gun into the back of his jeans and grabbed her so her arms were pulled behind her back. He drew her wrists together, cuffed them the way they'd been earlier, and then he unceremoniously picked her up and shoved her into the back of the double cab, as though she weighed nothing at all.

In seconds, Kell was next to her, Reid was in the driver's seat, the doors closed and locked.

She tried to lunge forward as a sudden attack of claustrophobia overwhelmed her, needed out of the car, the cuffs . . .

"She's hyperventilating," she heard Kell say, and there was rustling—at the same time her hands were freed, a paper bag was placed over her mouth. The truck began to move, the windows opened and fresh air poured in.

Breathing became easier and she felt less closed in. After several minutes, she moved the bag away from her mouth, realized Kell was watching her, but he'd shifted, so they weren't touching.

That was good, because she realized she did not

want him near her. "What happened back there?" she asked finally.

"Don't worry about that now. Come on, sit back and try to relax," he told her, his voice slightly hoarse, his face bruised, and she realized how close they'd both come to being seriously hurt. Again.

She complied with his request, as if in surrender. But she was far from actually doing so. Reid continued to peel down the streets, finally merging the truck in with the light nighttime traffic on one of the main streets.

"How did those men know you?" she continued.

Kell didn't answer her and she pressed, "Those men weren't after me, they were after you. I'm in more trouble with you than without you."

Or it could be in equal amounts, but still. She'd known that since she'd heard them fire their rifles earlier, when she'd first stumbled into them.

Neither man said a word to her as the truck whipped through the streets, although Reid made a cryptic phone call that she assumed was about the attack. Her gut tightened and the abrasions on her arms and palms began to sting. Her muscles were sore and tight from the running and the stress and she was sure she'd see a mess of bruises when she took her clothes off.

She wanted out, but she had nowhere to go. "I know you killed people when you had me handcuffed in the Jeep—I heard the shots. Who was it then? Was that connected to this?"

Kell gave her a long look. "Better you don't know a thing, sweetheart. You're in enough trouble of your own."

"You need to answer me. Who were those men in the alley?"

"No clue," Kell said finally, and she didn't know if he was lying.

"What did they want with you?"

"Seemed like they wanted me dead," he said mildly, infuriating her further. "I know what you want—but I don't owe you an explanation."

"I saved your ass," she spat, and Reid snorted.

Kell drew closer to her and suddenly the backseat seemed far too small. "You think your little stunt helped matters? I told you to run—you put yourself in danger by not doing it."

Then she wouldn't have seen what she had. These men were deadly. She knew that, but watching Kell single-handedly take on the three in the alley . . .

The violence had been mind-numbing. And still, he'd saved her life. Again. "I didn't want you to get hurt." That was the truth, spilling from her before she could stop it.

In the light that shone in from the storefronts and street lamps, she swore she saw his expression soften, but his tone didn't reflect that. "What do you want? You want us to bring you someplace where there's no danger? Right now, for you, that simply doesn't exist."

The implication that it might never wasn't lost on her.

"You have no idea what I want."

He turned to face her. "You think you're safer without us. You're wrong. You might even be thinking you're safer with the marshals right about now. You'd be wrong again."

She would be wrong—because Kell was the better choice to keep her safe from the men who'd murdered her family.

It took like to fight like. And right now she needed that on her side.

CHAPTER
5

Dylan took Riley to dinner, and then instead of heading straight home, he took the route past the Adirondacks, telling the woman he planned on spending the rest of his life with that he had a quick errand to run.

Partial truth, and Riley was full and happy from dinner and wine, so she turned up the radio, put her feet up on the dashboard and didn't question him. The truck strummed along the open road and his stomach tightened with the knowledge of what he was about to do.

He'd met Riley years earlier, when she'd been hired to kill him. Instead of holding it against her, he'd ended up in bed with her—and ultimately fell in love. Their road here hadn't been easy, but after Riley had gotten herself into trouble again, she and Dylan had worked together, and they'd made their peace.

Since leaving Delta Force years earlier in order to do private contracting—akin to spy work but without the yoke of the CIA around his neck—Dylan had helped his friend Cam successfully leave the military behind and had finally gotten to a place with Riley where they were working with and not against each other.

She was as good at the spy game as he was.

This past year had seen an awful lot of things come together and some others fall apart for the group of men he considered friends. His best friend, Cam, had found love himself. Cam had saved a woman he'd fallen in love with on a mission. Her name was Skylar and she made Cam the happiest Dylan had ever seen him.

Dylan's youngest brother, Zane, had also found love, with a doctor he'd saved from the clutches of a terrorist group after finding her in Sierra Leone and facing his own personal demons. And Dylan's middle brother, Caleb, had suffered a devastating blow on a mission with his Delta team, which included Reid and Mace and Gray—lost a friend and teammate and most of his memory as well.

It had returned—along with a woman who loved him, Vivi—thanks to both her and Mace's help.

Mace, another former Delta Force operative from Caleb's team, had battled his own losses and helped Paige Grayson, the stepsister of their murdered teammate Gray. And he'd fallen in love with her.

Definitely a pattern there, with the men letting the torture of their souls go and finding love.

Cam and Sky had tied the knot months earlier, at Mace's bar before the construction started. It had seemed fitting to give the place a happy memory before rebuilding. Now the bar it was in the middle of full-fledged construction, with the majority of the work being done by Caleb and Mace, since they needed to do all kinds of special security wiring. When Cam returned from his honeymoon, he'd moved in to help Mace, while Paige and Vivi moved into Sky and Cam's house for the month, since their soon-to-be home was unlivable.

Vivi was thrilled to have access to Cam's bank of computers and the three women bonded during the month-long sleepover. They also got closer to Riley, as she moved back and forth between Sky's house and some jobs she needed to complete. And while the women hammered out their roles in this new organization, Dylan began to make some plans of his own.

The first party in the rebuilt bar would be Mace and Paige's wedding. Mace had proposed soon after he'd rescued her from her from her biological brother—the man had escaped from prison, intent on killing her, and had almost done so, right in Mace's bar. Mace and Reid and Caleb had all helped to save Paige. Now Mace wanted to wait until the construction was finished to christen the new bar with a happy memory, the same way they'd honored the old bar with one.

But just as things were settling into place, with Cam, Mace, Caleb, Kell and Reid all agreeing to work together with Dylan and Riley—taking charge of their own destinies and leaving the military behind—Dylan caught wind of some unsettling intel.

When Vivi mentioned that there had been action on their names, meaning that someone had been looking them up and actively searching for information on all of them, Dylan did some checking on his own. Although he wasn't one hundred percent certain, he had an idea of who was behind the searches and he felt his past coming back to haunt him in a way he'd never worried about before.

Kell and Reid had finished their mission in Mexico, but not without bringing along some added trouble. After he'd gotten Reid's call, Dylan had put Vivi on figuring out who the hell was behind the attack on Kell. He assumed the attackers were tied into the searches Vivi had stumbled upon.

It was all starting to make sense in an absolutely terrible way, and Dylan, always a realist, wouldn't admit that it was true—not yet.

Before anything else blew up in their faces and despite the late hour, he knew it was time to take action on the plan he'd been putting into place for the past couple of months. He'd wanted things to be perfect.

Dylan turned right at the stop sign—the road was private and poorly lit, but he knew where he was going. He'd been here a few times before.

But this time, it wasn't a dress rehearsal, this was the real thing . . . and the woman sitting next to him was that as well.

"Where are we?" Riley asked for the millionth time. He'd been holding her hand for a while across the console and she was curled up in the truck's seat, looking even more gorgeous than the day he'd first seen her.

She'd tried to blow him up, had only succeeded in ruining his car, and they'd been fighting—and making love—ever since.

But for the past eight months they'd been together. Working, living—and he wasn't about to let anything come between them. "Almost there."

She sighed a little, but she wasn't complaining.

The fact that she trusted him enough to go along for the ride made him even more firm in his decision. When he drove up the long driveway and parked, she turned to peer out the window. He got out and went around to open her door, and she looked at him with a million questions in her eyes.

"I'm guessing if I needed to bring my gun, you would've told me, right?" she asked.

"You're fine unarmed. Come on." He took her hand and led her toward the small, private house.

Richard was waiting on the porch and he waved as soon as he saw the couple approach. The porch had several lit candles scattered around it, which Dylan had to admit was a nice touch.

He didn't have much in the way of traditional romance in him, but there was almost a primal need to do this right.

"You must be Riley," Richard said, introducing himself to her, and Dylan told him, "She doesn't know anything."

"Maybe you should take care of that. I'll set up in the meantime." Richard smiled and Dylan was surprised Riley waited until he went inside before taking her hand from his.

"I know you're not always big on sharing intel," she started, but he'd already begun to get down on one knee.

Her mouth opened, then closed. Her eyes got moist

and she barely got out, "Dylan," a whispered breath more than anything.

It was all she could say.

"Have I finally managed to surprise you?"

She nodded, her free hand over her mouth. He reached into his pocket and pulled out a ring. It was a band of white gold—because Riley rarely wore more jewelry than a watch. This was elegant and simple, and it suited her. She watched him hold it out to her and she nodded again.

"Is that a yes? You'll marry me?"

Finally, she found the words. "It's a yes, Dylan. It's always been a yes for you."

He stood then, pulled her to him, kissed her as the passion flared between them. Always hot, but this time there was a sweet tenderness, an easiness that belied all they'd been through to get to this point.

When they broke the kiss, she asked, "Why now?"

"I want to be tied to you, Riley. I want forever and I want everyone to know it."

He'd always been traditional in that sense, had wanted what his parents had. They'd married young, did everything together. They'd even died together, doing the adventure hunting they'd enjoyed so much, and while their death had been a devastating blow for Dylan and his younger brothers, there was no denying the positive influence their marriage had had on their children.

Dylan especially believed in marriage and its sanctity, thought it should be private—the more so, the better. His vows were for Riley's ears alone.

It was also safer if no one outside their immediate circle knew of the marriage. Bad enough if word got out they were together. It would make them equal targets, but actually Riley more than him. And although he hated that work would mar this occasion, he'd always been a hell of a realist. "Ready?"

"Ready." She smiled and he led her inside, where Richard had everything set up for the ceremony, including his wife, who would be a witness. The ceremony was brief, but Riley loved the fact that she and Dylan spoke their vows each other, promising in sickness and health and all the other things that could possibly happen over the course of a lifetime.

It was easy to make the commitment because, in so many ways, they'd already been to hell and back. And they'd survived.

When Dylan kissed her as her husband, it was her life coming full circle.

It was everything.

After saying good-bye to the pastor and his wife, she and Dylan made out like a couple of teenagers, leaning against the car for a while, until Dylan murmured, "Gotta get you home before we do something to shock Richard."

"What, no honeymoon?" she teased.

"Oh, there's a honeymoon, smart-ass. Get in the car."

She did so with a smile, and her phone began to ring before they'd left the driveway of the pastor's house. She dug it out of her pocket, didn't recognize the number, but with the women rapidly becoming her friends, her family, and her responsibility while the men were out of town, she picked up. Fiddled with the ring with her thumb, enjoying the smooth newness of the jewelry. Watched Dylan playing with the matching band on his finger as well.

But after she said hello, the male voice that greeted her stole away the sense of contentment she'd been sure would last for days, if not weeks. "Riley Sacadono."

A statement, not a question, and she remained silent. Wondered if she should put the phone on speaker, but Dylan was on with Mace already and so she steeled herself for a conversation she was certain would not be fun.

"I'm sure Dylan hasn't mentioned me," he continued. "He knows me as Crystal. Perhaps you can mention this conversation to him."

"Why not call him yourself?"

"Because this is much more fun. Like the old days . . . Dylan will remember the old days. And then he's going to wish they never existed."

Crystal hung up first and Riley shut the phone and fought the urge to throw it to the pavement speeding by. Dylan had many more enemies than friends, but her gut told her that this phone call was a much bigger deal than a simple enemy's threats.

No, it sounded too personal to be strictly business.

"What's wrong?" Dylan asked her, and as much as she wanted to leave this behind for the night, there was no way she could.

"You need to tell me about Crystal," she said, saw Dylan's hands tighten on the wheel and knew it was as bad as she'd feared.

Kell hated the look on Teddie's face when she realized just how damned dangerous he actually was, but he'd resigned himself to it. She was safe and that was what mattered, although it would've been a hell of a lot easier if the three guys in the alley had been after her.

No, it was him they'd goddamned wanted, and he had the bruises to prove it.

When he'd finished with the men in the alley, he'd rousted them of their wallets and weapons before throwing the bodies into a nearby Dumpster, all the while, Teddie's look of horror flashing in front of his face.

If she hadn't known what he was before, she did now. She had every reason to be afraid of him. Much better that way. Maybe she'd come to her senses and demand to be taken to the marshals before this got more out of hand.

Because none of the men in the alley was looking for Teddie. They'd come for him, and now he and Reid needed to figure out why. But he wouldn't discuss any of this in front of her, and so he willed himself to calm down and focused on their brand-new stolen vehicle, a big pickup with a double cab.

While Teddie curled into a corner of the back and closed her eyes, he leaned into the front seat. "Maybe we could be more conspicuous."

"You want safe and reliable, it's going to be conspicuous." Reid said. "But Cruz bought a shitload of these last month. We'll fit right in."

"Except theirs are bulletproof," Kell grumbled.

"We can do the phone book trick, but hell, we barely had enough time for me to grab this. We do have OnStar, though. And Sirius."

"You do realize this isn't our car, right?"

"Kinda is. Consider it a business expense," Reid

said, and Kell decided not to question him further, mainly because Reid had bought bags of food too— empanadas and tacos and burritos and chips—and Kell was starving.

He grabbed some of the wrapped tacos and handed them back to Teddie, was surprised when she accepted them readily.

"Did she really save your ass?" Reid asked, his voice low. Kell just snorted his response and Reid said, "I told you I liked her."

Kell wanted to say, *Then you deal with her*, but Reid would and *he* wouldn't have stopped with a strip search.

"Shut up," he said, unable to control the irritation radiating through his body and shoved a taco in his mouth. For now, it was safer to let her eat in the comfort of this luxury truck while Reid brought them to their new safe house, which Kell hoped he hadn't somehow purchased too.

Dylan would skin Reid's ass—and Kell's, by association.

"Dylan would have to catch us first." Reid said, reading Kell's mind and his reaction as he pulled up to a driveway with elaborate gates and punched in a security code. "Besides, I got tired of living in a hovel."

Fuck it. Kell was officially done arguing and trying to rein Reid in. He just hoped this mansion had actual beds and wasn't simply an empty shell.

He let Reid deal with getting Teddie inside, slid out of the truck and walked into the house and stared up at the huge chandelier as Reid passed by and said, "It was some movie star's place. Couldn't get out of it fast enough after that swine flu scare. It's been empty for a year—caretaker comes once a week. He was here yesterday, so we're set for now."

Teddie brushed by Kell and he made the mistake of glancing at her, noted that her arm was bleeding and her cheek was bruised and, shit, he'd forgotten that one of the men had gotten a stranglehold on her.

"You okay?" he asked, his voice much harsher than he'd intended.

She nodded, took a few steps away from him. "I'm just, ah, tired. Think I'll rest for a little while."

She was lying, but it would suit his purpose. Reid came up next to her and guided her into a den right off the kitchen, got her settled on the couch with a blanket and then he came back into the kitchen.

Kell spread the IDs he'd taken off the men in the alley onto the kitchen table while Reid scrolled through the GPS Kell grabbed from their truck conveniently parked beside the alley, for no other reason than it had been there and might come in handy. It would.

Teddie was in Kell's line of sight, pretending to be asleep on the couch. That was good, because she'd be trying hard to listen, which meant she'd stay put. Even so, he still had the urge to handcuff her to something. Like himself.

Yeah, way to get your head in the game, Kell.

The first ID was for a man named Juan Feliz. Arizona driver's license. The second was Gavin Slater. No license, but rather a military issue ID card.

Another vet. Shit. The third man had no identification on his person.

"I don't recognize these names," Reid said after staring at the IDs, and Kell agreed.

"DMH?"

"Could be, but that's pretty quick for them to regroup and track us. There's been no chatter to that effect either," Kell said as Reid turned the GPS screen to him.

"I've got two addresses that come up multiple times. We should probably pay a visit," Reid said.

"Let's feed all this to Vivi first," Kell suggested, and Reid nodded.

Kell called Vivi, put the phone on speaker, and he and Reid gave her the names and addresses they had retrieved.

"I'll get right on this," she told them. She was a better hacker than anyone who worked for the major Intelligence agencies.

"What did you find out about Teddie?" Kell asked.

"Not much," she said and that didn't bode well.

"Her story doesn't check out?" Kell asked.

"Her story doesn't exist," Vivi clarified. "At least not that I've been able to find."

"With witness protection, you might not," Kell said.

"Unless the story never existed in the first place," Reid added, and Kell gave him a sharp look, then let his gaze drift to the couch where she was curled up.

He couldn't get a read on her—she'd spent enough time hiding and lying, had managed to sharpen her skills to the point where she could easily throw someone off track.

Concentrate. Forget about the softness of her skin, the vulnerability in her eyes that made him want to gather her up and protect her in a way he'd never known before. "I need more details."

"I know, Kell, I'm still working it. I've hacked into the U.S. Marshals' database, so let me poke around more," Vivi said. "In the meantime, I've got some intel on one of the men in that photo. His name's Conner McMannus—honorable discharge from the Army three years ago, Rangers. He was injured badly in Mosul, lost a few fingers on his right hand and sight in his right eye. After he came home from rehabbing his injuries, his marriage fell apart. He sold his house about a year ago and no one's heard from him since."

"Credit cards?"

"Haven't been touched. His bank account was closed out and there's not a new one in his name," Vivi said. "He's disappeared."

"He could do that easily," Kell murmured. "Any of us could."

"Dylan's checking with his CIA resources to see if McMannus is running ops for them, but so far, nothing," Vivi added.

"He thinks McMannus could be working undercover?" Reid asked.

"He's not ruling anything out," Vivi said. "I'll be in touch as soon as I learn more. Dylan said to be careful."

Kell cut the line, and for a long moment the men just stared at each other, both knowing that Teddie had heard everything, including what Vivi said about her story not existing.

It was time for Kell to work on her.

Teddie kept her eyes closed tight even as the words *her story doesn't exist* echoed through her mind. Witness protection had buried her well and it was frightening to think she might not be believed because of it.

She hadn't been tired at all when she'd gotten out of the truck—she was practically jumping out of her skin—but she'd forced herself to lay on the couch and pretend to sleep so she could listen to Kell and Reid's conversation.

What she hadn't heard was Kell walking toward her, so she jumped when he murmured into her ear, "Guns. Spying. Quite a repertoire."

She opened her eyes, because there was no point in pretending. Looked into those silver-rimmed eyes and stared for a long moment, trying to find something in there to hate.

Again, she came up empty.

"If you wanted to know what we were talking about, you could've just stayed in the kitchen," he told her, looked sincere about that, and she wished her emotions weren't getting in the way of everything.

It had been so much easier when she came into Mexico with only one thing on her mind. She'd been so intent on revenge that she'd let it blind her into thinking she could do the job alone. "Do you think I'm telling the truth?"

He sat next to her on the couch and studied her. Reached out to brush some hair from her face. "I think you're scared. You believed you'd thought all this through but it's falling apart." His voice was almost hypnotic and she really hoped he couldn't read minds.

"I am who I say I am. I'm in witness protection. I'm sure if your friends look hard enough, they'll find me."

"They'll look, trust me. If there's anything else I need to know, it'd be a good time to spill it."

"Are you all right?" she asked instead, noting the bruises on his cheek and the side of his neck. She was sure there must be a lot more under his clothes, but he didn't move like a man who'd been on the receiving end of a near kidnapping recently.

"You're worried about me?"

She was, couldn't help it, any more than she could help the way she responded when he looked at her. He'd practically seen her naked and her body seemed to vibrate when she thought about it.

She reached out and ran a light finger along the bruise on his cheek and almost pulled back when his eyes flashed with desire. Desire, from that simple touch—and the flare ran through her too, made her fear melt a little. "I did come back to help—you chose to yell at me instead of thank me."

"How rude of me to try to save your life. I didn't want you to have to see any of that. Not because of what you'd find out, but that violence . . . it stays with you. And it sounds like you've lived through enough of it already."

She drew her legs up to her chest at the mention of her family's murder.

It takes like to fight like. "Are you? Like those men?"

He leaned his head back and closed his eyes, answered, "Yes," with little hesitation.

So much for reassurance. "Then yes, I'm scared. Really, really scared."

He looked over at her. "I figured—hyperventilation's usually the first clue."

"I was hiding it well until then."

"Yeah, you were," he said quietly. "I'm like those men, but I also work hard to not be like them."

She couldn't imagine anything scaring him . . . but maybe sometimes he scared himself.

"Those men in the photo . . . they were like ghosts—no one could find a trace of them. If I hadn't seen them, no one would even know who to look for," she said. "I was put into protection but I couldn't do anything but hide. I thought I'd go crazy."

No human contact, and that had never bothered her before. This time, it left her time to think about everything that was missing from her life. Too much time to wonder if things might've been different if she'd told her father about the night Samuel had tried to rape her . . . if that would've kept him away from their family and from framing her father . . . or if it had been inevitable.

It was too soon to reveal any of that to Kell, though. And it might always be.

"What did you do before you went into protection?" he asked.

"I was a photographer. If you Google me, you'll find my work." She didn't want to brag but she was proud as hell of what she'd accomplished. "I took photos in poverty-stricken countries—I was a good-will ambassador for the UN as well, combining the two in order to bring attention when and where it was needed." She'd traveled to more places on her own than she could remember—could document her entire life through film. The only thing was, it was through other people . . . never herself. Outside, looking in; actually, she preferred it that way.

But who really liked being an outsider?

"Did you always take pictures?" Kell was asking.

"My father bought me my first camera when I was eight." From that point on, she'd been enthralled with being able to capture moments in time, forever. "The whole idea fascinated me. With a picture, sometimes you get to see beyond the surface. That's the best part."

"And probably why so many people are uncomfortable with having their pictures taken."

Smart man. Why did he seem to get it—and her—so easily? Was this part of some game he was playing . . . or was he sincere? "Giving it up was really hard. The marshals told me I shouldn't even own a camera, that I might unintentionally expose myself that way."

"They've hidden a lot of people successfully."

"I wouldn't call having to give up everything a success."

"They kept you alive."

"You don't understand—I had to give up my career and I loved my career. Taking away my camera was like cutting off an arm. I still ache from not being able to take photos." She stared at him, willing herself not to cry. Why she was trying so hard to make him understand was beyond her.

"Why wouldn't I understand?"

"You love what you do?"

He didn't answer that but emotion crossed his face—anger and pain—and if she'd had her camera she would've captured it, taken her time studying it until she could figure it—him—out. But just as suddenly as it came, it passed and his expression looked like it always did, serious and fierce.

A warrior's face. Different than some of the soldiers she'd met over the years, and yet still oddly similar.

"You were safe for a year. Why expose yourself now?"

"I had to," she said fiercely. "Wouldn't you, for your parents?"

"Never." The word came out equally fierce.

The look in his eyes stopped her from questioning him further.

Kell waited for Teddie to really fall asleep, watched her slow, easy breaths and figured she was good for an eight-hour crash.

Reid had heard everything. Kell had nothing to hide, but the attraction Kell felt for Teddie . . . there was no denying it.

"You think she's bullshitting us?" Reid asked, turning up the radio so they couldn't be heard as easily as before.

"About some things, yes. But about the main part of her story—who she is, no way," Kell said.

"It's those little things that could get us killed."

Reid was right, Kell knew that.

He sank into the kitchen chair opposite Reid and his friend slid a soda can across to him. He opened it and drank half, needing the sugar. He felt old tonight. Older than he had in a long time.

This was his first mission back and he was slowly wiping aside the heavy cloak of vengeance with its heady scent.

You love what you do, Teddie had asked him, and he'd wanted to tell her that he hated it as much as he loved it, and that was something he'd never thought would happen. Not until last year, when he had walked into an empty hotel room in Sierra Leone, took in the scene of what had obviously been a struggle and looked past the mess to zone in on a note, left in a small pool of blood on the floor.

An eye for an eye, Kell Roberts.

His hands shook hard, even when he fisted them, and he stared at the words, letting the rage flow through his blood one last time before he quelled it.

Anger wouldn't help him now, no emotion would. DMH—short for Dead Man's Hand—a homegrown terrorist group turned extremist and international with ties that Delta Force was determined to cut, had taken Reid and three other Delta operatives captive during a mission cloaked in complete secrecy, something Delta Force operatives counted on for survival. The mission was fraught with danger, as they all were, and as always his four teammates treated it as such.

What the team didn't know at the time was that they had been tracked from the moment they'd landed in Sierra Leone.

The operatives' food was poisoned and DMH took full advantage of their weakened state, kidnapping all four of the Delta soldiers. And then they'd contacted

Kell, who'd been off on another mission, and taunted him with what they'd done.

Kell spent the next three weeks burning and killing and torturing anyone remotely related to DMH in order to find his missing Delta Force teammates. Refused to think in terms of before it was too late. The men were trained to know how to stay alive, to save themselves. Kell was counting on that as the hours ticked away, and finally, after a relentless search, there was a ray of hope.

He'd gotten intel on where his team was being kept. He'd slit the informant's throat ruthlessly, refusing to leave any live trail behind.

None of the DMH men would survive his wrath when the time came. But first, he made it to the underground prison in time to save three of his four men.

He boarded the chopper that brought them to Morocco, as the U.S. Embassy made arrangements with the local hospital to get Mace the urgent help he needed. Mace wouldn't have made it farther than that without emergency surgery. As it was, the flight seemed to take forever, the blades beating the air in time with Kell's pulse and the throb in his head.

It was controlled chaos. Gray's body, tucked in the back, a medic hovering over an unconscious Mace, Caleb passed out and Reid . . . fuck, Reid had been so still. When he'd first seen his best friend and teammate, Kell had been sure he was dead, lying facedown on the dirty floor.

He'd picked the man up and felt the warmth of his body—an unnatural heat of fever or infection, but it still meant life.

It wasn't until they started to strip Reid on the chopper to look for wounds that Kell saw the swollen bite marks on his calf from the poisonous snake. That bite had ultimately, ironically, saved his life.

Learning he'd fucked up and gotten made had chilled Kell to the bone. Now the remnants of his mistake surrounded him—dead and broken and none of them would ever be the same again.

His conscience ached as he visited them in the hospital, one by one before he left to smoke out the missing DMH kidnappers and any other men in the organization who'd been left alive to rebuild.

Mace's eyes were open, although he couldn't talk yet. He would live, thanks to Caleb's quick thinking. They would later discover that the rescue attempt caused the DMH men to try to kill Mace at that moment.

Another scar on his conscience.

Caleb was also awake but confused, the memories wiped from him as seemingly easily as shaking an Etch A Sketch.

Kell had almost bypassed Reid's room. Reid would see right through him, would know how he felt.

The worst part was, he would understand.

Kell didn't want forgiveness. Didn't want his conscience to pulse with the white hot throb of a heartbeat. But he opened the door to his friend's room, he forced one foot in front of the other until he was next to Reid's bedside.

Reid had just been told about Gray's death—their CO had taken on that burden. Soon, the three remaining operatives would be transferred to Germany before going back to the States.

"They knew you were coming, because of me," Kell told Reid bluntly. "Gray's dead because of me."

There was no blame in his friend's eyes at all. But the guilt settled on Kell the way it had from the second their CO, Noah Wright, explained that the DMH had chased them down purposely because of Kell's assassination of one of their most influential members.

And even though Reid asked him to stay, Kell refused, didn't make the trip to Germany with the men. No, he left Reid that afternoon and lost himself in Sierra Leone and beyond, tracking anyone who had even the remotest association with DMH, hunting, burning down, killing anyone and anything to assuage the guilt until the only place he felt comfortable . . . normal . . . was in the jungle, alone.

He hated himself for it, despised what he'd become. And three months later, he'd come out of the jungle with great reluctance—and mainly because Reid had asked again.

He wasn't ready for this, didn't want to be dragged back into society or into this woman's problems.

He was back, with both feet in, and Reid and the others relying on him to not fuck up, and he didn't like it at all.

Reid, who'd been watching him intently, no doubt knew Kell had just gone down memory lane. "Welcome back," his friend said with a small smile.

"I don't want to do this, Reid."

"So we'll turn her in and get out of Mexico."

His friend was saying all the right things and that was exactly what they should be doing, but . . .

He'd already smelled her fear, understood her desperation. He'd been there for so long himself.

"You're invested in this woman," Reid said finally, after a long moment of silence.

"What the hell do you want from me?" Kell asked, all the while knowing the answer to that.

Reid wanted Kell to be the way he was before all this shit started.

If Kell had stayed away, he probably never would've found his way back . . . and that would've been fine by him.

"Kell, come on, man, this is me you're talking to."

But Reid and Kell hadn't done much talking at all lately, beyond mission planning and banter, because all that was at least familiar, if not easy.

It hadn't been easy from the first moment he'd walked back into Mace's bar and agreed to work with Dylan as a merc.

Before that, he'd been gone for three months, intent on his personal mission of revenge. He'd returned only after finding the DMH kidnappers, with Caleb's guidance as to where he'd buried them. And then he stayed close to home, traveling between his place in North Carolina and Mace's for the next six months because he hadn't felt ready to return to anything more strenuous. During that time, he'd felt horribly removed from everyone and everything. This disconnect hadn't been lost on Reid—but thankfully he'd known Kell long enough to let his friend pull out of it on his own.

And Kell had, in a small sense, by coming out of the jungle and going to Mace's house in the Catskills.

Meeting his team, deciding he was done with the old and ready to dive into the new.

But he wasn't. The teamwork, saving innocent people when he'd failed to save his own team.

"You shouldn't count on me," he'd told Reid, who in turn had told him to "shut the fuck up."

"I don't think I can do this," he'd told Dylan earlier that afternoon when he'd first showed at the bar after months of being away.

"Then why are you here?"

Because he still had some semblance of humanity left, something he couldn't erase completely. Something Dylan seemed determined to bring back to him before it was too late.

"You stay out there alone, after a while you lose yourself," Dylan said.

"You stayed out," Kell pointed out.

"I came back just in time."

Kell wasn't sure he had—the look in Reid's eye when he'd returned haunted him. His friend took his absence as a personal affront and Kell hadn't fully regained his trust. And although they still worked together like a well-oiled machine, Kell knew it would be a long time before Reid stopped expecting him to disappear again without a word.

"Go if you want," Reid said irritably as he settled in on his own cot in the back room of Mace's bar.

And Kell had simply unfolded his cot and slept, because he owed his best friend at least that, and so much more.

Beyond that, his actions against DMH had nearly gotten his best friend and teammates killed, although Reid always called bullshit on that.

"Any of us would've done the same thing, given the opportunity," he would argue.

"You'd have made sure you didn't get made," Kell would shoot back. DMH had traced him, probably ended up knowing more about him than Delta did.

The damage had been done. Whether or not he was beyond repair remained to be seen.

All of this would be so much easier without a conscience. And yet he'd never been able to push his down for long. After a while, Kell would simply pretend that none of it bothered him, because things went much easier on him when he did.

"I fucked up, Reid."

"It could've happened to any of us."

"But it didn't."

"You've done everything you could over the past months to make up for it, even though you didn't need to."

It hadn't helped. It scared the hell out of him to look back and see that he was becoming, someone he—and Reid—didn't recognize. "I can't do this, Reid. Can't risk fucking up again."

"You walked away from me. You're trying to do it again without giving me a goddamned chance to help you." Reid paused. "You haven't lost your edge, Kell."

"Maybe I want to."

"And what? Move to a log cabin in the woods and take up fly-fishing?

"I have a conscience, but I know what it's like to bury it. I thought I'd have to live my life that way. And after DMH—even before—I was like a fucking machine. I don't want to do the job anymore."

Reid could understand but he wasn't done . . . he had more to do, to make up for.

"We've been doing this a long time. Nine lives, guardian angels . . ." Kell said.

"You think our luck's running out?"

"You think we're lucky?" Kell responded and Reid snorted. "I feel like the walls are closing in. And here we thought Teddie was bringing the danger to us. Looks like she's as screwed with us as she is without us."

"Maybe she'll want to go back to the marshals," Reid said. "She's scared shitless of us."

It was true, but for reasons he couldn't yet explain, Kell knew that Teddie belonged with him. For now, he'd comfort himself with the fact that he'd managed to keep her safe this long.

Yet, they were both hunted. And if he and Reid continued to help her, they'd open themselves up to even more trouble.

Reid wanted to alternately punch his friend square in the jaw and hug him, and fuck it all, Dylan had warned him that Kell's transition back to the land of the living wouldn't be easy.

But shit, Reid hadn't had an easy time of it either. Typically, Kell was there to pick up the pieces, and this time no one had.

Most of those pieces were still scattered for him. He remembered the food poisoning, being dragged from the hotel into the van and waking up in the darkness of the cell.

He'd been halfway to breaking out when the puff

adder got him in the calf, where he still had a scar that ached most of the time. After that, it was all a big blank until Kell gave him the antidote on the chopper and he woke up to find he'd been to hell and back.

Mace's throat healed with some vocal cord damage. He would've been cleared medically if he'd wanted to be, but he hadn't. Caleb's memories had come back; a mixed blessing, as he would no doubt always be as haunted as the rest of them.

But still, they'd gotten some closure.

For Reid, his life was an endless cycle of escaping in death-defying ways and leaving behind others who weren't so lucky. "I'm trying to go easy on you, bro, but I don't like what's going on here."

"I know you're still pissed at me."

Well, yeah, that was true, but Reid was pretty sure he'd get over it. Eventually.

"I stayed away because—"

"Don't go there, Kell."

Kell turned from him and Reid sighed as the wall went up between them again, a barrier that fourteen years ago hadn't been there after a mere seventy-two hours of knowing each other.

Kell hadn't wanted to talk about any what had happened with DMH. And so Reid shut down a little more himself and waited his friend out, but that seemed to close Kell off more.

But his reaction to this Teddie chick—that was interesting, to say the least. Reid would roll with it because if this woman could bring Kell's soul back, Reid would be grateful as hell.

He and Kell had had brief relationships over the

years, mainly for the sex, as neither man was in any one place long enough to make things work. Truth be told, Reid hadn't been all that interested in making anything work. Neither had Kell, and that's why the connection between his friend and Teddie fascinated and confused Reid. He could see the way they were circling each other.

Even though Teddie was scared of Kell, she couldn't look away.

There were even bigger problems on Reid's mind now, though. Something else was going on: Vivi was fielding all their calls—including his earlier one after they'd completed the mission—and there was nary a word from Dylan himself.

"I'm going for a swim," Reid announced to Kell, who just stared at him. "What? I'm not letting a heated pool go to waste."

Kell didn't try to stop him and Reid stripped as he walked outside into the cooler air. The gates were high here and the nearest neighbors' houses were also vacation homes—deserted ones.

Naked, he dove into the warm water, did a few laps to burn off some of the tension and realized if he wanted more relaxation, he'd need to literally swim through the entire night.

So he paused and rested his arms on the decorative concrete around the edge, and thought about what the hell he was actually still doing out here in the first place. Because they had completed an important mission, and because keeping Kell's head on straight was the hardest thing about working with him these days.

He was risking a lot with the black ops missions in

the first place, knew it and didn't give a shit. He owed the Army another six months of service and then he was done. He'd stick with Dylan, do black ops until he was ready to retire.

You'll be fine if Kell leaves.

Not that he was particularly fine before meeting Kell, but Reid knew things now. And it's not like he hadn't been solo on missions before. Calling him capable was severely underestimating him.

To be honest, if Kell dropped out of the game, it would be something of a relief. Because Reid had been waiting for the other shoe to drop, for Kell to be taken from his life the way anyone who got close to Reid seemed to be.

So yes, better for Kell.

Shit, he couldn't keep his mind off the swirling mess of memories that threatened to envelope him. It rarely caught up with him this badly; the circumstances over the past few months were definitely to blame.

His life had been very much about loss, but he'd been lucky to find the group of people he had. Losing Gray, his teammate and friend, while he himself was lying unconscious in a cell—thanks to a snake bite— and his whole team was being tortured around him . . . well, some days, some hours, it was just too much.

Sometimes, he could still hear the screams of his parents, his brother and sisters. Could feel the fireman's strong arms hoist him up and out of the house through the thick smoke that burned his lungs and made breathing nearly impossible. Those same arms stopped him from going back inside for the rest of his family, even as the house collapsed onto itself, killing everyone left inside.

He'd never forgive that fireman for saving him. It was a ridiculous sentiment, he knew, but if only he'd died that night . . .

Ah, fuck it. The guilt would be the death of him.

Reid had picked up skills quickly in the orphanage he'd been placed in as a temporary measure. He was fourteen and as he was shifted from one temporary place to the next, he'd learned as much as he could about the art of thieving and survival.

He'd never had to worry about those things in his old life. But that life was dead and buried, along with his family. And if he couldn't be with them, he didn't want any part of anyone else's family.

The six-foot-one football player with all-American, blond-haired, blue-eyed good looks could've had a shot at a good family, despite his age. But his new-found aptitude for theft and snarly attitude toward anyone or anything that looked like help put an immediate stop to that.

He'd made sure of it.

The first house he was placed in, he locked himself in his room, cut the electricity because he'd just learned how, stole money from the mom's purse and snuck out the window.

He was back in foster care within three days.

There were the psychologists, the doctors, the nice people in the foster care system who tried to tell him that good behavior was his best friend.

He wanted to tell them that there was no way he could do that, that it just hurt too damned much inside. That he was pretty sure the pain would never subside and that he didn't think he'd ever be able to hang on to anything good ever again. And so he'd promised himself that he'd never really try.

Now he was really trying. He climbed out of the pool, dried off and stayed out by the pool in the dark, readying his weapons. He'd wait the night for Kell to let him know if they were leaving Teddie behind . . . or if Kell was simply leaving altogether.

CHAPTER
6

Reid came inside long enough to tell Kell he'd take the first shift watching the house. Kell didn't sleep particularly well at all, although he noted Teddie had no problem in that area.

He switched off with Reid a couple of hours earlier than he was supposed to; Reid didn't argue, just went inside muttering under his breath, which Kell knew was aimed at him.

They wouldn't leave the house again until nightfall, and it was only six in the morning. This particular place had a pretty detailed security system setup, including cameras that caught the roads surrounding the property, so score one for Reid.

He prowled the house restlessly, unable to stop his mind from running scenarios that made his head throb. He'd cleaned his cuts and taken ibuprofen for the other aches and pains he'd gotten in the alley . . . and made a promise to himself to get his shit together.

When his phone rang, he was eager for the distraction. He glanced at the screen before answering and saw it was Vivi.

"Tell me you've got some good shit for me," he said, not doubting that Vivi had worked through the night.

"I've got a few addresses on the GPS—restaurants, stores, a motel in Juarez. Other than that, it's brand spanking new, bought a week ago," Vivi said. "The men who attacked you are hired guns—mostly low-level stuff."

"How did they get that intel about me, then?" Kell asked, more to himself than her. He'd known for sure that the men hadn't been at the top of their game.

Sending them after him had been akin to murder. Whoever employed them had been on a fact-finding mission, and Kell had no doubt given them what they wanted. When the men didn't return, their employer must've guessed that they'd found Kell, and Reid, by association.

If not for Teddie, they'd be out of Mexico and well hidden somewhere in the States. "Anything on Samuel Chambers or the men who killed Teddie's family?"

"McMannus's a wanted man, for sure—he's being looked into for the murder of Teddie's father because of her eyewitness statement. Samuel Chambers was investigated as a possible accomplice to the crime because of his close friendship with Teddie's father, but he was cleared."

"Why?"

"I haven't gotten that far yet."

"But McMannus's mercing, not CIA."

"Appears to be. Chambers was part of the diplomatic community until about ten years ago. Then he retired. He's had a place in Mexico for years, mainly a vacation home, since his passport shows he continues to travel most of the time. I've got an address for you. His bank account's not anything impressive and his record's been clean until now," Vivi said, but they both knew that meant nothing. "I'm checking for hidden bank accounts."

He wondered if Teddie knew what Chambers was involved with and decided he needed to find out immediately. After he got the rest of the intel.

He headed for the room where Reid was sleeping. His friend woke up as the door opened and Kell put the phone on speaker so Vivi could relay her information to both men.

"I also managed to get into the marshals' database, and yes, they're actively looking for Teddie. Not just because she escaped witness protection. There are other reasons. She wasn't lying about being in the restaurant or about shooting someone," Vivi said. "She shot two men—one at point-blank range and the other . . . witnesses say it looked like she tried to take him hostage and then she pushed him away and shot him instead. Someone videotaped it on their cell phone."

Kell blinked. "Sure they don't have that mixed up?" he asked, even though he knew they didn't. Because he'd known she was hiding something, and he couldn't fucking wait to hear her explanation.

"After the other guys came in, she got spooked,

shot the hostage in the shoulder in order to make her escape," Vivi continued.

"So the marshals and the local police are after her, not to mention McMannus," Kell muttered.

Reid shrugged. "She's in a hell of a lot of trouble."

"So are we, if we're caught with her." Kell checked down the hall into the den where Teddie was still curled up on the couch.

"I'll call back with any updates," Vivi said before hanging up. Kell did the same as Reid rolled off the bed and stretched.

"You'd better get some answers," he told Kell.

"Why me?"

"You're the one who seems to like kissing her," Reid commented, and Kell fought a strong urge to punch the shit out of him for guessing that correctly.

"We've got an address for Chambers," he said instead.

"Sounds like he had something to do with Teddie's father's murder . . . and that she suspected that, according to what Vivi says about witness's evidence, right?"

"Teddie told me herself she met Chambers in the restaurant." Kell looked grim as he glanced toward the couch. Teddie was sleeping restlessly now, her long, bare legs tangled in the blanket Kell had gotten her from a closet.

"Either way, she's in deep shit," Reid commented.

But they were in deep shit too, and were they shouldering Teddie's burdens now? "What the hell is going on here?"

"I could take a run by Chambers's place when it

gets dark," Reid offered. "And you can question the hell out of her before we make any decisions."

"You want to turn her over to the marshals and watch her rot in a Mexican prison?"

"No, that's not what I want." Reid turned to face him. "But you need to decide what the fuck it is you want."

"You think I'm going to bolt, leave you behind again and not take your calls." Because he'd done it before.

"Yeah, I do. I've been waiting for it for the past week," Reid admitted.

Reid always did know him better than anyone. "I'm not going anywhere for now. But after this . . ."

"We'll talk about it then, okay?" Reid cut him off, and Kell nodded.

When night fell, Reid went to Chambers's house, said he'd pick up a ride along the way. Kell told him to keep in touch and then paced a hole in the floor waiting for a call. Teddie had gotten up once to eat something and then went back to the couch, the past days obviously taking a toll on her, and goddamn, what the hell was he doing here, with her?

The old Kell would've called the marshals to pick her ass up, no matter how pretty she was.

She's not here because of her looks.

And, if he was honest with himself, the old Kell would've had second thoughts on calling the marshals on her too. But the past was such an easy thing to rewrite at a time like this.

Finally, after an hour, Reid called.

"I'm outside Chambers's house," he said.

"And?"

"He's got a bandage and a sling on his arm," Reid said. "And a hell of a lot of security."

So the eyewitness reports must've been correct—she had shot two men, not one, and she'd conveniently forgotten to tell him. "What's Teddie's game?" he muttered, more to himself than Reid, but his friend responded anyway.

"The real question is, how far do you plan on taking this?"

Kell rubbed at the tension in his forehead but it did no good. "I'm going to talk to her now—I'm bringing her to Chambers's for a little truth or dare scare tactic, so stay put."

"And then?"

"If I believe her . . . I'm going to help her."

When Kell didn't say anything else, Reid gave a soft, *what the fuck?* whistle but he didn't say another word about that, asked instead, "Want me to head inside and have a look around? Chambers's going into the shower—I'll have a small window of opportunity."

It would be for the best. "Don't get caught."

"Fuck you. And don't take too long to get to me," Reid admonished, and Kell hung up and went to rouse Teddie. He handed her some soda when she sat up and rubbed the sleep from her eyes, and she muttered something about being hungry.

She went to the kitchen and rifled through the fridge. She made a sandwich while Kell watched her, and she sat and ate looking out the window, as if wanting to avoid both his gaze and his conversation.

"Where's Reid?" she asked finally, but he didn't answer her question.

"Tell me more about Samuel Chambers. How and when did you contact him?"

"I tracked down his number through another family friend in the diplomatic community—I wasn't supposed to be in contact with anyone, but there were people who remembered me . . . they felt sorry about what happened. They thought Samuel would want to help. And so I called him about a week ago."

"When you called him, what did he say?"

"He was freaked," she admitted, looking resigned to having this discussion. "He asked me not to share his address with the marshals."

"And you didn't find that odd?"

"I know better than anyone that diplomats make a lot of enemies." She pushed her plate away from her. "Look, I get it. You think this was a really stupid thing for me to do, coming to Mexico on my own to see Samuel. And it was—I admit it, okay? But I was very short on options. No one was trying to bring the men who killed my family to justice."

"How do you know that?"

"I couldn't get any answers from the marshals and Samuel himself confirmed it, told me there hadn't been any new leads on the case. He said he'd been looking into it as well. Don't you see—he had leads and that's why the mercenaries were following him."

More lies, but he went with it. "Did he say he was being followed or threatened?"

She shook her head. "We didn't talk on the phone long. He told me he had info, that it wasn't safe to talk on an unsecured line, that I should meet him at the restaurant." She paused. "If a marshal had been with me, he might've been killed."

"If a marshal had been with you, you'd never have been allowed to go." He paused. "Why the restaurant and not his house?"

"He said it was safer for me."

And the song remains the same. "But it wasn't."

"No."

"So according to you, the mercs came into the restaurant and started shooting and you just left Chambers and shot at the mercs and then ran?"

"Samuel was shot. I saw him go down and I thought . . ." she trailed off, as if not wanting to tell the rest of the lie, because she knew Chambers wasn't dead.

Kell stared at her as if willing something close to the truth to spill out. She wasn't completely lying, though—just not telling the whole story.

And although she was doing a hell of a job, he knew the lies were beginning to trap her. She didn't let on, still appeared a little shell shocked from the earlier incident in the alley. She was looking at him as he stood and walked toward her, gasped when he turned her chair roughly to face him.

"Are you bullshitting me?" he demanded, and it was so easy to let the animal in him rise up, to forget that he was supposed to be calm and civilized at times like this.

It was so much better when he was alone with his weapons, his mind only on the mission. Women got in the way. More so when they were lying.

"I'm not."

"You are fucking with our lives here," he growled.

"Every bit of intel you give me needs to be the absolute truth or we could all die."

The harshness of his words broke through her tough exterior and the fear he'd seen in her eyes last night returned.

Good.

Even though it made him wince internally. Also good.

"You think I've been lying to you?"

"Yes," he told her bluntly, and instead of getting angry, she nodded.

"I don't know how else to make you believe I had nothing to do with these men. And I certainly had nothing to do with the murder of my family—my God, who would do something like that?"

He didn't want to tell her that money and revenge did strange things to people.

"I had nothing to do with the murder of my family," she repeated when he said nothing.

"But you were left alive."

"And I live with that guilt every day," she said fiercely. "Do you have any idea what that's like?"

He did, but he sure as hell wasn't telling her that. "Come on," he said, then walked over and opened the door leading to the garage.

"Where did Reid go?" she asked again, more warily this time—and that's right, keep her off balance. She was ready to spill, and when she saw what he planned on showing her, she would.

"Come on." His voice was impatient. She followed him, let herself into the passenger's side of the truck, and for a long moment he thought about cuffing her but decided against it. For now. But he had them in his pocket, just in case.

They rode in silence. He knew Chambers's house was twenty minutes away, thanks to the stolen GPS system now sitting on the dash of the truck.

When they drove up the steep hill that allowed them to look down on Chambers's house, Kell cut the lights and the engine and looked through a pair of binoculars before handing them to Teddie.

"What are these for?"

"Look into the lower windows," he said.

"What's this about?" she asked as she brought the binoculars up to her eyes and trained them where Kell had directed.

When she stopped cold, he knew he didn't have to answer her, but he did anyway.

"It's about the truth," he said. "Maybe you want to knock on the door, say hello. Apologize for trying to kill him."

She looked into the window for a long moment, completely silent, her body language not changing. And then, finally, she lowered the binoculars to her lap and turned to look at him. "If I'd wanted Samuel dead, he would be. I had plenty of opportunity."

"Since you're such an amazing one-woman show, maybe I should just leave you here to fend for yourself."

She didn't answer, but when he leaned across her to push open her door, she was most definitely surprised.

"Go," he told her. And he wasn't kidding.

———

Could she call his bluff?

When Teddie looked into his eyes, she caught a flicker of the dangerous beast that lay underneath. Well hidden and ready to strike. She had a feeling it was the end of the line for her evasiveness. She'd pushed it too far already, and it was as stupid as prodding a sleeping lion.

She pulled the truck's door closed. "We shouldn't stick around here long. I'm sure he has surveillance."

"We need to wait for Reid. But you have five seconds to start talking or you're out."

"Reid's here?"

"Four seconds."

He wasn't kidding. "My father told me something about Samuel."

"Let me guess, the marshals don't have the info you're about to tell me?" Kell asked, and she did hate him right then, would hate him even more when he knew everything. She didn't doubt he would pull every last secret from her, and to think about bending like that made her ache in strange places.

She'd never told anyone what Samuel had tried to do to her when she was just seventeen—the sexual assault she'd fought off—and she couldn't start there with Kell. It wouldn't provide proof of anything anyway. Instead, she'd admit why she really went to meet Samuel in the first place.

"My father told me not to say anything to anyone, that it was too dangerous, but he'd discovered that there was a rash of kidnappings of wealthy Americans for ransom that happened every time he moved to a new place for diplomatic service. He believed Samuel was actually masterminding the kidnappings.

And I think Samuel murdered my father because of it."

Kell punched the steering wheel and swore. "You think Chambers set up your father?"

"Yes. My father had believed for a while that it had to be someone in the diplomatic community aiding and abetting in the kidnappings of wealthy and influential Americans. Typically, they would register with the embassy in case they needed something."

"So someone who had that information would know when they'd be arriving."

"Right. And they were being kidnapped right from the airport—no signs of struggle, so it looked like they went with the kidnappers willingly. They probably thought they were getting into a waiting chauffeured car that would take them to their destination. It happened in the last three countries where my father worked. He felt targeted. He worried for our family. He suspected he was in danger and wasn't sure he was getting help from the authorities, because at that point, nothing had been done. The night after he told me, he was killed."

She blinked a few times but didn't cry.

"Why did your father think Chambers was behind the kidnappings?"

"My stepmother was having an affair with Samuel." She whispered it, but it didn't hurt any less to say it that way. "She was the leak."

"But you have no proof."

She knew about Samuel's manipulation of the women in her family—for her, that was enough. "My father had no reason to tell me all this, no reason to lie. Samuel and my father went to school together, with my mom. The three of them were extremely close." It made the betrayal that much worse, and her voice broke. But she swallowed the sob—she would not cry. Tears hadn't helped when her mother died or after her father was killed, and they would do nothing now but weaken her resolve. Weaken her.

"My father's killers needed to be brought to justice," she insisted.

Kell didn't look as convinced. "You're in deep shit, Teddie."

"Tell me something I don't know," she snapped. "What's Reid hoping to find?"

"Something that proves what you just told me."

"Yeah, I'm sure Samuel would just leave that evidence lying around." She crossed her arms and turned away from him, but Kell wasn't having that. He physically turned her back to face him, holding her by the shoulders.

"I don't understand what you were thinking."

"I was going to force Samuel to confess."

"You didn't think he'd bring the mercs in to get you?"

She had. But her plan had involved using Samuel's attraction to her, even though the thought repulsed her. "I had a plan," she said weakly.

"Your plan blew up in your face—and consequently, ours."

"Sorry that I'm not as experienced in covert operations, but I still managed to find out what I needed to. Because Samuel would never have called those mercs into the restaurant if he hadn't been involved with them—that was no coincidence."

"We've got a little more experience in shit like this

than you do, so you might want to give a little less lip and a little more thanks."

"Thanks? Thanks for what? When you made me strip down for you? Or when you got me involved in a fight that wasn't mine? This is your game, Kell, and I don't know how to play it."

"I don't know about that, Teddie. You've been playing it pretty well since the second we met."

"I'm not playing you," she insisted. "I'm saving my own ass, the way I've done since Mom died. I'm sorry if that doesn't suit your needs, but it sure as hell helps mine. I can't play the sad little victim for you—can't and won't. So do whatever you have to do to me; I can take it."

"You sure about that, honey?"

Kell's voice was gruff, his eyes wild, the way they'd been whenever things got heated between them.

"You're just pissed because you're attracted to me, because you felt something when you touched me," she told him, and she'd surely felt it, too. His fingers had practically seared her skin and she was both angry at him and left wanting more.

The heated anger had more than a slight edge of lust to it, on both their parts. And he was so close, his touch hot where his fingers brushed the bare skin on her neck where the too large borrowed T-shirt pushed off her shoulders.

She wanted more, but to give in now . . .

Kell didn't let her make that choice. He moved closer for just a moment and then he pulled away, broke the contact between them, but the sizzle didn't leave this time.

He was still too close yet she put her hands together

on the console between them as if prepared to move into his seat, his lap, and finish what he'd started.

And then the door opened and Reid popped his head in. "Sorry to interrupt this special moment, but we need to get the hell out of here."

"Fuck you," Kell muttered under his breath as he moved away from Teddie.

Still, Reid's timing couldn't have been more perfect. Without asking, Teddie moved into the back of the cab to let him sit next to Kell, and Reid stared between the two of them and shook his head.

Kell backed slowly down the slight embankment without starting the truck up and she said a silent prayer that they'd escape Samuel's notice.

Apparently, someone was heeding her prayers, because they got to the main road and beyond without incident. There was silence for most of the ride, beyond Kell and Reid talking in short bursts in acronyms she didn't really understand.

Within half an hour, they were back at the safe house—but their conversation was far from over.

R iley didn't ask about Crystal again until they got home. Dylan locked the door behind him and put on the security alarms and set the cameras, and yeah, this would take away any chance of a honeymoon for right now.

The last thing he wanted to do was talk about Crystal. "Can we enjoy our first week of married life without drama?"

"Apparently not," she mused. "And be honest, you wouldn't have it any other way."

Most of the time, that was true. Tonight, losing himself in Riley was all he had on the agenda. But Crystal's call had ruined all that.

How long had it been? At least five years since he'd seen him, ten since they'd first met, and at some point in there, Dylan recognized Crystal for the sociopath he was. Learned from him, screwed him over but good and then moved on.

Apparently, Crystal held a hell of a grudge.

Dylan was able to put Riley's questions off a little longer when a call came in from Vivi, who was checking in for Kell and Reid. He'd known she'd be giving the men intel, and hearing the plans for their next moves eased his mind slightly.

An earlier call from her had confirmed his worst fears. Kell had been attacked by men who knew his record, and in conjunction with Crystal's phone call, it was too big a coincidence to actually be one.

Crystal was working his magic and Dylan needed to conjure up some of his own.

It had been a long time since he'd had to play as dirty as he would have to with Crystal. But since he'd been taught by the man, he'd picked up more of his tricks than Crystal would like him to know.

"Okay, so," Dylan started, and then the alarms blared and both he and Riley had their weapons out and trained on Cam, who'd broken in—probably right after Dylan called him—and stood in the hallway, pissed as hell and prepared to help Dylan explain this shit to Riley, maybe, or maybe it was to kick Dylan's ass for not preparing for this eventuality.

"Should've fucking killed him when you had the

chance in Jakarta" were Cam's first words to him, and yeah, this was going to be a long night.

"Can we get this over with so I can consummate my marriage?" Dylan growled as he lowered his weapon, and Cam broke into a smile and then said, "No."

Riley said no at the same time and Dylan groaned and sank into the couch.

He noted that his new wife was still holding her weapon, and a little too close to him for comfort.

"He hasn't told me anything about Crystal," she told Cam, and proceeded to fill him in on the phone call she'd received.

"Why don't you tell her about how he nearly killed you—and when you got the upper hand, you let him walk?" Cam prodded.

"I didn't exactly let him walk," Dylan reminded him. He'd been hoping the Albanian Mafia could do the job for him.

"Start at the beginning, you two," Riley said with a hard knock of her palm on the table to focus them on her. Her ring made a noise and Cam looked between it and Dylan and made a *well, get to it* motion.

"John Crystal was my mentor," he started. "I did my first black ops mission with him. For him. And I liked everything about it. At that point, Crystal was an honorably discharged former Force Recon Marine. He was a few years older. Had a lot of contacts. Gave me enough money to keep Cael and Zane in good shape for a while. For a few years, things were fine, until his older sister was raped and then murdered by three men while we were on a job in Bosnia. He wasn't the same after that. He started playing God. Hell, he was probably always a sociopath. Maybe I was one step away myself—maybe we all are. But I was starting to realize I wasn't a team player."

Cam snorted and Dylan shot him a look.

"What? You had to come to that realization?" Cam asked, and Dylan ignored him. Damn, he'd been young. Hungry and so eager and Crystal had been a willing teacher, for a price. Crystal had a ton of contacts. Experience Dylan wanted. He'd promised Dylan the world, if Dylan would continue to work with him.

But, like Crystal himself, following orders was never in the cards for Dylan Scott. At least not for long. "I tried to just walk away, but he wouldn't have that. Instead, he set me up, told me he'd let the Albanian mob think I'd stolen three million dollars from them. He stole the money, of course, and was already halfway to pinning it on me and so I turned it around on him," Dylan admitted. "It forced him to go into hiding." Not before Crystal had confronted him, though.

"Should've killed him," Cam muttered again, and Riley was simply staring at him.

"He came back wrecked after his sister was killed."

"When an animal goes rabid, you put it down," Cam persisted.

"We're all one step away from that on any given day," Dylan said evenly. "Killing him then would've made me just like him, dammit."

"And turning him over to the Albanians wouldn't?" Riley asked softly, the way his conscience always did when he wondered if killing Crystal would've been more humane.

In those days, Dylan had been anything but. And so

he poured himself a Scotch before he answered Riley, albeit indirectly.

"It was a good life. Money. Women. Action. It was perfect for someone like me. I think even Caleb and Zane couldn't have held me back, especially once they were old enough to fend for themselves. The lure of that lifestyle—when you want it—can be the most seductive mistress in the world." He took a long swig of the Scotch, letting it burn a deliciously slow path to his belly. "I've hurt a lot of people. I'd like to think most of them deserved it. But I might've started to love my job a little too much. I started . . . no, I was an island. But you dragged me back, you and Cam and now . . ."

"Are you happy, Dylan?" Riley asked him quietly. "It's hard to leave that solitary life behind."

Riley had, easily, because she'd never really wanted it in the first place. Her life in the spy game had focused on revenge, and while she was good at what she did, having a better reason to do it suited her.

These days, when she helped people, she practically glowed.

"I'm happy, Riley—in a way I never thought I could be. But back then . . . I couldn't kill Crystal. I could see it in his eyes . . . I thought he deserved another chance. Everyone does."

Cam didn't say a word and neither did Riley, at first. And then she said, "Sometimes, they don't take the opportunity, no matter how good it is."

"That's why I'm not giving him another chance," Dylan said firmly. These days, he had everything to lose, had never before understood more than he did right now why spies hid their families.

With his brothers—both by blood and choice—Riley and the other women circling his orbit, he realized how vulnerable they all were.

He had to find a way to protect them.

"He's formidable and deadly," Dylan confirmed. "I have to be more so."

"You can't take this on by yourself."

"I brought it on by myself—I have to be the one to end it," Dylan told her. "Besides, he's not going to stop until he has me—he just plans on going through all of you first."

Crystal had called in a few favors, even ones he hadn't been owed, and played his theory that Kell and Reid were in Mexico, sent in to take out a gang leader turned drug lord. The information had been difficult to get, shrouded in mystery and rhetoric, but when the agent he'd been utilizing knocked on his door with a worried look on his face, Crystal knew he'd played his cards just right.

"I have an update on the men sent in to grab your targets." This guy was so young and earnest.

He'd never survive.

Crystal stepped aside and let the man into his house, which doubled as his office. "Tell me what you've learned."

"They're . . . missing."

This was no surprise to him, although he pretended it was. "Care to elaborate?"

"We're checking morgues and hospitals."

"Christ." Crystal scrubbed his face with his palms to hide his grin. He'd known from the start he'd have to work hard to get to Dylan Scott, that there was only one person capable of carrying out his plans.

"There's more," the young man continued. "Wires are reporting that Rivera and Cruz are dead." He spoke flatly, as if he wasn't sure if it was good news or not.

Crystal wasn't sure either, but the fact that his agent had a bead on Dylan's men showed him they weren't invincible.

The fact that he could get to Dylan's girl, even more so. The contact with Riley Sacadano had been enough to keep him smiling for a good, long while.

That little shit Dylan thought he could learn what he needed to and then throw Crystal away like a piece of garbage he no longer needed. Thought he could torture him by forcing him to run and hide from the Albanians and figured that he'd never surface again. But that wasn't the case at all, and Dylan was about to learn that Crystal wouldn't give up until he got even.

He was a very patient man when it came to revenge. Waiting until he'd been able to give the Albanians their money back—complete with interest—had taken time. But it was just as well, as now Dylan had a life in place—something he would not want to see destroyed—and that made getting revenge even sweeter.

Crystal would pull Dylan's life apart, brick by brick, and force him to watch.

The fact that Dylan's retreat still bothered Crystal these years later pissed him off the most.

Crystal had never been the touchy-feely type. Most of his life, that seemed to work against him, an ingrained fault always pointed out to him by girlfriends.

Until he'd found the military, that is. There, being a hard-ass worked very much in his favor.

Now, being self-employed, it was working even better.

He only had one real regret and he stared at her picture now. He hadn't thought his sister needed protection, and while she hadn't been killed by anyone he knew, she had been brutally murdered.

To this day, he'd been unable to bring those men to justice and it hadn't been for lack of trying. He could do most anything he set his mind to, hunt down some of the most wanted men in the world, but he hadn't been able to find the scum who'd raped his sister before killing her.

It haunted him, woke him out of semi-sound sleeps.

"I'm sorry," he whispered to the picture now. And then he put it away and stared at the photos that were spread out in front of him. Dylan Scott. Caleb Scott. Zane Scott. Mace Stevens. Kell Roberts. Reid Cormier.

It was hard to track Dylan and his friend, Cam, and Kell too, but Reid had been a bit easier to track because he was still in the military system, and Crystal had inroads to those files. And Reid's life story was an interesting one—he'd been able to pull some early records on the man, and he'd certainly discovered something that intrigued him.

He finally found his pound of flesh. So yes, Reid would be his first target, followed by Kell. In half an hour, he'd be on the last flight to El Paso.

By tomorrow, he'd be on his way to being the worst thing that had ever happened to the last two men on his list. If he wanted the job done right, it was time to do it himself.

"Sir, would you like me to continue to track down the missing men?" the agent asked Crystal.

"Too hard. Besides, there's going to be a third missing very soon," Crystal said, and when the man looked confused, Crystal leaned forward and wrapped his hands around his neck.

The kid slumped to the floor and Crystal hauled him over his shoulder and left the house with the body of the would-be agent who'd been just short of being a good enough protégé. None of them measured up anymore. None of them were willing to do whatever it took to be the best.

From this point on, he would do his own dirty work. After years of grudge work, it was finally time to have some fun.

CHAPTER
7

The drive home was quiet, save for Reid letting him know that he'd pulled some intel from Chambers's house, and that he hadn't been spotted. That was good—it would give them an advantage if Chambers thought Teddie was out there alone and scared.

Once inside the safe house, Teddie walked out to the balcony.

"I'll give you guys some time alone," Reid told him. "That's best."

"I'm going to call Vivi to give her the phone numbers I copped from inside Chambers's house. I also pulled some intel from the hard drive of the man's computer that Vivi can no doubt hack into, although none of it promises to clear Teddie's father," Reid said before retreating to the privacy of a closed room.

Kell had a really bad feeling about this. Any father

would want to protect his daughter from his faults—blaming the stepmom was an easy out.

Moreover, when all was said and done, Teddie was still hiding something. Something extremely personal, maybe something she wouldn't even admit to herself except in her darkest moments.

To push her now would do nothing but drive the confession inward. Besides, he had a feeling what she was holding on to would do nothing to alleviate or accelerate the danger of the current situation.

No, it was just a part of her overall emotional minefield. He just had to hope it wouldn't blow at the wrong time.

Teddie was a strange combination of take-no-bullshit and softness. She intrigued him, but he'd let her go her own way after all this was over.

He should've let Reid handle this. But it was too late for that now.

Teddie was out on the balcony overlooking the pool and he went out to her in order to finish what they'd started in the truck. He stood next to her, looking down at the pool and the lush plants surrounding it.

This place was paradise, so he wasn't sure why it felt like hell.

"I feel so trapped" was all she said.

He understood her desperation in a way she probably didn't herself. It was something he'd lived with on a daily basis, the knot in his stomach when his parents discussed a new con, one that could still form easily if he thought back to those days.

"You don't know what I'm dealing with."

"Bullshit, I don't. Stop fighting me. I'm the only chance you've got."

"Then I guess I'm out of luck."

"I never said that."

"I didn't want to kill Samuel," she admitted. "I was going to make him talk. And then everything got out of hand and I needed to get away. I knew my father hadn't been lying, and when those men who killed my family came into the restaurant and I saw it all with my own eyes, I knew I had my proof. But I still have to prove all this to the marshals."

"Teddie, this is something too big for you to handle alone."

She had no one left and nothing left to lose. "The way I've been living this past year is not really living."

"Having nothing to lose makes people do stupid things."

"And sometimes it helps you think a lot more clearly." The agitation that came with her earlier lies had burned off, leaving behind pure anger and frustration burning in its wake.

She was a beautiful girl who had been living a life involving lots of travel and perks. She'd been independent, living life on her own terms. Having all that come to a screeching halt in such a horrific manner would've shaken the strongest of people. But Teddie was still strong, still fighting.

Granted, he'd prefer she fight him a lot less, but you couldn't have everything.

"The marshals want me to continue hiding indefinitely. I don't want to spend the rest of my life like this."

He could understand that. Living in fear was really

no way at all to live, she was right about that. And he knew all too well what it was like to be shoved someplace without your consent. What it was like to have no way out.

But he also knew Teddie was trouble with a capital *T*, and he wasn't at all sure he was ready to handle it.

His body argued otherwise.

Soft skin under his fingers; she'd been wet through the lacy fabric when he'd searched her in the warehouse hideout and it had been all he could do not to fall to his knees in front of her and lick her until she came against his face.

"Please don't turn me in. I'll do whatever you ask," she told him softly, touched his cheek and moved closer to him. He turned, allowing her to do it, and she took full advantage, pressed her body to his.

She was goddamned trying to seduce him. And it would work if he let it. He wanted her lips on his, so when she moved against him, he didn't stop her—not physically anyway.

"You should never make an offer like that to someone you don't know."

She drew in a harsh breath but didn't back down. "You said I was safe with you."

She wasn't even close to being safe with him. Whether she was choosing to ignore that or had momentarily forgotten it in light of her confession regarding Chambers didn't matter. Kell burned for her and it had nothing to do with the heat. No, his body pulled to her . . . he wanted to strip her down to her bra and panties and finish what he'd started the other night.

And from the way she was looking at him, she wouldn't argue.

Kell had her backed to the balcony wall, yet wasn't touching her at all. Maybe six inches separated them and it was as if he radiated a force field that kept her pinned. Her knees trembled a little and she couldn't be sure if it was from fear or something else . . . that flare of desire that shot through her every time she was near him.

And she hadn't really been out of his sight for days.

"Your pulse is racing," he noted. She didn't answer. Couldn't. Because she wasn't sure a moan wouldn't escape. "What are you afraid of?"

Everything. You. But again, she couldn't trust herself to speak.

He moved, an infinitesimal amount, and she instinctively went to back up.

But there was nowhere to go. Her breath sounded harsh to her own ears and she fisted her hands at her sides, wondered how she could be so angry at someone and want him all at the same time.

He brought a hand up to her cheek, teased her earlobe with a finger then ran his thumb along her jawline. Her heart jumped, her nipples hardened . . . all her body's way of screaming at him to notice her.

And he had, judging by the fire she saw in his eyes.

"I've got to kiss you," he muttered.

And he did, his mouth unforgiving on hers. In response, her hands went to his face, touching lightly as if afraid to break the moment. His scruff was rough on her fingertips, his mouth hot, his tongue searching . . . teasing . . . tempting.

His hands were nowhere near as tentative as hers. They were under her shirt, playing with her nipples, and she melted, went wet between her legs.

Resistance had been futile from minute one with this man. If it had been a different time under different circumstances, she knew this attraction would still be there, because in spite of everything it was there now.

She shouldn't want to be in his arms, but that's the only place she did want to be.

Kell could take her right here. Probably would have too, if he didn't hear the not-so-subtle clearing of a throat and fought a combination groan and growl, with his mouth still on Teddie's.

He pulled back, noting the confusion in her eyes, and asked, "What's up, Reid?" without bothering to turn around.

Teddie put a hand to her mouth, her cheeks reddened.

"Not as much as what's up with you, *Kell*," was Reid's reply. "Dylan's on Skype, needs to talk to us both."

"Give me a minute, please?" he asked as Teddie continued to stare at him.

"Sure thing."

When he heard Reid walk away, he addressed Teddie. "I've got to go talk to Dylan."

"Who is he?"

"I work with him. He might have some information

we need about the men who are after you." He left out the part about investigating her. No need to piss her off when he had some of her trust.

"He knows about me?" The panicked look in her eyes had returned.

"Yes. He's on our side, okay?"

"Is he going to turn me in?"

Kell had no goddamned idea. "No, he's not. Come on inside."

But she pulled back from him. "I need some air. I think I'm going to go down and swim."

He started to shake his head but she pointed out, "It's gated. I'm not going anywhere. I get it, okay?"

It *was* heavily gated—she couldn't go anywhere unless she decided to scale twelve-foot walls. But still, "I don't think you get it at all." It was then that he pulled the picture she'd had in her bag out from his back pocket and held it up to her. "These men are mercs, like you said. One of them was American military."

"Do you know him?" She looked like she wanted to back away from him, but didn't. Couldn't, actually.

He pointed to McMannus and she shifted uneasily. "Not personally. His name's Connor McMannus. He was discharged on medical a few years back. An IED caught his Humvee in Iraq. He lost some fingers on his right hand, sight in his right eye."

She blinked. Took the picture and stared at it. "He was wearing long sleeves in the market, but . . ." She shook her head. "His vision. He could've seen me, should've. Makes sense now."

"Hard to compensate for that, especially in close

quarters," he said quietly, trying not to sound too soldierlike. Those close quarters found her family killed. "I know you're trying to reconcile me and Reid with these men. In some ways, I'm sure we're like them. But Reid and I—our friends—we don't murder innocent families," he said shortly.

"The men from the alley . . ."

"That had nothing to do with you and everything to do with us," Kell confirmed. "You're not safe with us, but you're not safe on your own either."

"Why are you telling me this now?"

"Because you need to make some hard decisions."

"I don't care about the danger. But I have no way to pay you," she admitted.

"But you're not going to give up searching?"

"How can I? Would you?"

He didn't answer that, not for a long time, because he wasn't sure of anything these days. "I can't make any promises longer than twenty-four hours at a time, and I sure as shit can't do anything for you if you lie to me again."

"That's fair."

Goddammit, she looked so sad and so strong all at once, and she took his rough hand in her soft one as she said, "Thanks," in a voice filled with more emotion than she'd previously shown.

Such a loaded word . . . such a loaded situation.

He didn't want her thanks, didn't want her depending on him, and why did she make him want to act like a freakin' hero?

He turned away and headed downstairs before he agreed to anything else, heard her follow him him until she got to the door to the pool. She went outside and he went into the kitchen, where Reid had the computer set up and was already talking with Dylan.

Kell pulled up a chair next to Reid. "Hey, D."

"Where's your girl?" Dylan asked.

"She's not—Forget it. Teddie's out by the pool."

"And her problems are screwing everything up."

Kell couldn't argue with that. He was tangled up in her, unwilling to extricate himself, and Dylan seemed to be all filled in on that regard.

Strangely enough, he wasn't trying to talk Kell out of it. "She's all alone," Kell said finally, avoiding Reid's gaze.

"And she's told you everything?" Dylan asked.

"Yes," Kell lied. Because she had—mostly. "She thinks her father was set up by Chambers. He's got to be in bed with the mercs who killed her family—they showed at the restaurant where she met with him.'

Reid nodded in confirmation. "Vivi got back to me with the numbers I found from Chambers's phone. They trace out to two of the men in the picture Teddie had. So he's definitely a part of all this."

"From what I could find out, the authorities believe Teddie's father was the mastermind behind a kidnapping ring," Dylan said without further hesitation. "It's probably the reason he got killed. He had access to the rich Americans traveling in and out of Khartoum. They think McMannus and the other two men were working for him and that they turned on him in the end."

"So nothing points to Chambers as his partner," Kell said, and Dylan shook his head.

"Nothing. Either Chambers covered well or Teddie's dad was behind it all. Maybe he just got greedy.

Or else he was on the verge of getting caught and the people he was working with decided to finish him off." They heard Dylan drumming his fingers on the table he was sitting at in his house in upstate New York. "You have to tell her—now."

"I know, D." He stared at his friend and then glanced at Reid, who remained silent, taking all the information in. "She won't believe it. She'll want me to investigate it further."

"Gotta do what you gotta do." Dylan was cryptic as usual; he rarely gave an exacting answer unless they were on a job. Then he was precise, the way they all needed to be.

Everything else was a gray area, and Kell had been swimming upstream in the gray for most of his life.

Dylan continued, "I contacted the Mexican police station earlier—have a contact there who gave me some more intel. Found out that Chambers told them Teddie was on drugs and she'd come to him for help in kicking a coke problem. Said he was as surprised as anyone when she shot him. There's video from inside the restaurant and a few people came forward after catching the action on their cell phones."

"So he's not pressing charges?" Kell asked, and Dylan shook his head. "That doesn't mean he's going to leave Teddie alone."

"Is helping her something you're both comfortable with?" Dylan asked, and Reid shrugged.

"Don't act like you don't have a choice," Kell told him.

"Do I?"

"You two need to work your shit out, and fast, or I won't send you out together again," Dylan said.

"You might not have to worry about sending Kell out again ever," Reid said, and Dylan focused on Kell.

"Something to tell me?"

"No." Kell's jaw clamped tight after he ground out the word.

He knew what Reid was doing—trying to force his hand, press him into making a decision about whether he was staying or going.

Reid's way of saying, *If you're staying, get your fucking head in the game.*

No, he wasn't being fair to his friend, and that hadn't happened before Teddie appeared on the scene. "If you're not into this . . ." Dylan continued.

"I'll make sure you're not the last to know," Kell said, which could easily earn him a right hook from Dylan if they were in person.

But the man let it go without seeming ruffled at all. "Fix this," he told them, ran his hand through his hair as he spoke. "All of it. I don't give a shit how, just do it."

For the first time, Kell noticed that Dylan was wearing a wedding band. "That for cover?"

Dylan held up his hand and stared at it, used his other hand to roll the band around. "No."

Both Kell and Reid stared at him until he finally admitted, "Riley and I got married today."

"Well, that's something I thought I'd never see," Reid commented.

"Me hitched?"

"You finding a woman willing to put up with your ass for a lifetime. Now, what else? You didn't have to see us on Skype to tell us about Teddie's father, or your marriage."

Reid never minced words. But Dylan never talked before he was ready.

"What the hell's up with the house I saw you bought?" Dylan asked, then took a long sip of the beer. "You'd better be able to sell the place fast."

"It's a great safe house under a dummy corporation."

"We don't need one with a hot tub."

"Speak for yourself."

Dylan muttered a few curses and then said, "Someone's been running our names. I had Vivi do some checking. She came up with a few possibilities, but then the guy came forward and made it very clear who he was and what he wanted."

Dylan looked so damned serious and both men instinctively stilled, listened intently as their friend and mentor told them about his own onetime mentor, a man named John Crystal, who'd come back to haunt Dylan, and probably his friends.

That type always made for the worst kind of enemy, and Dylan looked wrecked as he told them about Crystal's sister, which appeared to have been his undoing, and then the three-million-dollar screw job that got Crystal in trouble with the Albanian Mafia.

"We've got a problem. It's mine, but unfortunately it's spilling over and I'd do anything to be able to tell you this in person. I don't want you dragged into my shit, but it can't be helped. Crystal's come out of hiding and he's evidently been watching me. Apparently, he pulled my credit card statements last month and found I'd purchased a ring. He made his contact through Riley. He waited until my life was as close to perfect as it's ever been, and it's going to be his joy to take it all away from me."

"We won't let that happen," Reid said fiercely. "What's his ultimate game?"

"He wants to take that money out of my hide, literally," Dylan explained. "Even if I paid him, it wouldn't be enough. He wants my debt in blood, he wants me to suffer. I don't live my life any differently because I have an enemy, but I've already put you both in danger and I don't want to risk leading Crystal to your new house. He's already tracked you to Mexico somehow. I have no doubt he sent those men in the alley."

"Shit," Kell muttered, ran a hand through his hair.

Dylan looked frustrated as hell. "He's playing cat and mouse. His favorite game. Crystal does it by using psy-op moves. He'll comb your background looking for any kind of angle he can use to persuade you to do jobs for him—he used to like playing judge and jury, and no doubt he's come even more unhinged during his forced isolation. He also finds out what makes you tick and uses that to fuck with you." He pointed at Kell. "I think that makes you a prime target. If I'm right, he might've already talked to your parents."

"Can we take him out, or does he have safeguards in place?" Kell asked, because a man like that sounded like he'd have things set up to continue to haunt Dylan in case Crystal was killed before his job was done.

"I don't know who he's working with, but I'm assuming he does."

"So we capture him, then," Reid said. "Save him for you."

"I'm going to make sure I'm the one who finds him first. You guys need to get the girl across the border any way you can and figure her problem out from a safer place. We're dealing with two separate shitloads of trouble and I'm not happy about either scenario."

Kell felt sick instead of that usual rush of adrenaline at the threat of danger. Dylan looked grim and Kell knew that leaving the team wasn't an option now. "We're with you, D. You know that."

"We all have a past. Figured you weren't a Boy Scout, and we don't run from shit like that," Reid said, and Kell knew it wasn't a dig at him at all, just an honest statement of their code.

Dylan didn't smile, didn't curse either. "Time to close ranks" was all he said, with a nod. "Take care of yourselves. Stay in touch."

He turned his monitor off and Kell knew it was serious as hell, because Dylan was not the type to give news like this over a computer screen.

But the plan was in place. The men would remain scattered, with Mace and Caleb together with Sky and Vivi and Paige, and Dylan with Riley and Cam, and Kell with Reid. They'd decided months ago that this would be the best solution when a major threat hit them.

And Crystal was bigger than a major threat.

When Kell turned off their screen, Reid looked pointedly at him, "You get how dangerous she is, right?"

"Yes." He wanted to help her anyway, would live on the edge for her, because it felt right. "You don't trust me?"

"No, you don't trust you," Reid seethed. "Look, fuck her or don't, but find me some reason we can trust her."

He stormed away from Kell, and Kell stared up at the ceiling and then decided to go check on Teddie and—if possible—find what Reid was asking for.

He walked upstairs, rather than heading straight outside, and looked out the sliding glass doors, to see her sitting on the edge of the pool with her legs in the water. He wanted to join her, couldn't for so many reasons, chief among them that breaking the news that there appeared to be strong proof her father had been in charge of the kidnapping schemes and was pushing the blame on others would ruin any mood. She'd never believe it anyway. Actually, at this point, he didn't either.

Instead of going to the pool, he took a shower, tried to keep his mind off her and failed miserably. Used Reid's iPad to search for photographs she'd shot before she'd taken a leave from the business to recover from the loss of her family.

At least that's what the statement that witness protection made her release before she went into hiding.

They'd left an opening for her to slip back into her old life—they hadn't killed her off. Explaining how you managed to come back from the dead was apparently a bitch and a half.

Her name and photographs were all over Google. He studied them. She was really good at what she did. There was heart and soul in there, passion.

There were some landscapes, but mainly faces. The children. All the pain, and still some of them were smiling.

It reminded him of Reid when the were younger—they had rarely been photographed but when they were, their eyes were so full of secrets, too old for their faces, so much so it was almost painful to see.

The photographs—some color, some black-and-white—were beautiful. Stark, stripped down, devoid of any subtlety. They were in your face, meant to make you start. She'd made it so they were hard to look at, but impossible to look away from.

A-fucking-mazing.

And she hadn't been able to touch a camera in a year. It must be killing her.

As she'd told him, her camera was as vital to her as a limb—it was the way she related to the world, to herself. Her comfort, her joy.

No wonder she was so completely lost.

He had no doubt that if she tried hard enough, she could see right through him.

He'd been lucky that she'd been distracted so far. But she wouldn't be forever.

Could he offer to let her see through him? See everything? He didn't even want to do that himself, and so he shook that thought off and slid outside to the balcony to check on her again. He wasn't expecting to find her swimming naked, the soft moonlight making the dark water look incandescent as she dove under again and again, moving from one side of the pool to the other. The water was dusky but the pool's interior lights illuminated the shape of her body better than the noon sun.

Holy Christ. It was a waste having her behind the camera. She should be in front of it, posing naked. For him.

Right now.

He gripped the balcony's railing, hard, rather than fist his cock.

She looked beautiful—perfect—and he watched the sleekness of her body, her wet hair break the surface, and wondered if she could feel him watching her.

She had to know one of them would be.

He stood there, letting himself get lulled into her peace.

What was it about her? She might still be hiding things about her life from him—and he was betting she was—but hell, he'd been lying to himself for years for survival. After all, that's what survivors did. They didn't ask themselves what they wanted from life, because it was a question they might never be able to fulfill.

What *did* he want from life?

He'd never asked himself that. It would be a long time until he got an answer, because he had no clue beyond *stay alive and keep moving,* not necessarily in that order.

When she'd come outside by the pool, Teddie had been both relieved that Kell had agreed to help her and angry that she needed his help. After letting her legs dangle in the water for a while, she stripped down and started swimming.

It was in the pool that all the grief and pain and guilt slid away, until it was only about the slight chill in the air, the smell of bougainvillea and the heated water welcoming her body. She dove under, swam as far as she could until she needed a breath. Broke the surface, the only sound the rippling of water and her soft laugh of delight.

That laugh reminded her of her old life and everything it had entailed.

The last time she'd gone swimming, she'd been on a shoot in the Amazon rain forest. She'd been called there to assist in a photo shoot with a well-known photographer whom she'd considered an idol. He'd been a bit of a prick, but still brilliant, and she'd gotten some wonderful shots—as well as amazing publicity from the deal.

Her room had been a private guesthouse with its own pool. After finishing up in the makeshift darkroom she'd created in the large bathroom— she still preferred the traditional method to digital photography—she'd stripped down and gone swimming, and she'd found peace, just like she did now.

Her old life had been about travel and adventure and helping others—she'd been wrapped up in her career and she'd thought she was completely happy with that.

Now she realized she'd been both fulfilled and lonely during those years and the profundity of that acknowledgment—and the fact that it took a tragedy to force her to admit it—made her sad.

And still Kell wouldn't rest until he'd pulled everything from her.

If she as honest with herself, she'd admit that might be a relief. Until it happened, though, it would simply keep her on edge.

When she glanced up at the balcony where she and Kell had kissed earlier, she saw a figure standing there.

Kell. She could tell by his stance. He was watching. Staring. Maybe thinking of the way he'd kissed her.

She wasn't used to being put on display like this. She was always the one behind the lens, ready to capture the picture, manipulate the space.

But she was the one being manipulated here, and she found herself liking it, wanted to give up control to this man.

He's as hurt as you.

Why had it taken her so long to see it? Tapping into people's emotions was crucial to her job. And if she thought about it, she'd clearly seen the vulnerability in his eyes, hidden well behind that stony glare, and she remembered the way his mouth felt against hers, the kiss welcoming and desperate all at once.

In response to that thought, she touched her lips. Thought about his touch on her body and wondered if he'd join her.

Wondered if maybe she should invite him.

But she'd courted enough danger for one night. And so she simply swam, content knowing that his eyes were on her.

CHAPTER
8

Grier spent the morning poring over Teddie's file. She started by looking at some gruesome pictures of the murder scene from Khartoum, then she read Teddie's interview.

Now she tapped her finger against the glossy print of the three men in the marketplace. Teddie had fingered them for the crime. She didn't have any leads on Teddie yet, and although it hadn't been more than seventy-two hours, a woman with no training of any sort shouldn't be able to give them the slip for long.

She hadn't used credit cards, touched her bank accounts or gotten in contact with anyone from her past as far as they could tell. If she'd made calls, it probably had been on a throwaway cell phone that was now long gone. And she had left behind almost everything in the small room she'd called home for the past year.

The room really sucked. And although she'd never met Teddie personally, Grier sat on her bed and imagined what things were like for her here.

Grier dealt more with fugitives than witness protection candidates, but she'd had enough experience with both to know there were many similarities between the two. Teddie straddled that line now. Whether or not she'd meant to shoot anyone was irrelevant. She had. And Grier needed to catch her.

The marshal who'd been in charge of Teddie's case was a fourteen-year veteran named Al, and he was pissed.

"She never gave any indication she'd run. She followed the same routine the entire time she was here," he told Grier now, having met her in Teddie's room.

"Phone calls?"

"A few here and there that came filtered through her manager. People begging her to come out of retirement. She hasn't touched a camera in a year."

"You got too comfortable with her. It made you sloppy," Grier told him. "She was gone twenty-four hours before you noticed."

"She's got no family, no real place to go," the marshal pointed out, trying to cover his ass.

Grier got it. Budgets were tight and they were all spread too thin. But this was a major fuckup, pure and simple, and it was all going to rain down on her head. It was time to start tracking Teddie, culling cell phone numbers from her records to see what they found. They'd tried to give her some privacy while the Khartoum authorities looked into the killing of her family.

Apparently, that wasn't going well, if at all. Teddie

was most likely frustrated, but she hadn't given any indication that she'd try taking matters into her own hands.

Grier mused on Khartoum's lack of progress on the drive back to the office, asked Jack to pull all Teddie's records so she could do a read-through in order to really get inside the woman's head.

She was in the process of doing so, emotions getting the best of her when she went over the details of Teddie's family's murders, just as Teddie's emotions would've taken *her* over, when she spotted someone heading toward the glass door of her office.

He didn't stop to knock.

The man was tall, with tawny-colored hair and amber eyes. The gaze and gait of a predator, albeit a very attractive one.

And he'd zeroed in on her.

How he'd simply been allowed to waltz through a restricted area was another story entirely, but she supposed he exuded a confidence that would've gotten him through easily enough with a military or law enforcement ID and a smile.

"I have some information you need on Teddie Lassiter's case," he said with no greeting.

Grier kept her voice and her expression neutral. "Why don't you have a seat and let me take some general information from you?"

His mouth quirked to one side. "I don't think so. I'd grab a pen and paper and start writing, because I'm only saying this once."

She didn't take her eyes off him as she pulled out a small notebook and pen from her back jeans pocket. "Go."

He gave her an address outside of Ciudad Juarez. "She's with two men—Kell Roberts and Reid Cormier—who are armed and dangerous."

"Mercenaries?"

"Worse. Military."

"Like you?"

There was that grin again. "No one's like me, sweetheart. And don't bother trying to follow me—you'll never get close enough to catch me . . . unless I want you to."

His dipped his head at her before he strode out like he didn't have a care in the world—or a reason why he'd given her this information.

Or an explanation of how he'd gotten it in the first place.

She motioned for Jack to follow him and then stared down at the address for a long moment before turning back to her computer to do some investigating.

Mexico had always been a haven for men and women looking to escape their old lives—for many different reasons, very few of them above the law. She didn't doubt the man who'd just left her office was one of them, or that she'd see him again, and too close to the address he'd given her for comfort.

Her cell rang—Jack's number. "Talk to me."

"I lost him." Jack sounded pissed, and impressed as hell.

"Come on back in. We're headed to Juarez."

"I take it we're not going on vacation."

"Not even close."

Teddie stayed in the pool until the skin on her fingers puckered and she began to shiver, despite the water's warmth. She wrapped her naked body in a towel and showered in the downstairs bathroom rather than parading through the house. She'd pushed her luck far too many times over the past days.

After her shower, she slipped on a puffy white robe that smelled freshly laundered and was folded on one of the shelves as she wondered who this house had belonged to previously.

She padded up the stairs on bare feet, her clothes in hand, until she found Kell, sitting on a bed in the first bedroom on the left, the one with the sliding glass door that overlooked the pool.

He glanced at her, heat in his eyes. "You can sleep here. I brought you some clothes to wear," he said, and she glanced at the black T-shirt and pants he'd laid out. "They're mine—they'll be way too big, but they're clean."

"No laundry service in this house?" she asked wryly.

"No laundry soap," he said. She'd wash her shirt and jeans out in the tub as best she could anyway, but for now, his T-shirt would do. She slid into the bathroom and pulled it on. It came to mid-thigh and she pulled the robe on over it forgoing the pants for now.

"Did you learn anything new from your friend?" she asked when she emerged.

"Yes." He didn't look happy about it.

"Just tell me."

He waited a beat and then said, "According to the CIA, they believe your father was the mastermind.

They were investigating both him and Chambers at the time of the murders and they weren't able to find anything on Chambers. That's why you're being offered protection, since you can identify the actual men who murdered your family, but the investigation is at a standstill beyond looking for them. They're still actively looking for the men, but only so they can't hurt you."

"They think he brought this on himself?"

"Our source—"

"Is wrong," she finished for him. "Look, I came to terms a long time ago with the fact that Samuel isn't who I thought he was. You will not take away my father from me like that. No way." It was the closest she'd come to revealing what Samuel had done to her when she was a teenager. And it was the closest she would, for now.

"I'm sorry, Teddie." He sounded like he really hated being the one to break this news to her.

"Please help me prove otherwise. Before McMannus finds me—or the marshals. Either way, I'll be dead, literally or figuratively."

He didn't argue with her last statement, just told her, "Chambers hasn't said anything to the police about you or why you tried to hurt him, beyond the fact that you were on drugs and he was trying to help you. He's saying you came to him for help kicking a cocaine habit. The marshals know what happened, thanks to video surveillance and eyewitness testimony, some of which was corroborated and captured on cell phones, but Chambers's not cooperating with them. He's refusing to press charges; still, that doesn't mean he's going to leave you alone."

"I can't let him get away with what he did."

"You also can't prove it." Kell's words were harsh but his tone wasn't. "Is there anything your father told you that you could verify through diplomatic authorities?"

"Suppose they're in on it?" She crossed her arms as though creating a shield, as if that would prevent whatever he told her from sticking, and then she could pretend it wasn't true. "I have no way of knowing if Samuel was working alone."

"The kidnappings happened in every country your father worked in over the last seven years," he said gently. "Can't say the same thing about Chambers."

"Samuel set him up."

Kell didn't say anything for a long moment. "That could be true, but it would be a hell of a thing to prove. Is this something else you already knew?"

"No, they never told me my father was a suspect in the kidnapping ring. Don't you see—Dad found out Samuel was using him and my stepmother and they were killed for that knowledge."

"Suppose your father was . . . is . . . guilty of this?"

"He still didn't deserve to die like that. And my stepmom and half sisters didn't either." She couldn't keep the bitter anger out of her tone. "I need to be alone for a while."

"Not going to happen."

"Please."

"You can turn the lights off. That's all I can give you."

"You let me outside all by myself."

"That was before Dylan shared this intel with us. Based on past and recent experience, combined with this new information, you must want to take on Chambers even more desperately now. I can't let you do it alone."

She didn't answer him, mainly because he was right, and she was tired of being as transparent as one of her photos.

Instead, she walked to the bed and switched off the lamp, bathing the room in darkness. With that being the only barrier between them, it felt strangely intimate to be in the room with him like this.

Would he stay the entire night, watching her sleep? *Yeah, like you'll sleep at all tonight.*

But everything was so much simpler in the dark, and even though she didn't want to talk to him, he didn't share the sentiment.

"Why'd your father take his family to some of the most dangerous places on earth?"

"He said somebody had to."

"You don't think he might've finally gotten frustrated? Realized they weren't paying him enough for shit like that?"

She took a deep breath so she didn't snap his head off when she answered. "That's not who he was, Kell. If you could've seen him, when he told me what he thought Samuel had done . . . the man was his best friend. It would be like finding out Reid betrayed you."

A pause, and then, "How'd you know Reid is my best friend?"

"It's pretty obvious." She smiled in the dark. "If I told you he'd betrayed you, you'd never believe it. You'd go to your grave trying to prove otherwise."

"So why wasn't your father taking that approach?"

"He said he had proof. He'd lost thirty pounds since I'd last seen him and he hadn't needed to diet. He was a mess."

Kell had to believe her. That was the most important thing right now. Someone had to believe her, because as much as she would do this alone if she had to, she knew her chances were slim to none that way.

Could someone who'd aroused the kind of feeling inside of her the way Kell had be that dangerous to her? Could he really hurt her?

She had the phone number to Al, her handler, and the means and opportunity to call him at any time. Neither Kell nor Reid was stopping her. "I could go to jail for shooting Samuel—especially if he decides to press charges. If the CIA has nothing on him, I just look like a crazy person out for revenge."

"You're a dangerous woman, Teddie," Kell said.

She hadn't thought about it like that, but she guessed—according to the marshals, at least—she was. "I don't feel that way. I feel like I'm making deals with the devil."

He snorted at that. "We're the lesser of two evils. I can promise you that."

She believed him, for no other reason than she was still alive. She pulled the blanket around her, leaned against the headboard and rubbed her temples. The peace from the swim and the shower following was long gone, replaced by a throbbing tension headache that tightened around her head like a band.

There was no possible way her father had anything to do with the murders. But she wondered if Samuel's bitterness over what had happened with her had anything to do with her family's deaths.

Had her father paid the price when Teddie refused Samuel? Is that when he began the kidnapping scheme?

The possibility was enough to make her physically ill.

She needed air. Water. Something.

She got out of bed, stumbled, went the wrong way, and Kell's arms were around her, both steadying and stopping her.

"What's wrong?" he asked.

"I don't feel well."

He brought her back to the bed. He'd been so close before; his kiss, his scent had lingered on her before her swim. It would now again and she didn't want that temptation. And so she pulled away, and he watched her as she wrapped herself in the blanket as if he'd been planning on ripping it away and taking what he wanted.

"If I'm so much trouble, why did you kiss me?" she asked.

"Because I wanted to. Why did you kiss me back?"

She hesitated, just long enough to come up with the lie. "You didn't give me any choice."

"Bullshit." His voice was tight and he was next to her in the dark, making her blood boil and heart pound. "Is it easier to give in that way? Because I can play pretend as well as the next guy," he murmured, a finger tracing along the side of her neck.

She shivered involuntarily. He chuckled. Her nipples hardened.

"Tell me you don't want to kiss me again. You don't want me to run my fingers over your nipples. They're hard and you're just thinking about it, right?"

She nearly touched them herself, that's how badly

they ached. "I didn't mean to accuse you of anything."

He pulled back. "Of course you did."

"You're doing all this on purpose, to keep me confused."

"And you're still holding something back. I'll know
what it is by the time this is all over."

She was hot and cold at the same time. Wanting his
touch. And still so very angry. "Go away."

"Not a chance." He paused. "You were the one
who asked me for help originally. Fucked up my op.
My life. You don't get the luxury of backing out
now."

With that, he pressed her to him again and he kissed
her, his mouth punishing on hers, just the way she
wanted it. Her body trembled, more from anticipa-
tion, but she couldn't deny that there was some fear
there too.

She was vulnerable in so many ways. Kell had already taken her out of her comfort zone—and promised to do more of the same.

His kisses grew more insistent, and she opened for
him, resistance both futile and waning fast. Her
hands, which had shot forward against his chest when
he'd leaned in, were trapped between them and she
was helpless . . . and it was how she wanted it.

The responsibility of all of this was too much.

She was warm now, all over, her blood boiling as
his tongue played against her, finishing the kiss that
had gotten interrupted earlier. Her robe had fallen
open, slipped off her shoulders, and her T-shirt had
ridden up. One of his hands slid along her bare thigh

as the other splayed along her lower back to keep her pressed close to him.

She tried to close her legs, didn't want Kell to know how wet she was for him, but his hand was insistent . . .

He pulled back as she kept her thighs closed. "You wet for me, baby? I can tell even if you don't let me touch. But you're going to let me, right?"

His head dropped and his mouth suckled a cotton-covered nipple—hard enough for her to loosen her body and grab at his head, and then she no longer cared if he knew the truth.

When his fingers found her core, she froze for an instant, and then couldn't help but move as he circled her clit with his thumb, another finger sliding inside of her, his hand twisting and turning in order to give her the most pleasure.

He was taking none for himself.

"You were teasing me in the pool, weren't you?"

"No," she said, but she realized she was lying. Knowing he'd been watching her had been a heady experience and she hadn't exactly reacted by being shy and covering up. She'd continued to swim, feeling his eyes on her. She'd even thought about letting her hand stray between her legs while doing so, letting the water cover the indiscretion.

And if she'd touched herself, she would've been thinking about Kell and no one else.

This was an interrogation of sorts, without the handcuffs or the harsh words. He was forcing her to open to him, to give him everything of her, and she was complying with his wishes.

"I knew you were watching me . . . yes," she managed,

punctuated by a low moan of pleasure as his tongue laved a nipple and then he sucked hard, the zing going straight to her womb.

"Feel good?" he asked, surely knowing it did. He only had to feel the wet on his hands to know his skill had made her slick and ready.

He pushed her back on the bed gently so she was fully exposed to him, and he dragged the T-shirt up with his teeth to bare her breasts.

Her hips moved as if she had no control over her own body—her nipples tightened almost painfully under his tongue, and then it all gave way to pleasure as her climax came long before she wanted it to be over.

But as she crested along the contractions of her orgasm, she realized he wasn't stopping. If anything, Kell seemed more intent than ever. He was moving down, his face between her legs, and she tried to sit up.

This act was so intimate that she'd never allowed it. She'd never had a long-term or even short-term boyfriend, and while she'd enjoyed sex, this seemed to be something to save for the right person.

Kell obviously believed he was that person—his lips met hers and she felt as if she could come again, right then and there. He spread her, took her with his mouth, and a need so raw and fierce overtook her that she surrendered to him completely. Trusted him with her body, with this act of sex—and she'd been so right about him. This man was dangerous as hell. And she knew that danger would fast become addicting.

She let the intense sensations of his tongue on her

sex wash over her. His hands reached up to tweak her nipples and she found herself clutching at his arms as her body writhed against him.

She should be embarrassed by this, by the fact that she was being put on such display. But she'd teased him and she'd wanted this—it had been building from the moment she'd pulled the gun on him.

Her orgasm gripped her, shuddering through her like a storm out of control and she was pretty sure she called out, but had no idea what she'd said. She was lost in the hot throb, where her pulse seemed to be inside her sex, and Kell was still there, laving and sucking, albeit with less pressure. Everything became highly sensitized and her thighs had small tremors she couldn't control.

When he finally pulled back, there was a predator's gleam in his eye. He looked so damned . . . satisfied. So very in charge, and she wanted to slap him and kiss him at the same time.

He stood and she pulled her shirt down to cover herself, because his hot gaze still licked her like fire and she was afraid she would beg him for more if she opened her mouth.

So she didn't.

"We're not through, Teddie. Not by a long shot," he told her, his voice raw. He left the light on when he walked out, not closing the door behind him.

She wondered why he hadn't tried anything further. He'd obviously been aroused, as any man in that position would be, she supposed, and the thought that he hadn't wanted her enough twisted her gut.

A day ago, she'd wanted nothing to do with this

man and now she was wondering why he didn't want
her.

She was far more messed up than she'd thought.
Maybe the isolation over the past year had done a
number on her. But tonight, with Kell and her orgasms, she'd felt freer than she had when she was
traveling the world, doing her photography.

Kell left the room, dick hard, wiping his mouth on
the back of his hand—and he saw Reid waiting at the
top of the stairs.

His friend was pissed off, and all of this was too
long in coming.

He was angry that Reid had pulled him back to the
team. Angry that Teddie was pulling at him too.

Mostly, he was angry with himself. "I told you I
was better off alone."

"Then you should've stayed gone," Reid said bit-
terly.

"You called. You asked. You knew I wouldn't refuse you."

"Yeah, that's right. I'll take that blame, Kell. I was
trying to pull you back from that goddamned cliff
you were hovering over for too damned long."

"The mission."

"It started before the mission," he said, a sharp
edge to his tone that stopped Kell cold. "You were
becoming a machine."

"I liked it that way." And he had. It was much easier to retreat inside that familiar shell of coldness than
to feel. And he'd started to feel way too much—it ate
at him, came up hard at odd times, made him unable

to sleep or eat, and maybe his parents had the right idea.

Life was a hell of a lot easier when you didn't give a shit about anyone but yourself.

"Good for you. Then you should go," Reid said furiously. "I'll finish up here and you go do whatever it is you need to."

The pain in his friend's eyes . . . Reid was hurting as much as he was and Kell was helpless to stop it. Everything he did made it worse. "I won't abandon you in the middle of a mission."

"You were never here to begin with."

"Reid—"

"Go. It wasn't a suggestion, it was an order."

"I don't take those from you," Kell told him.

"I said, go. Right now. Walk away, like you want to. I'm not helping you with this woman if you're head's not in it. I'll deal with her."

That made Kell snap to. He'd been fighting himself for so long it was almost a relief to transfer his anger onto someone else, no matter how misplaced.

They'd fought like this only once before. When they were seventeen and Kell had attempted to leave the foster home for good without Reid.

Now he rammed into Reid, his head down like a charging bull, pushing his friend against the wall in the hallway. Reid didn't let Kell keep the upper hand for long, used the momentum to propel himself at Kell. They both went tumbling to the ground, arms swinging, fists pounding. There were grunts and curses, months of pent-up anger and frustration behind every hit.

At some point, they rolled into a bedroom. Reid

brought a small table down on Kell and Kell in turn used the leg to hold Reid in place by the neck. Reid drove his leg up into Kell's kidney, and he howled in pain, hit the wall where Reid practically threw him.

"Son of a bitch," he cursed, and Reid went at him.

"That's you, not me." Reid landed a blow and Kell attempted to stand. Reid pulled him back down again and rolled with him until Kell was under him, pinned.

"Please stop."

Teddie's voice barely registered at first, not when his hand was locked across Reid's throat. Reid had him in a similar hold and their free hands were alternately blocking and punching. Reid was still on top of him, but Kell brought up a sharp elbow directly to Reid's side.

It was Reid's turn to go down in an angry howl of pain. Kell shifted to grab him again but Teddie moved between them, shoving herself in the small space that separated the men.

It was a stupid move, and a brave one.

"Stop it—you're killing each other," she said, a hand on both men as if she could keep them apart like that. Reid was looking up at her, his face bloodied, his eyes still glittering with a fierce anger.

"Move," he told her. "Or I will move you."

"Try it," she snapped back, pushed at him a little. And he did, went to pick her up by the hips and physically move her out of the way, but Kell stopped him by holding up his hands as if surrendering.

Reid dropped Teddie and stumbled out of the room, muttering. Kell turned away from Teddie and made it to the bed before collapsing.

He knew she'd be there when he opened his eyes,

and so he did, sooner rather than later, surveyed the damage to the wall, the table. Felt it on his face and body and fists.

"Christ," he mumbled, wondered if Reid would accept his apology now and then realized he wasn't ready to give it yet.

Fucker. And he was right about everything. Always had been, and that was the most unnerving thing about the man.

"Want to tell me what that's about?" Teddie asked.

"You wouldn't understand."

"I understand anger all too well," she said. Left him for a second and came back with a wet washcloth, proceeded to wipe his face where he'd been cut and bruised.

Reid was a hard opponent, as fierce as he was. If they'd wanted to, they could've done some real damage to each other. "We haven't fought like that since we were kids."

"How long have you known him?"

"Since we were sixteen." He shifted, winced. He'd still been sore from the fight in the alley. Reid's beating on top of it just served to remind him that he was being an asshole. Pulling away from the very men who always had his back.

For good reason. You're responsible for fucking them up. "Reid's still pissed at me for leaving," Kell explained. "It's a long story—a lot of shit I can't tell you. And some I just won't."

Would it be that way between them forever? And why was he thinking forever with Teddie when he'd long ago trained himself to think only about today—

that minute, that house, only thinking ahead so far as a mission required him to.

But he couldn't stop seeing Teddie there, with him. "I assassinated men from DMH—a terrorist organization. I hunted them down one by one. I felt like no one could stop me, and no one did. Instead, they got four men from my team. And they tortured them. Killed one of them. The three that survived will never be the same. And Reid's one of those three."

The kindness in Teddie's eyes nearly killed him, but he didn't turn away, not even when she said, "But they don't blame you."

"Reid's angry. I left him when he needed me to just be there, the way I've always been. But seeing him . . . seeing all of them like that . . ." He shook his head. "I took off without waiting for orders from my CO."

He'd spent a month or two turning every rock, rattling every cage, the panic growing to a point where there was only one way to stuff it down. He let the cold, calculating part of him seep back in—just a little, he told himself—and it had worked. He focused. Killed anyone who'd gotten in his way. "It wasn't good enough. If I'd been faster, more careful . . ."

"You found them."

"One of them died because I wasn't quick enough."

"The God complex is not a good look for you." The words slipped out of her mouth before she could stop them and she was sure they would turn Kell angry and cold. Instead, he looked at her, an animal awakened, savage—and yes, she could see the pain there. Wanted to smooth it away with a word, a touch, a kiss . . . all the while knowing it could never be that easy.

Or could it?

She leaned in and touched her lips to his. He responded instantly—hungrily—reached for her. Pulled her close as blood coursed hot through her, a rush like a sudden fever, a clawing, all-consuming need. It didn't seem to matter to him that, minutes earlier, he'd been fighting.

It was as if that had brought his blood to boil, but she didn't care what did it. She felt as if a wall had been broken, as if she suddenly understood him.

She wanted to know everything about him and she wasn't sure how or why it happened, but it was too late to stop it.

"You want to fix me, don't you?" he whispered against her neck, and she nodded.

"You want to fix me too," she whispered, and he snorted a little, kissed his way up her neck as his hands wound around her waist. And then he just stopped, like he knew she had more to say. "I've turned into someone I don't recognize. I hurt, all the time, and when I'm not thinking about the people I've lost, I'm thinking about revenge." She paused. "I guess you understand."

"Better than you know." Kell splayed his palm along her lower back to pull her in close. "You want to feel, right? Something—anything—besides hate and fear."

"Yes."

"Do you really?" he asked, tilting his hips toward her, his erection jutting against her, a hot, wet heat between her legs that made her press back against him, lighting a fire in his eyes.

"Yes. Why are you doing this?"

"I'm doing it to get what I need," he growled, before his mouth covered hers and she didn't have to ask any more questions. Just needed his skin on hers, his big, strong hands gliding over her body, stripping her down. Letting her come apart.

"Wait . . . what about Reid?"

"He'll know to stay out," Kell said against her mouth. "You want to do this even though you're scared of me?"

"Because I'm scared of you."

Then it was all heat and moans as he moved down between her legs, tasted her through her underwear until she arched against his mouth.

She'd had sex before, a few one-night stands, even in countries with men who seemed wild—but compared to Kell, they had all been tame.

Kell was not—his body poised over her like an animal in full predator mode, stalking every inch of her, until she ached to be held down and taken.

"Kell . . . yes . . ."

"Yes what?"

"Yes to everything."

But then, just as suddenly, he pulled away. Stopped to listen to a sound she couldn't hear at all.

"Get dressed—get your things," he told her, didn't explain further, and she didn't need him to. As Kell went down the stairs and she headed to the room where her clothes were, she saw Reid standing at the door, rifle in hand.

Her heart pounded and she raced to her bathroom, tearing off the robe and putting on the black pants Kell had left for her, tying them up as best she could and grabbing her own clothes and stuffing them into her bag.

She shoved her feet into her sneakers and went down the stairs quietly, not wanting to disturb the men. She sank onto the bottom step and waited for Kell or Reid's next direction. Watched as Kell collected the mens' things as Reid stood guard.

"Come on, Teddie." Kell finally motioned to her from the doorway leading out to the garage.

She got into the second seat of the truck's cab—it seemed way sturdier than the Jeep and she figured the safest spot would be in back. Ducking. Although she doubted it was bulletproof.

"Are you any good at shooting?" Kell asked, and yes, she'd learned when she'd been traveling in dangerous places. She'd honed her skills this past year, only leaving her gun behind so she could cross the border more easily, then buying one in Mexico.

"Didn't I prove that to you already?"

He arched a brow. "You proved you're willing to shoot. What I want to know is, how good's your aim?"

"I wouldn't have missed."

"Good." He handed her his gun, butt-first. "Keep your eyes peeled. Don't shoot me or Reid, no matter how tempting."

She laughed in spite of herself, nearly horrified at what a foreign sound it was. "Where are you going to be?"

"Reid will be here, with you. I'm going to scout outside so we're not driving into an ambush."

That should've made her feel safer. Instead, she was terrified. "Don't get hurt."

"That's the idea," he told her as Reid got into the driver's seat. In seconds, Kell shut the door and disappeared as both she and Reid waited in tense silence, staring at the garage door in front of them.

"We'll be fine, Teddie," Reid said after a long moment, his voice calm and oddly reassuring.

She'd thought he was as angry at her as he seemed to be with Kell, but from the tone of his voice, she suddenly knew that wasn't the case at all.

There was no one outside the house. Kell checked the entire perimeter twice, moving silently through the thick bushes that kept the place private from passersby.

Reid said the security cameras hadn't captured anything. But if he and Reid were coming at this house from the outside, the cameras would never have captured them either. It was why he only put stock in his instincts.

Maybe his instincts and Reid's were all fucked up from the threat Crystal posed. But no matter what, staying in the house was no longer an option.

"Come on out, Reid," he called. "I'll check around the front gate, but it looks all clear."

The garage door opened almost silently. What happened next wasn't even close.

When the bomb and the flash-bang grenades went off simultaneously, Kell was far enough away to get hit with only part of the blast. The full brunt would've surely killed him, as the partial was still close enough for him to get thrown to the ground hard and to—

hopefully temporarily—take away the majority of his hearing.

And then Reid was kneeling over him, his lips moving and Kell tried to tell him he was fine but must've been yelling because Reid slapped a hand over his mouth to shut him up.

The aftermath of an explosion was always eerily quiet, but his lack of hearing made it far worse.

"Don't move, don't talk," Reid was saying, and Kell nodded, but fuck that hurt. He saw spots and knew he'd pass out soon, tried to get up so Reid wouldn't have to carry him to the truck. But he got halfway up and Reid mouthed, *"Stubborn bastard,"* and then everything went black.

Teddie heard the explosion, felt the heavy truck actually rock when it was halfway through the garage door, and she pressed a hand to her mouth so she didn't scream.

Instead, she moved to the front seat after Reid abandoned it to look for Kell and tried to see through the front window.

The night was too dark, the smoke too chokingly dense, and she fought the urge to leave the truck and run to see if the men were all right.

They had to be.

Finally, after what seemed an eternity, she saw two figures emerge through the haze, one carrying the other. She scrambled to the back of the truck and opened the doors. Reid set Kell down and crawled in after him.

"Is he . . . ?" she asked.

"He'll be fine. Can you drive us out of here?"

"Yes," she agreed without hesitation, moved behind the wheel and got the truck moving, her heart beating a tattoo in her chest.

Reid couldn't have been lying to her—Kell was okay. He'd been breathing, and that was always a good sign.

The road outside the house was quiet and she sped along the dirt and rock as fast as she could manage in the large vehicle, which was surprisingly smooth. For about four miles, there were no problems. And then she caught sight of something in the rearview mirror.

It was a car coming up behind them with its headlights switched off, and it was moving fast.

"We're being followed." She willed herself to stay calm, listened to Reid telling her to bank a hard left and floor it. As she followed his directions, she heard him readying a weapon, the truck bouncing more than she'd like it to because of Kell. But Reid reassured her she was doing great, that he would take over as soon as he could.

"Teddie, lose them," Reid instructed.

She would because she knew for certain she needed these men, needed to prove to them she could be an asset. She shoved her fear down and let a more productive and empowering anger take over. It pushed her to maneuver the heavy truck easily down the back roads.

She'd had the good fortune and privilege to meet all kinds of people over the years, spent some time learning to drive race cars, and now she let those underutilized skills come back to her.

"Hang on," she called as she swerved hard and watched the car behind her shake on its wheels. She slammed the brakes and doubled back, letting the other truck careen past and into the ravine on the side of the road. She wasted no time savoring her victory, instead punched down the gas until they were flying down the road again and then cut across to the main road, trying to avoid being spotted.

When she was done she didn't hear a single complaint, just an appreciative whistle and Kell saying loudly, "Where the hell did she learn to do that?"

"I don't care where you learned, I'm just glad you did," Reid said, a note of surprise and approval in his voice. Instead of taking over, he directed her down back roads, and even though no one was following them now, she used a series of circle maneuvers, just in case. Held her breath until she realized they were no longer being followed.

Then she exhaled, nearly every part of her body shaking, and continued driving to keep them in the clear.

"Teddie, we're going to the border," Reid said.

"But Reid, I—"

"Don't worry about it," Reid told her, and she heard him talking on his phone to someone about needing a special dispensation to cross back into Texas.

When he got off the phone, he told her, "Pull over when you can and you and I need to switch."

"Will do." But she wanted to make sure the danger was truly behind them for now. And she needed to make sure that the scared girl she'd left behind wouldn't return anytime soon.

Now was the time for strength, for keeping her shit together. She would do it if it meant staying safe.

She drove for another half an hour at top speed, and so far, so good. When she caught sight of a hidden spot along the road, she pulled over and killed the lights, then quickly switched spots with Reid.

Reid turned the lights back on and gunned it. "We're ten minutes from the border," he said. "Just hang on—it's going to be rough."

She was sitting mainly on the floor and letting Kell take up the majority of the backseat. Her limbs were like jelly, thanks to the adrenaline and the tight hold she'd kept over her body during the driving.

"Is he going to be okay?"

"Yeah. He had a double whammy with the flash-bang grenades," Reid explained. "They blur your sight and take your hearing temporarily. They toss you down hard, worse if you try to fight it. These took him by surprise. He was lucky as hell—his sight came back fast." Reid paused for a second and then asked, "You all right?"

"Yes. Where are we taking him?"

"We're going to get him checked out. Lose the truck and get to another safe house. One that lives up to its name," Reid muttered that last part angrily.

She touched Kell's cheek gently, relieved to feel the warmth, reassured by the steady rise and fall of his chest. "Is he unconscious?"

As if to answer her, Kell squeezed her hand. *No.* Good.

"How'd you cross coming in?" Reid asked.

"Easily." She'd been worried the whole time, but

they'd let her pass without incident, viewing her as a single woman headed for a vacation adventure.

Getting out would be a different story—something she'd planned on figuring out later. The marshals had taken her passport and IDs last year when she'd gone into hiding, issuing her a new one under a false name, which is what she'd used. "Reid, I don't have a passport," she reiterated. "I have no ID or tourist card—I left them at the motel by accident when I went to the restaurant to meet Samuel."

"Don't worry about it. Just stay where you are and don't open your mouth," Reid said as they pulled up alongside a border guard carrying a big gun.

He looked in and saw her and Kell holding hands, told Reid, "I'm collecting on this favor."

"Can't blame you for that," Reid drawled.

"Try to stay the hell out of Mexico for a while." He tapped the side of the truck, called, "All clear."

Her heart pounded as they drove across the border, leaving Mexico in their rearview mirror.

But somehow, she realized, she was involved in far worse trouble than when she'd started.

CHAPTER
9

Reid had cut off Teddie's concerns about getting through the border. Taking a wanted woman with him out of Mexico had been of less concern than getting them all out of the danger that seemed to be closing in on them from all sides.

He'd called Dylan, got Cam instead, but he was just as good for what Reid needed. And he didn't curse Reid out, just made some calls and got Reid the contact. Now Reid followed the directions Cam had given him until he saw a new truck waiting for them, one with Texas plates. He pulled next to it and helped Teddie out. Then he carried Kell—who was fighting sleep by this point—putting him in the new truck.

He took off the old plates off and replaced them with another set that were stored in the back of the new truck. Tossed the old Mexico plates down a

nearby ravine off the side of the road, and then mo-
tored the vehicle the three hours toward their new
safe house.

Teddie was stoic—she didn't complain, merely
roused Kell every now and again once he'd finally
given in to sleep, to make sure he could come to con-
sciousness.

He did, and that made Reid breathe easier.

"You've done this before—saved him," Teddie said
finally from the dark of the backseat.

Reid glanced at her in the rearview mirror, catching
sight of the concern on her face. "We've done this
rescuing-each-other shit back and forth for a while.
Hell, he's saved a lot of people. It's his calling—he's a
natural."

"You know him well."

"I used to. These days . . ." Reid broke eye contact
in the mirror as his words trailed off.

"I figured. You can only fight with someone like
that if you love them."

Reid nodded, kept his eyes on the road.

"I hate to think I've come between you," she continued.

"You were the straw that broke the camel's back,
but it wouldn't have taken much," Reid admitted.
"You can't hurt him. He's been through too much
shit already."

"What's going to happen now?"

Reid wondered if Kell was listening to every goddamned word, then decided he didn't care. "He's gotten close to you, against all odds. I've never seen him
act like this."

"Is that a good thing?"

"He needed to let himself heal, and I'm not talking about physically, from these most recent wounds. He needs to forgive himself."

"Do you forgive him?"

"I'm close." Reid smiled in spite of everything, his face sore and bruised from the earlier fight. "We're family. It happens."

"What about your biological family?"

His face clouded. "They're dead. My family's Kell, my other teammates. It's a lot more than most people have."

It was true—because it was more than she had— and Reid didn't appear to feel sorry for himself.

"I can't believe you risked everything to get me across the border with you."

"Kell wouldn't have wanted you left behind, no matter what," Reid said. "I had to honor that."

"What's going to happen now? Do you think that bomb was meant for me, or for you?"

Good damned question. "It doesn't matter—we still need to deal with the mercs. Kell's the one to take you farther than this. I'll stay behind and distract the marshals."

"I can't ask you to do that."

"You didn't." Reid ran a hand through his hair. "When we were teenagers, Kell saved me for the first time. Like I said before, he was always helping people, even when he didn't want to. It's like he was born a hero." Reid smiled.

"A reluctant one," Teddie acknowledged.

"We pooled our money and left the foster home

when we were seventeen. Decided that we needed more funds if we were going to leave Alaska. So we took the highest-paying job we could find, on a crab boat. We were the lowest on the food chain, and Christ, it was such a shitty job, cutting bait, freezing our asses off. But after six weeks, we had more money than we'd hoped for."

"So you left Alaska then?"

"No, we went out on the boat twice more. I guess we were always gluttons for punishment." Reid glanced at Kell. "After that, we went to California. Got ourselves into some minor trouble and realized pretty quickly we had to find something more constructive to do."

"The Army."

"It kept us busy."

"Kell said he's not in anymore."

"Right. I am, although only until the end of the year." He paused. "I've never seen him like this with any woman, and like I said, I've known him since we were sixteen. I saw the way you looked at him, the way you've been with him since he got hurt. And I know you're afraid of him—you should be in some ways. But you'll have to get past that."

But you'll have to get past that.

Right now Teddie felt as though she'd promise anything as long as Kell was all right.

She'd held his hand the entire time Reid spoke, reassured once again by the warmth she felt there, and also from Reid's stories. After his more serious speech, he spent time telling her about some of the trouble he and Kell had gotten into when they were crabbing, and then in boot camp.

Finally, they pulled into a gated house with an attached garage and parked inside it. She nearly wept that they'd made it here safely.

"Teddie, are you all right? Can you get out and open the door so I can bring Kell inside?" Reid asked, and yes, she could. There was only one patient here—Kell—and she wanted to help.

She climbed out and opened the door, followed Reid as he carried Kell to the nearest bedroom and laid him down. She tried not to gasp when she saw the gash in his scalp in the light, and then she noted the blood seeping onto the pillow from what must be a wound on the back of his head. She hadn't noticed it in the truck. There were multiple other cuts and bruises as well, and she helped Reid tend to them all.

Finally, Kell was bandaged and Reid went to shower, since he was covered in smoke and dirt. When he came out in fresh clothes, she switched with him, not taking too long because she didn't like the idea of leaving either man.

As if she was the one who could save them or something. But still, she hadn't done a bad job of it today, she thought as she toweled off and put on some fresh clothes she'd pulled from Kell's bag.

When she came out of the shower, she noticed that Reid had stripped Kell of his shirt and tucked him into the bed using a blanket he'd found. He pointed to a closet, where she located some extra pillows.

"Why don't you get some sleep?" he said.

"No, why don't you get some sleep. I'll stay up with him," she told Reid, who shook his head.

"You stay here with him. Sleep if you need to. I'll be keeping watch." He left the room quietly, shutting the door behind him.

Hearing those bombs go off had been terrifying. Reid had working surveillance much of the night before. She'd had much more sleep than him, but she knew Reid would insist on remaining on guard no matter what she said.

She was grateful to be able to stay with Kell, watching over him. Letting him rest and recover. She got under the blanket, getting as close to him as she possibly could without putting pressure on his many cuts and bruises. Stroked his hair and smiled when he murmured and burrowed against her, his head to her breasts. Smiled, because he was murmuring her name.

Everything hurt. Staying asleep—unconscious, whatever—would be far easier than this, but he kept sensing movement around him. Not being able to hear yet was frustrating and scary and he needed to see what Reid and Teddie were planning.

When he opened one eye with a squint, he knew he was in a safe house and not a hospital, which was a start.

"You hurting?" Reid asked him then—Kell was reading lips, hearing a bit, but he knew Reid was yelling.

Kell shook his head and Reid continued, "Don't try to be a goddamned martyr."

Wishing he could punch Reid instead of nod, he settled for the latter, got a pill and some water and pointed to his ears.

"Only been a few hours. Give it time."

Kell nodded, willing the strong meds to work their magic. He didn't know where the hell they were, could've sworn he saw a border guard looking in on them, which could only mean that Reid was down with helping Teddie.

He owed his best friend a hell of an apology.

When he woke again, his head was buried against Teddie's breasts, and damn, that was the best thing to open his eyes to. Her nipples were hard through the thin cotton T-shirt she wore and he nuzzled against her, felt vibrations in her chest and was sure she was saying something, probably asking if he was okay.

He was about to be way more than okay.

His hands went under her T-shirt, tugged it up until her breasts were bared to him, the nipples a dusky rose color. He moved to tongue her nipple, then drew it farther into his mouth, her hands moved to his hair as if to hold him in place, the delicious laving making her squirm. The too big pants slid off her hips easily. She was naked now against him and he needed to be naked too. Like, right goddamned now.

She obviously agreed, since she was tugging at his shirt and pants. He felt like he was floating, and God, the drugs were kicking his ass.

He didn't let that stop him, worked her other nipple as his hands dipped lower, between her legs to finger the wet heat . . . which was all for him. He was swimming through the murk, because he had to have her, right now, needed to make her his . . . couldn't afford to let her slip away.

He vaguely heard some sounds—maybe she was saying his name, but his shirt was off and she was pulling him up toward her, unbuttoning his pants, helping him take them off and kick them away.

He pressed his lips to the base of her throat, feeling vibrations pulsate against them. His cock brushed her wet sex, her legs spread, and she would let him take her.

He'd lost total control and she didn't seem to mind, although he only had her body's responses to go by, like the slick between her legs, turgid nipples, the vibrations he felt when he kissed her throat. She smelled like flowers and honey and everything good.

He wouldn't open his eyes for fear this was just a dream. If it was, he didn't want to wake up anytime soon.

He slid against her, his cock brushing her sex, the sensations of skin on skin so intense, he could probably come against her stomach and again inside of her. His hands touched her face as hers twined in his hair and then moved down his back. Her legs wrapped around his body as if urging him closer still, and her hand reached down to circle his cock and guide him inside of her.

When he first entered her, he had to stop and breathe, fought not to take her as hard as he wanted to. She was so hot and tight, and holy fuck, he was shaking from the effort of not moving.

But she was moaning, loudly enough that he could catch the edges of it, and it urged him on to push inside her harder. When he did, her back arched, hands slid down his sides and nails dug in once he'd finally fully penetrated her.

He pushed up on his palms and rocked his body against hers. He moaned, couldn't judge how loudly, but it made him open his eyes to catch her smile and he nearly lost it then and there.

Her eyes were the colors of the jungle—browns with a hint of mossy greens, exotic—and he could crawl into her the way he had them and lose himself, the way he was doing right now. Her legs locked around him, holding him at the waist, urging him on, to take her without the usual slow finesse he would've given her if it had been a different time or place.

But it wasn't. This was what they had in the here and now and he was done trying to explain it or make excuses for it. He wanted her—had wanted to drive into her like this since she'd pulled the gun on him.

The fact that she appeared to want him equally as much made it that much sweeter as he pumped his hips and let her sex sheath his with its moist heat.

He was so deep inside her, she felt the spear of pleasure in her womb.

"Please, Kell" was all she could say, and she didn't know if he'd heard her or could read her lips, but he was taking her, pulling her body up to his, with his hands splayed across her lower back as if he'd never let her go. The strength of his body hadn't failed to surprise her over the past days, but even now, wounded as he was, she felt like he could still take on an army and win.

Strong, and yet so gentle. The combination turned her on so completely, she felt like she could come immediately. But she didn't want this to end that soon.

She hadn't realized how badly she needed this, needed him. Had never expected him to come out of his sleep this way, his eyes still closed and him so hurt and yet his arousal pressed against her belly, and she couldn't have stopped him.

No, that wasn't true—she hadn't wanted to, let him breathe a kiss against the side of her neck, allowed his hand to roam under her shirt to squeeze a nipple to a taut peak and then caress it so a straight shot of pleasure went from breast to groin.

That had been just the beginning of things. "Kell, I'm going to—"

"Come, Teddie," he murmured, as he took her with fast strokes and the orgasm came, hot and more intense than she'd ever experienced.

There was something to be said for the combination of sex and danger.

Kell hadn't stopped moving while she came, contracting around him as if the ripples would never end . . . and she just hung on to him and heard herself cry out again.

"You'll come again," he told her, like he could command the orgasms from her, and right now, she didn't doubt he was capable of anything. The way he made love to her was mind-blowingly pleasurable, the way she'd always dreamed it could be.

She didn't care about anything else, not when she was so out of her mind with need. None of it mattered except the brutal plunge of Kell between her legs, stretching her, making her whimper with pleasure as a white light shot across her field of vision and another orgasm rolled through her.

When she opened her eyes again, Kell was staring at her, so intently she knew she was lost, gone forever, no matter how badly he scared her.

Right now she wanted to be scared by him, every second of every day.

Teddie wasn't sure how much later it was when she fully woke from Kell's touches. She'd slept after he'd taken her, sated and exhausted, and now she was on her stomach, her head buried in a pillow and Kell was on top of her.

He put his forehead on her back, let it rest there. His hand was between her thighs, spreading them, caressing her, and she felt his arousal brush against her.

"Don't want to stop," he murmured.

"Then don't."

He pulled her to all fours and entered her from behind. Her breath quickened as her body readjusted to his girth. He left lingering kisses across her shoulders, and a nip or two, no doubt leaving marks.

She wanted him to leave marks, wanted them to linger on her skin with the same tingling sensations that were shooting through her now. She was spread and helpless against his thrusts and she cried out—his name, soft moans, louder ones, urging him on—and he remained above her, riding her until their skin was slick with sweat and they were both breathing hard.

Sex with Kell this time was like a fight, a battle they were both winning. And when they came, almost simultaneously, the victory coursed through her, hot and fast and sweet, left her trying to catch her breath long after they'd both semi-collapsed on the bed.

She turned her head to look at him, as he was still half lying with his chest on her back. "You were supposed to rest. Relax."

"That was relaxing," Kell murmured, his hearing obviously restored. "Nice driving, by the way."

"Jealous?"

"Impressed." He turned and winced. "Christ, don't let Reid give me any more of those painkillers."

"They forced you to make love to me?" she asked, and he just smiled.

"Where are we?"

"Texas."

"And you're not out of danger. But you will be," he promised her. "You have to trust me."

She was more than halfway there. "I'm here, aren't I?"

He got even more serious then. "I'm sorry you had to see that."

"The bombing?"

"The bombing . . . the things in the alley . . . at the drug house. All of it."

She held his gaze steadily. "I'm not. You saved me."

"What changed?"

"I don't know. Me, I guess." She shifted, suddenly feeling quite vulnerable, which made her insecure. "I know what side you're on right now. But what's to stop you from changing your mind?"

"Nothing, except my word. It's always been the one thing I've had, so I don't fuck with it."

"You almost died."

He nodded.

"I almost . . . in the alley. Before that too . . . I almost died, Kell. And it's not the first time in my life that I escaped death. How many chances do I get?"

"What scares you the most?"

"That maybe a part of me wanted to die. It would be much easier."

"That's a coward's way out. And you're anything but."

"I'm tired, Kell. For a long time, I didn't know where to turn or who to count on."

"You know now. And you refuse to give in. That stubbornness is what's gotten you this far. Now it could be the thing that does you in."

"I didn't mean to lie about what happened with Samuel in the restaurant or why I came to see him. I knew he was a bad man."

He pulled her close, stroked her hair, and she'd never felt so safe in her entire life.

"If anything had happened to you back there, Kell . . . I was so scared. And I'm tired of being scared."

"So don't be," he said simply.

When Kell woke again, it was light out and he was under the covers, with Reid sitting on a chair next to the bed.

"Teddie's showering. She didn't want you to be alone. She hasn't left your side," Reid told him. "Guess she has a thing for moody bastards."

Kell would've hit him but that would've taken effort, and right now he still felt weak as shit. "We're definitely being set up," he muttered instead and Reid nodded in agreement.

"This has Crystal's name all over it."

"You called Dylan?"

"He's well aware of the situation," Reid confirmed. "The entire situation."

Kell paused for a long moment, then said, "You know taking her across the border means we're in more trouble—you were reluctant to do it when I mentioned it, but I guess something changed your mind."

"She's all alone in the goddamned world," Reid said, and if nothing else, both were far too sensitive to that for their own good.

"I told her we'd help her."

"And then?"

"And then what?" Kell asked impatiently, the pain making him irritatable, despite his earlier relaxation.

"Are you only with her to get your rocks off?" Reid threw that last part out calmly. Baiting him, the same way Dylan had earlier on Skype.

It worked. "What the fuck, Reid? You jealous, wanting some?" Kell asked, all the while knowing that wasn't the truth at all.

"Jealous? Yeah, I guess I am," Reid told him. "Not because I want Teddie, but because I want someone to look at me the way she looks at you."

"She doesn't look at me like anything. She's scared of me."

"Means she's smart." Reid paused. "I'm going to

throw the marshals off track, lead them back into Mexico. And then I'm going to send Chambers to you and let you have the pleasure of dealing with him."

Kell stared at his friend, realizing he hadn't apologized for fighting him earlier. Or thanked him for saving his life. "You're doing this for her?"

"I'm doing it for both of you," Reid said. "I can handle Chambers. I can handle the marshals. If Crystal comes at me, I'll fuck him up too."

Kell had never seen his friend so worked up.

"If you still want out after we clear Teddie, I won't give you any more shit about it," Reid promised.

"We should stay together."

Reid cocked his head and then told his friend, "I won't let you lose her."

Kell didn't know what to say to that. It was a simple yet poignant statement, and Kell was overwhelmed by it.

Maybe he would be with her after all was said and done. And maybe he'd end up in jail.

It was where he'd always thought he'd be anyway. But he didn't think Teddie deserved that.

"I have to clear her," he told Reid. "I don't know why it's so damned important, but it is."

Reid eyed him calmly. "Of course you know."

"My innate need to help people."

"You don't help everyone" was all Reid said, but his words didn't hold a trace of bitterness. "Maybe it's time you let someone help you."

When Kell didn't say anything, Reid continued. "Something changed you. You've always taken the weight of the world on your shoulders while you wait for your bad genes to take over. Hate to tell you, man, but if it hasn't happened by now . . ." He trailed off, shrugging.

"What if she really thinks I'm like the men who murdered her family?"

"Then keep proving to her you're not."

The road was blocked off. Grier parked her truck and got out, showing her badge to the Mexican police who were surveying the area.

"What happened?"

"Looks like a bomb." The officer rattled off the exact address she was headed toward and Grier got the oddest feeling she was being watched. She fought the urge to pull her gun as she walked up to the property, saw that the gate had been blown off its hinges.

"Where are the people who were staying here?" she asked.

"Gone. Neighbors saw a truck take off down the road," the policeman told her.

"Who owns the house?"

"Ma'am, you'll have to take that up with the Department of Records. Looks like a recent sale." He pointed to the real estate sign, which was now partially blown to bits on the side of the road.

She dialed the number on the sign and got voice mail. Left her message and got interrupted by call waiting, and a number she didn't recognize.

That happened quite a bit—she gave out her number to informants and criminals alike. Now when she answered with, "Marshal Vanderhall," the man on the other end said, "They've crossed the border. They're in Texas, practically under the nose of your people back there."

How did he know she wasn't in Texas now? She wheeled around to survey the small crowd of people and emergency workers surrounding the house. Some were on their phones, some were taking pictures of the house, but none were the man who'd come into her office the other day. "And you're giving me this info out of the goodness of your heart?"

"My civic duty."

She bit off a laugh, although his voice was devoid of sarcasm. It wasn't often she couldn't get a read on someone, but with him, all she got was cold. Icy. "Thanks for your help. Got an address in Texas?"

"Marshal, I can't do all your work for you," he said before hanging up.

"Asshole," she muttered.

"And here I thought bringing you coffee would get me on your good side," Jack told her.

"Not you. That guy called." She relayed the conversation to Jack. "Could easily be a setup. But I don't think so."

"He's got us running around Mexico," Jack pointed out.

"Where Teddie was, until very recently," she mused, surveyed the destruction around them. "Think that guy is capable of this?"

"I think anyone's capable of damn well anything," Jack said.

"Call the office. Have them do a search—we'll stay here and try to get more of a read on our informant."

"Guy's gotta have some kind of ulterior motive."

"Of course. I just have to decide if I care." Running a check on the men Teddie was with could be a real problem. Going in cold could be as well.

She'd have to chance it. Getting Teddie back would get her team off the chopping block. "Come on. It's time to catch our girl."

CHAPTER
10

It was a day later and Kell was up and about, moving as if he hadn't been nearly blown apart. Aside from the bruises that marred his handsome face, he looked like he had when she first met him.

And he moved with purpose.

"We're getting out of here." He dumped a driver's license onto the table where she was finishing breakfast, having watched Reid pacing the first floor of the house like a caged lion for the past hour. She flipped it toward her, saw her picture and the name Kara Lindsey.

"What about Reid?"

"He's staying behind to keep the marshals away from you." Kell's words confirmed what Reid had promised her. Her stomach tightened at the thought of how much trouble she was really in.

It had been easy to forget, since it appeared that Kell and Reid were in far worse trouble than her.

"When are we going?"

Kell glanced out the window. "Little while. I'll let you know when it's time."

A screech of cars outside made her look out the front windows. A man wearing a U.S. Marshals jacket got out of one of the two cars. It was her handler, Al, and he couldn't be too happy with her.

The man in the other car was a marshal too—she recognized him as Al's backup, although she'd only met him a couple of times over the past year.

Al had a megaphone with him, and he began speaking into it, calling her name and telling her to come out of the house.

"Time to go," Kell said from behind her, handed her bag to her.

"It's too late." Her voice trembled a little, but her face was set in firm lines. "Let me go out there and end this."

"Reid, leave from the back as soon as I'm gone," Kell said, never taking his eyes off the front window. She turned in time to see Reid nod, then the pair fell silent as if the rest of their plan was already set.

She had no doubt that it was.

Kell took her, pulled her back against his chest and started to open the front door. Guns trained on her and her hands automatically went into the air as she said, "Don't shoot. Please."

Then Kell put his revolver to her temple and she froze.

What was he doing? She actually trembled, and for

a split second, she doubted everything she'd come to trust about this man.

Of course, having guns pointed at her didn't help. She realized she was struggling a little against Kell's grip, but that only served to make him hold her more tightly, her back snug to his chest.

"Please don't shoot," she heard herself say in a weak voice that she didn't think carried more than an inch from her mouth. She tried to lift her hands into the air but they were trapped.

"Stand down," her handler, Al, called out when he saw Kell holding her. "Sir, put the gun down and put your hands up. I'm a federal marshal and I need to take Teddie with me."

God, no. She'd much rather go anywhere with Kell, even at gunpoint.

Kell snorted under his breath at Al's words, then called out, "She's coming with me."

"Let her go," Al ordered. "You crossed the border with her. You're both in some trouble, but it's nothing compared to what will happen if you don't leave here with me," he said, his voice sounding so reasonable, and it was all such bullshit.

None of the marshals had any intention of helping her.

"You're not going to shoot her—we both know that," Kell told the marshal, his voice an icy calm.

"What do you want with her?" Al asked.

"She's valuable to me. What do you want with her?" Kell asked.

"She's wanted for questioning in a shooting death and an attempted kidnapping. But I know we can work something out, and no one needs to get hurt in the process," Al reasoned.

Kell kept the barrel of the Sig to her temple and she felt the cold press of steel dig into her skin . . . sweat trickled between her breasts and her heart pounded and she wondered what he was thinking. But she didn't dare ask.

"I'm taking her out of here," Kell said.

"We will hunt both of you down, sir," her handler promised.

"You can try" was his answer as he started to move away from the men in front of the house, taking her along for the ride backward.

She attempted to walk but he was moving too fast and she was basically dragged unceremoniously along the walkway and then through the grass. Kell still held her once they were out of sight, and before she could ask him what he was thinking, the truck they'd driven to Texas in flew by her at top speed, and she heard the marshal yelling orders and their cars screech away after Reid.

She realized that Reid had kept his promise to her, that he was going to help Kell keep her safe, and at great risk to his own life.

She couldn't speak and so she just stood there and waited for Kell's direction.

After they could no longer hear the sirens in the distance, Kell peeked around the corner, then left her behind for a few moments. Long moments.

When he returned, he said, "Come on, let's move," and tugged her along the back of the house, through the backyard directly behind theirs.

"Are we stealing a car?" she asked.

"I prefer the term *borrowing*," he said. "They're on vacation, won't report it missing for days."

"How do you and Reid find these things out?"

"Maybe one day I'll tell you." He used some kind of key to open the side door of the garage and motioned her inside. There was an old Tahoe with tinted windows in there, and Kell fiddled with it for a few moments. It started easily and she hopped in, held her breath for something horrible to happen when the garage door opened and the truck eased out.

They seemed to be in the clear, but she couldn't relax yet. Kell didn't say anything for a long time either and Teddie let the drive calm her. Kell went off road and she knew he wouldn't stop for a long time, in order to make sure they truly hadn't been followed.

"I'm sorry I didn't tell you how it would go down," he said after about twenty minutes. "I needed you scared. It was the best way to convince the marshals you were being held against your will."

"And get yourself in trouble."

"At this point, Teddie, that's not an issue. I have bigger and badder on my six."

"You could've walked away, to save your own skin. You wouldn't be the first person to do that, and I wouldn't have faulted you."

"No, you would've expected it," he said, slamming his hand on the wheel. "You'll let me help you, let me fuck you, and you still think so goddamned little of me."

"I don't . . ." She stopped. "I'm sorry, that's not true."

"I helped you because I couldn't not help you. Why'd you let me help you instead of going back to the marshals? Because I know I scare the hell out of you. Or does the possibility of jail scare you more?"

"Because I couldn't not." She echoed his earlier sentiments sincerely, her eyes wide, and everything else was stripped away in that moment.

"At least we have that in common."

"I have a feeling there's a lot more than that." Over a year ago, her life had been so completely different, and yet she'd been around men like Kell for most of her childhood, circling her but not actually getting close. "It's nice not to be alone in this. For a long time I thought that was the best way. The only way."

Kell nodded. "I've been where you are."

"That's why you told me not to seek revenge. You knew what it feels like," she said quietly.

"It can ruin your life if you let it." His voice was grim. The dust blew up around the car wheels and she longed for the cover of night. "I don't want that for you."

She wanted to reach across the console for his hand, but she didn't. They'd already shared intimacies, and yet she'd never felt shyer around him. Like nervous butterflies were in her stomach and the something that had broken inside of her so long ago was well on its way to being repaired.

A few hours later, Kell pulled over into a used car lot. Teddie remained in the car and he came back half an hour later with new plates.

"We've got a new ride."

"That was fast."

"Cam already bought the car," he explained.

"You guys have quite the network."

"It's good to have friends," he told her, and she realized that it certainly was.

"Have you heard from Reid? Think he's gotten across the border yet?"

"He texted—he's back in Mexico."

She collected her things and he grabbed his own bags and together they walked over to the new SUV, parked in the corner of the lot. She got inside as Kell fixed the license plates and then he leaned into the opened window, saying, "I'm going to grab us some sodas and food," before heading across the street to the convenience store.

She familiarized herself with the truck, in case she'd be driving, and while doing so she turned on the radio to find out what was going on in the rest of the world.

A hurricane bearing down on Florida seemed to be the only thing the reporters were talking about. It sounded like it was going to be a really rough one—a Cat 3 that they thought would go down to a Cat 2 by the time it hit landfall.

It was supposed to hit within the next thirty hours. Evacuations were rampant.

She shivered. She hated storms like that—hated hearing about them, watching their aftermath on television. She turned the radio off and played with the GPS, wondering if it was some kind of sick joke that it was set to the very area of Florida that was expecting the hurricane.

Kell came back about ten minutes later with a stash of snacks and sandwiches and sodas. "We've got to keep stops to a minimum—we're on a time limit."

"So where are we going?"

"Florida."

Her stomach tightened. He'd been the one to set the GPS. "Have you not heard about the hurricane?"

"Who'd ever think we'd be driving into it? The perfect cover."

"Or suicide," she muttered.

"We'll be hard to chase or find. That's what matters."

She tried to keep her tone light when she said, "Did I mention I'm scared of bad storms?"

"Yeah, but you didn't have me," Kell murmured, right before his phone rang.

That sentiment—and the knowledge that they were still a day away from their destination—allayed a bit of the impending panic. Besides, she couldn't say anything else on the subject, because Kell was driving, phone to his ear, and he was doing a lot of listening, interjecting a few words every now and again; when he hung up, he put the radio on.

The music played and the miles passed at a good pace. She was far too keyed-up to sleep, and she let the soft breeze from the open window play on her face and in her hair as she downed sugary sodas.

If she thought really hard about the fact that she was a fugitive from justice, hanging out with a merc and driving into what promised to be at least a Cat 2 hurricane, she would instantly become a babbling mess.

But, for her father's sake, she couldn't. She needed to get to the bottom of things—and a little voice inside of her told her she could do it.

———

Reid was in his element. The truck drove like a dream to begin with, and between OnStar and Sirius he was all set. During the six-hour drive, he caught up on the news, downloaded some new music and spoke with Zane, shooting the shit with the SEAL as he drove, getting lost on purpose for a while.

Because it was time to have some motherfucking fun, even if it killed him. And hell, it just might.

And then it was time to stop playing cat and mouse with the marshals and lose them for good. That was accomplished too easily and he cursed the fact that no one knew how to track anymore. Fucking economy was ruining training.

Still, today it worked in his favor and when he zoomed toward the border, he knew the plan had gone well.

Although he hated to ditch the truck, it had to be done. He managed to trade it for some fast cash just outside the border patrol, canceled the registration as he walked across the border on foot, getting through easily thanks to some creative passporting. Found himself a shitty motel room, and now he had a lot of work to do. First order of business was making contact with Chambers, then staying alive was running a really close second.

At least now they knew who was fucking with them, but that wouldn't put a stop to it. Whether or not Crystal wanted to shut them down or simply kill them remained to be seen, but either way, Dylan had his work cut out for him.

Reid got his CO's *Where the fuck are you?* text, and ignored it. But he couldn't ignore Dylan's call, which came about twenty minutes later as he was headed to the restaurant where Teddie had originally met with Chambers.

"Ya."

"You need to get out of there," Dylan growled. "Decoy's not a good look on you."

"Safest for everyone," Reid said, well aware of the potential sacrifice he was making on Kell's behalf— and Dylan's too.

"When does your leave end?"

"Six days."

Dylan swore, but Reid didn't bother to. He'd used up all his allotted curses for the century on Kell.

"I'll get it done, D," he promised. "You heard from him?"

"No."

Shit. "Any leads on Crystal?"

"Last seen in Mexico."

"Good." Let the fucker come for him.

"Jesus, Reid, just try to stay out of trouble," Dylan said.

"You realize I came back here to create some, right?" Reid reminded him, and Dylan began to curse again, a fluent string that lasted at least two minutes. The familiar gesture was oddly comforting, as if nothing had changed, even though it felt like everything was about to. "I gotta go—got some female trouble on my tail."

He hung up on Dylan's curses, which was a shame, since he always managed to learn a few new ones from him—and in varied languages as well—and waited for the woman to catch up.

She'd been on his six for the last ten minutes and

he'd let it happen, because he wanted to know what the fuck she wanted.

Plus, she was hot.

He lost her around a corner to see if she was decent at tracking. And she was, because she caught up to him about five minutes later, while he waited against a wall outside an open bar, leaning there like he didn't have a care in the world.

She sidled up to him, her bright blue eyes never leaving his own. "I've been wanting to talk to you."

"I'm not interested in company tonight," he said casually, hands in his pockets. "Besides, I never need to pay for it."

For a brief second, she looked horribly offended and then she leaned next to him, pulled out her badge. "U.S. Marshals."

"And you're trying to make extra money?"

Fuck a damned duck—he'd thought he was done with marshals for the day. Well, well, this would make things interesting, because even though her badge was Texas and she had no jurisdiction here, the Mexican police would work with her unofficially. They backed each other up, since they were frequently after the same fugitives.

She was hot as hell, take-his-breath-away hot, and she was also the law, which was a big freakin' bummer, since Reid typically didn't like to date women in his own profession. Not that he actually dated—it was more like sleep around, don't get attached, because that was way easier.

"You're quite funny."

"So I've been told." He looked inside the bar, which

housed a few locals, who were already half in the bag, judging by the bad karaoke. "Up for a drink?"

"I thought you didn't want company."

"I said I didn't need to pay for it."

"Who says you won't?" she asked, and he bowed a little to her, because nothing turned him on like a sharp woman. "What's your name?"

"Reid."

"Reid what?"

"Reid Cormier."

"I'm U.S. Marshal Grier Vanderhall."

"You like that marshal part a lot, don't you?"

"I earned it."

"True that." He studied the badge she still held in her hand by taking her wrist and holding it up. "Not a bad picture either."

He memorized the ID number for future reference, because while this was all chill right now, it was going to go badly very soon. He hoped she wouldn't take him in for questioning tonight, since he still needed to find exactly where Chambers did his business and get in on it. He suspected all it would take was a little scratch thrown around.

"If it's a no go for the drink, I think I'll head in and have one by myself." And slip out the back.

"I'd rather you not go anywhere just yet—I have some questions for you."

Reid was going to make this fun. And she meant fun in the most *un*fun sense of the word.

Grier wanted to strangle him, among other things. But she needed to tread lightly. Beyond an informant, who'd been reliable until this point but gave her no indication of who he was or why he was involved in this, she had absolutely no proof that Reid had been anywhere near his friend Kell when Teddie was abducted.

"Why did you give my men the run-around earlier and then leave your truck at the border?"

"I don't know what you're talking about," Reid said.

He'd led her marshals on a wild-goose chase for a good six hours. There was no record of him crossing the border and she still had guards there on the lookout for Kell and Teddie, although she suspected they weren't heading this way at all. "Why did you leave your car at the border in Texas?"

"I'm aiming to live a simpler life. It's a new Zen thing I'm trying out."

This boy must've given his mama hell. "Cut the shit, Reid. I want to know where Teddie is."

He frowned a little. Looked semi-adorable doing so. All-American, blond, blue-eyed, built like a football player, and his hands were big. Capable. "Not familiar with anyone by that name, ma'am."

Ma'am. Ouch. "Why are you lying?"

"You hurt my feelings."

She caught the slight Louisiana drawl in his last statement. "If I catch you with her . . ."

"You'll haul me in?" He opened his hands. "It's not going to happen. But what did this Teddie do?"

"She's in witness protection—you know that. You also know she's wanted in conjunction with a shooting and a murder, although that's possibly in self-defense. And your friend kidnapped her. Or maybe it was all a show."

He shrugged and let his gaze wander away from her like he honestly was bored with the entire conversation. "None of this is my problem, trust me."

"I don't. You're lying to me, sugar."

"I like it when you call me pet names," he drawled, and my Lord, he sent shivers through her, and here she thought she was quite immune to charm in all its pretty packages.

But this man had the combo of being good-looking and highly trained. He could probably kill her with his pinky.

Yeah, there were those shivers again. "I'd like you better if you told the truth."

"No, you just think you would. Trust me on that."

He was probably right, but still. "I'm going to have to put a tail on you."

"I won't mind you on my six. 'Course, I'd rather be on yours, but no one ever said life was fair."

"I know you're military."

He didn't say anything but a small grin played on his lips, like he didn't care if she had that information.

"Maybe if I contact the DoD and show your picture around, they'll be interested in helping me."

"Maybe. They're pretty busy these days with the wars and all," he pointed out, like he was being helpful.

"I'm too busy for more of your crap."

"So take me in. Interrogate me."

She pictured him all bound up, and if that happened, she would not be talking. Well, no more than saying his name repeatedly and very loudly. "You could just share what you know."

"Out of the goodness of my heart?"

"Yes."

"My heart's a wicked place, Grier."

"I'll bet," she muttered.

She had no real evidence that warranted taking him in, beyond the fact that he knew Kell. She'd been monitoring his cell phone and no calls to Kell had come in or gone out, but all that meant was he was using a throwaway.

She could search the estate he'd supposedly been staying at again, of course. She'd already been through his financials, but all that seemed to be on the up and up. "Give me something, Reid."

He looked her square in the eye. "I'd give up the ghost, Grier. Kell's too good—you'll never find him. But she's safer with him than she'd ever be with you."

"Because he's former Delta?"

"Because he's in love with her," he said bluntly before pushing off the wall. "See you around, sweetheart."

Well, she couldn't say he'd never given her anything.

CHAPTER
11

Pretending to take Teddie hostage had been the only way out. It had allowed him and Reid to split up and now they could claim to have no knowledge of the other's plans.

The marshals would attempt to follow Kell back into Mexico. Except they'd really be following Reid and the wrong car crossing the border, which would make Kell's life easier.

Once back in Juarez, Reid would put the plan to catch Chambers in motion. Reid was also responsible for keeping an eye out for Crystal, as was Dylan.

And although Kell hated to leave Reid alone, he knew his friend was up for the job. Once Chambers was taken care of and the evidence collected, Kell would untangle the mess with the marshals.

With Teddie's help, they made the drive without stopping beyond quick bathroom and fast-food breaks.

He kept the news of the hurricane to a minimum on the radio because he could actually feel Teddie tense up when she listened to it.

It took them thirty hours altogether to get to Riley's house in Florida, because Kell was driving the speed limit, so as not to draw attention to himself. Besides, even with the back-road shortcuts he used, the traffic was still snarled.

But at this point, his was one of the only cars traveling *into* the area.

"We're lucky—we've made it just in time. In a few hours, they'll close down this road and stop traffic from coming in."

"Lucky," she echoed, stared at the darkening sky and paled.

"Stay with me, Teddie," he told her. "I'm going to get us someplace safe within the next half hour."

"A hotel?"

"Better," he said. Finally, he pulled off the main road, toward a sturdy-looking house, and up a slight incline into a garage that locked behind him. "This is a friend's house. We're far enough away from the ocean that we won't have surge. It's new construction, built to withstand the brunt of storms."

Add to that the shutters a caretaker had already locked in place and Kell felt they were in good shape.

They'd fly up to New York as soon as they could—or drive, or whatever, and they'd hide along the way. But waiting out the storm here was one of Dylan's strokes of genius.

Of course, not knowing about Teddie's storm phobia had been a slight fly in the ointment, but holing up in Riley's house was as safe as they could be under the circumstances.

They were not only hiding Teddie from the marshals, but Kell from Crystal, and for at least the next seventy-two hours, he and Teddie would both be unreachable.

He used the code to open the door and went in, with Teddie behind him, to check the place out.

It was cool and quiet and dark. He switched on the lights—no one from the street would be able to see them, thanks to the shutters. Riley had a generator here as well, so they'd be good for quite a while.

Now, if he could just get more than a minimal text from Reid, he'd feel better. The man had to be wreaking havoc with the marshals—it was what he did best and he was often the Delta sent out to cause such disturbances so the rest of the team could work their magic.

Reid was a natural for sure.

Teddie was pacing around, unable to relax as the storm began to pick up a bit. She switched on the TV and he hoped she'd watch a movie instead of The Weather Channel, but he had a feeling that was a pipe dream.

"They're doing evacuations of this area," she called out to him when he went toward the kitchen to call Cam.

"Not mandatory, just a recommendation. I doubt the storm'll hit landfall as more than a Cat One. We'll be fine," he told her, and she harrumphed. He pretended not to hear it, opened his phone and noticed he didn't have any signal. Riley had to have a sat-phone in this place somewhere, and he snuck past Teddie, who was glued to the TV, and went to search the house for it.

Teddie remained rooted on the floor by the large TV, watching The Weather Channel like it was her lifeline, even though it was currently scaring the hell out of her.

The wind howled through the shuttered house. Kell was in the kitchen trying to get a signal and she wasn't sure how much time had passed. She dragged a few pillows off the couch and lay down on the floor.

She might've fallen asleep for a little while, only to wake to the sounds of a vicious whistle of wind. It sounded angry and she swore the house shook a little.

But the lights and the TV were still on and Kell was still in the kitchen and they would be all right.

The reporter was talking about gusts of wind up to seventy miles per hour in their area. The perky woman trying to stand out in the middle of a beach warned her not to go outside.

"Don't worry about that, honey," Teddie muttered. And she was starting to lie down again when the effects of the storm began to really hit the house.

The TV fizzled out first. She saw it as the last vestige of normalcy before the world ended and felt the panic rise in the back of her throat. She tried to distract herself, until the lights went out a few minutes later, leaving the room dark, although not pitch-black.

Not yet.

She opened her mouth to call for Kell, but no sound came out. She was entirely too focused on the way the wind whipped the palm trees, how the fat raindrops had begun to pelt the house with bulletlike precision.

And then there was a loud sound, like an engine starting up, and seconds after that the lights came back on. They were dimmer than before, but it was still a very welcome sight. Literally.

"Teddie, hey." Kell was behind her with a battery-powered lantern he placed on the floor next to her and then he wrapped her in a blanket before settling in next to her.

She pulled the blanket more tightly around her. "Sorry" was all she could manage without fear that her voice would break.

"Nothing to apologize for," he told her. "The generator should work through the whole thing—the lanterns are for just in case. I guess you weren't exaggerating when you said you don't like storms."

"I thought I'd be okay." She was so far from that, it was laughable.

He moved away a bit to rifle in a low cabinet on one end of the couch. He pulled out a bottle of Jack Daniel's and held it up. "This could help."

"I don't really drink."

"Then it'll definitely help." He handed her the bottle after opening it, and she took it hesitantly, the scent strong enough to make her almost refuse it.

Still, she took a sip, bit back a cough as the amber liquid burned all the way down to her stomach. She let it settle and then took a longer drink and then another, until Kell liberated the bottle from her and took a long swig of his own.

"There's plenty of food we can eat. I'll manually light the pilots on the stove," he said.

"Do you cook?"

"Not well," he admitted.

"I can help." The edge was definitely off, but the fear of what the storm would bring remained.

"Good." He grinned. When he did that, he looked about seventeen. She could almost picture him and Reid in Alaska, at the foster home. On a crab boat.

"I hate that you and Reid are fighting," she said suddenly.

"It's not because of you."

"I know. But I'm not making it any easier."

Kell didn't answer right away, took another slug from the bottle. "Maybe you are and you just don't know it."

She didn't push for an explanation, let his words sink in for a few moments, allowing the warm fuzzies from both the alcohol and his statement wash over her.

"Would that be all right with you?" he asked finally.

Instead of answering with words, she leaned in, hesitating for only a second before kissing him, a sweet gentle kiss on the mouth first. And then she lingered a kiss on his cheek while her hand cupped the nape of his neck.

When she pulled back, he asked, "Are you trying to heal me?"

"Is that possible?"

"I don't know," he said honestly.

"I think . . . you could heal me."

"Is this the JD talking?"

"Maybe it gave me the courage I needed."

"You've already got that, in spades," he told her.

She wanted to kiss him again, but then she swore the house began to shake and she nearly jumped into his lap.

Once fully there, she did kiss him.

Kell needed to take all Teddie's clothes off. Immediately. Right here, on the floor by the couch as the storm began its lash of the coast. She'd wiggled against him, held his shoulders like she'd never let him go, and he'd like to think it was more lust than fear driving her.

He nuzzled against her neck, sucking the soft skin there and making her squirm more as his hands went under her shirt. But suddenly, she was intent on taking off his clothes, which could be just as fun. She tugged his shirt over his head, shifted so she could help him out of his jeans, which he somehow managed to kick off while she remained mostly on top of him, and then her hand circled his cock.

Fuck. Yes.

His head went back against the couch—couldn't really move his hips from the position he was in, but somehow, that made it hotter.

"You have too many clothes on," he managed, but her only answer was a nip on his shoulder as her hand stroked faster.

She continued kissing and licking her way down his chest, and then she was pushing him to lay down under her, and she continued to head between his legs.

He lay prone on the rug with the house shaking and his body following suit as she spent time on his nipples, with licks and sucks that went on a straight line to his cock, which was already way too sensitive; he fought the urge to grab her and take her.

This was her party. He'd had his way with her already—and while she hadn't minded, he wanted her to be okay with all of this.

She continued looking over his body—he wasn't as scarred as some of the guys he'd worked with but he could easily use his as a map of his life. The skin on his shoulder puckered, a souvenir from a knife fight in his first years on Delta Force. A fight that, for the record, he'd won.

A few, like the scar on the inside of his palm, were from a slipped knife on a crab boat—he'd been lucky not to slit any tendons. And that's when he'd learned to stitch himself up, because they were thousands of miles from shore and the crab boat wasn't going back in for a scratch, as the captain had called it.

Her fingers played gently along the new bruises he'd received over the course of the past days, circling them and then brushing them lightly like her touch could make them all better, and she couldn't know how close to true that was.

"These must hurt."

"Not so bad."

"Tough . . . going to borrow some of that." Her mouth pressed to his shoulder, a kiss and a soft lick of tongue on his hot skin.

"Anything you want."

"You're so beautiful," she whispered, looked at him with her eyes full of the compliment. No one had ever said that to him before—and holy Christ, she meant it.

He should tell her there was nothing beautiful about him, but he needed it to be true, didn't want her to see him as a danger . . . didn't want her to see the ugliness he'd been born with on the inside.

"Fuck me, Teddie," he told her, and she flushed at the dirty talk, mouth open slightly. But then she started to strip off her clothes, letting them drop all around him.

Stripped, then hesitated until he brought her back to his attention with a touch, a stroke. First, she uncovered her breasts—soft and firm, a perfect handful, slim torso, and when her pants came off she revealed the blond curls that rubbed against his cock. All he wanted her to do was slip him inside her, take him all the way in.

The wind gusted up, hard enough to shake the hurricane shutters. A loud boom from outside vibrated the floor under him and she started, looked panicked.

"Shit," she muttered, but he brought her back to the present again, his hands on her breasts, tugging the flushed nipples gently.

"I'll keep you safe."

"Does nothing scare you?"

You. The thought of not being with you. "Nothing right now." And that was the God's honest truth.

"Teddie, come on. Fuck me. Right now." He tugged her onto him, wanting to forget everything as badly as she wanted to block out the storm.

They would do it together.

It was as if the storm was driving them both—her seeking escape and solace but he didn't care. He wanted her again, the same way he'd been wanting her from nearly the beginning.

The other afternoon had only whetted his appetite. And he was grateful to the storm for allowing this, for giving them refuge.

"It's going to be a bad one," she whispered.

"Then let's make this good—balance it out."

She didn't want to think about the storm anymore, the tension she'd been holding inside needed release, and judging by the way Kell looked at her, he did as well. His smile made her stomach flip, because he didn't smile often. His hands molded to her breasts, made her arch and moan into his palms, rub against him for a few moments. Then she reached down and guided him inside of her.

She lowered herself slowly, letting him fill her, and it felt so good. Sex had never been this right, and Kell's strangled groan, his hands on her hips pushing her down the final length of him combined to make her a slave to the sensations.

For a moment, she remained still, feeling him pulse inside her. Her palms rested on his chest, her breathing quickening, and then she began to rock back and forth, taking him the way he'd done with her the other day. Making him writhe underneath her, begging for her to go faster, urging her on. Her belly tightened as she began to lose control, barely able to hang on to him, as he began to move her hips for her, bucking up so his cock drove more deeply inside, and she was hanging on for his ride now.

She couldn't take her eyes off him. He looked wild and beautiful and he was giving some of that wild beauty back to her. As her orgasm grabbed her, she threw her head back, her sex clamped around him, and he yelled something—her name, maybe, mixed with a curse or two—as he came hard inside her.

Grier had trailed him pretty well for the better part of the last hour. Reid lost her for good by letting her think he was staying in a motel across town. It was then that he doubled back and headed to the restaurant he'd been trying to visit that afternoon. He'd suspected that Chambers had asked Teddie to meet him in a place he felt comfortable and protected. The kitchen staff confirmed he had a regular table once Reid offered cash to them.

Reid was sure those men would let Chambers know an American had been asking about him, and that was exactly what he wanted.

Now he waited across the street until he saw Chambers pull his car into the small lot, gave the man half an hour to settle comfortably before Reid went in to try to get a job working with him.

It was for sure a dangerous move, but he supposed he'd always been dangerous. Foster homes were almost as good as juvie or jail in terms of learning to be a better criminal, and he'd been fortunate—or unfortunate—enough to get in with the right kind of crowd early on.

Delta had given him the opportunity to perfect his skills and now he used them to put his life on the line. He grabbed a beer from the bar and took a walk, found Chambers holding court in the back of the restaurant as if he were some kind of high-level mafioso.

In reality, the restaurant was a piece of shit, but

Chambers could play the big-fish, little-pond game here. Judging by the number of hangers-on, he was fooling a lot of people.

McMannus was the only security, sitting at a table to the right. As Reid advanced, the man stood, ready to turn him away.

"Need to talk to him about a job," Reid drawled.

"We're not hiring."

"I'm not interested in working for you—I want to hear it from him."

"It's best for your health if you turn around and leave."

It was going to end up like a bad B movie where Reid kicked McMannus's, the current bodyguard's, ass to catch the attention of the big boss.

In this case, it would be that much more satisfying, knowing that the bodyguard had murdered innocents.

"I'll give you one last chance to get out of my way," Reid told him.

McMannus smirked. Reid was only too happy to wipe that right off his face with a hard slam of his forehead to the man's own, sending him stumbling back, dazed.

Reid took advantage of that, advanced and knocked him flat with a punch that was more bar fight than skilled Delta but was damned effective and took very little effort.

McMannus fell and did not get up and the whole ordeal had taken under a minute.

Reid smiled and finished his beer, because yeah, he'd definitely gotten the crowd's attention—and

Chambers, too, since the man motioned for Reid to come closer.

Reid did, walking slowly past a few pretty women who looked him up and down. Whoever won the fight usually got to take home the best woman, but tonight, that wasn't his main goal at all.

A pity, really. His mind flashed back to Grier and he wondered how pissed she actually was right now. He guessed very and that nearly made him grin right in Chambers's face.

He pulled up a seat that magically opened right next to Chambers and the people who'd been sitting at the table slowly scattered.

Chambers took a sip of his drink—looked like Dewar's—and licked his lips as he put the glass down back on the table. Stared at Reid as if trying to memorize his face and Reid found the entire damned thing really creepy. "Was that performance for me?"

"Did it work?"

Chambers's expression didn't change. "I typically don't like show-offs, but that was impressive."

"It was nothing." Reid paused. "I'm looking for employment."

"How did you hear about me?"

"Let's just say I've got something you want. Actually, someone," Reid clarified, the danger of the game running hot in his blood.

Chambers sat back and considered him slowly. "And in return for this someone?"

I'm going to kill you. "I want in."

Chambers took another drink. "This person . . . ?"

"A woman," Reid clarified.

"I have plenty of those."

"But this one shot you." Reid glanced at Chambers's arm that was still in a sling and let that information settle in. For the first time that night, Reid caught a slight flash of anger behind the other man's bland gaze.

"For a man who's just come on the scene, you know quite a bit."

You'd better believe it, buddy. "Give me a call when you're ready to talk." Reid slid his phone number, written earlier, along with a few names and other numbers, at Chambers. "That's my phone and these are my references. Feel free to call and check up on me."

"What's your background?" Samuel asked. "American military?"

"Yes."

"And you're willing to do anything?"

"Always." Reid stood. "I want a job before I tell you where to find her. That's my deal."

"And if I don't play your game?"

Reid just drawled, "You will," and he walked out of the restaurant, knowing there could easily be a gun aiming between his shoulders or an ambush in the alley to the right.

The man he'd taken down had gotten up and gone out the back while Reid had been talking with Chambers. It was time to make sure he was no longer a problem—for Reid, and for Teddie.

Chambers would be all Kell's problem, though. It's the way his friend wanted it and Reid was more than willing to comply in order to watch Kell get back into the game, no matter how briefly.

He strolled as if to pass the alley that ran along the

side of the restaurant, his body taut as a wire. At the last minute, he stepped into the darkness, and found who he was looking for.

McMannus was still unsteady from the hit he'd taken. The head-butt move could be a real stunner if done correctly.

If not, you could end up knocking yourself out. Reid had only done that once. Now he said to McMannus, "You're a slow learner."

He wanted to ask him about Khartoum, press for a confession, but it would come back to bite him in the ass if the man survived, told Chambers.

The bastard reached out and Reid saw the glint of a blade. The knife caught him along his biceps, tearing the sleeve of his shirt. It didn't hurt—not yet—and Reid took that opportunity to pound the shit out of him.

First, he subdued the knife hand, pounded it against the wall until the weapon dropped with a clatter, and then he brought the guy to the ground.

"Where did you learn your moves? The Boy Scouts?" Reid asked him, pumped for a good fight.

Tonight, he'd find none. The man rolled too easily, and Reid had his arm across McMannus's throat in seconds while he lay prone and helpless.

Before Reid could do anything else, someone called his name. Female voice.

He took his arm off McMannus. "Run, you fucker. I just saved your ass—it won't happen again."

McMannus looked at him strangely and dragged himself away, half-hopping, half-running.

Chickenshit pussy. Reid touched his arm where the warm blood was dripping. Ripped some fabric from the bottom hem of his T-shirt to bind his wound as he heard light footsteps heading his way from the main road.

Grier. "Are you all right?" she asked. "I saw him come after you. What happened?"

"No clue. I guess he was just a mugger." He glanced at her. "Is this a lucky coincidence?"

"I don't believe in coincidences."

He snorted and pushed to his feet. "I lost you for a good long while."

"You're welcome for helping you with the mugger."

"I had it under control." He went to brush past her but she held a palm flat to his chest. He looked between her hand and her face, raised his eyebrows. "You want a piece of me now?"

"What were you doing meeting with Samuel Chambers?"

She didn't move her hand. He had to give her credit, because his death stare usually did the trick on both new recruits and tangos alike.

He'd obviously have to perfect it for female marshals. "I went inside for a beer."

"And you got into a fight."

"It happens. Especially when people touch me without permission."

She removed her hand but continued talking. "You just happen to have a meeting with the man who was once suspected of working a high-level kidnapping ring in three countries with Teddie's father?" She was way better than he'd given her credit for.

"Just looking for employment."

"Gainful or not, right?"

"Money's money."

She cocked her head. "I don't know you well enough to say this, but that's not what you're about at all. You're one of the good guys."

"Jesus, Grier, you really don't know me at all." He shook his head as he lied, because fuck it all, she seemed to. "I've gotta go lick my wounds."

She was going to put two and two together really quickly. "I've seen Teddie's picture from the marketplace in Khartoum and I've passed it around here—people have mentioned seeing the men, although they're too scared to tell me where. I've been over the file since she disappeared."

"Maybe you should've been on it from the second she went into protection," he countered, and now it was her turn to dole out a death stare.

It kinda turned him on.

Grier was caught between a rock and a hard place, because Reid was working really hard on what was really her investigation. He wasn't doing it for money—he'd already told her he was doing it for his friend. For love.

God, an operative with a romantic streak.

She knew what he was trying to do. By breaking into Chambers's world, he was trying to prove Teddie's father's innocence—and by association, Teddie's. But Reid's ass wasn't on the line with this missing WITSEC suspect. Hers was, and she needed to find Teddie, using whatever it took to get Reid to help her.

"Is the man you fought responsible for killing Teddie's family?" she asked, because she hadn't been able to get a good look at anything but his back jumping the fence.

Reid didn't answer her directly. "He'll come after me again. I can't be responsible for what happens."

She began to walk away and he followed her.

"Reid, you need to bring her in to me."

"She'll get there."

"On my time, not hers or yours."

"Do you always work inside the law?" he asked, and she had to stop and think about that. Because yes, she did. She respected the law, worked within its parameters—but often got frustrated as hell with the bureaucracy.

"I think everyone's safer that way," she told Reid finally.

"I think that you know you couldn't be more wrong." He began to walk away, still bleeding down his arm.

"How are you getting back to your room?" she called after him before he got too far away.

He didn't turn around when he called back, "My two legs."

She hesitated and then asked, "Want a ride?" before she could stop herself. But her words did make him pause, and she heard him sigh, saw him shake his head like he couldn't figure her out.

Half the time, she had the same problem.

He turned to her. "Is this on the record?"

"No. Does that mean you'll take the ride?"

He glanced at his bleeding arm. "If you've got a first-aid kit in your car, I'd rather that and then dinner, if you're up for it."

"Come on." She motioned for him to follow,

opened the back of her truck and had him sit there while she brought the kit around. He took over immediately, and she watched as he stitched himself up easily.

Military for sure—this would've cinched it even if she hadn't already known. He glanced up at her when he finished, grinned, like he knew she was nervous around him and that it had nothing to do with her job. "Hungry?"

She cocked her head as if attempting to figure out his motive, which, at the moment, he probably had no clue as to what it was, and she finally nodded. "I pick the place, though."

"I'm done. Lead on."

"It's back closer to your motel."

He raised his eyebrows but didn't say a word, just took the passenger's seat and they drove to the restaurant, making small talk about the city, the escalating violence and the problems with the drug dealers and gangs.

"In one border town, they have a single cop, a policewoman," she said with a shake of her head. "Who can win this?"

Reid shrugged and she continued, "Rivera and Cruz, two of the big ones, were found murdered a few nights ago. That's really shaken up the drug dealers, so it's been quiet since then. They're trying to regroup."

"I'm sure they'll find a way."

"I know you probably don't want to talk about this."

"I'd rather talk about you."

"My job?"

"No, you," he said, and she wondered if this was all a bullshit act, because if it wasn't, then he was really good.

She didn't say anything when she parked, and they walked into the restaurant and got their table, complete with tortilla chips and salsa and beers. "It's a hole in the wall, but that's the best kind of place," she offered.

He leaned back in the booth. "See, now I've learned something about you."

"You already did when you discovered I work within the confines of the law."

"So you agree they're confining."

She swished a chip in salsa. "Maybe," she said before taking a crunching bite.

That made him smile a little and there was a comfortable silence while they ate and she tried to think of a way to explain to her superior that this really was business. It just happened to be very pleasurable as well, and that rarely happened in situations like this.

"I've done some checking on you," she said once their food was served, in an attempt to regain the upper hand . . . any hand, actually. Although she really didn't get the feeling he was trying to one-up her—he was trying to do a job.

"Really? Find anything good?" he asked and then took a few bites of his food like he was relishing it.

"You barely exist."

"I tend to travel light."

"Because you're in the military?"

He sat back. "Why? Would that turn you on?"

Everything the man did turned her on and he knew it. "I think it's admirable that you're trying to help

Teddie. But she's in a lot of trouble and you and I both know it's in her best interest to turn herself in and let us sort this out together."

"No clue where she is."

"I'm supposed to believe that when your friend took her at gunpoint?"

His steel blue eyes pierced hers. "Grier, I've got enough shit going on—I don't need more."

"Then why are you actively looking for trouble?"

"People have been asking me that for years. I don't know why it's taken so long for them to figure it out."

"So what's the secret?"

He leaned forward, whispered, "It's a hell of a lot of fun. You should try it sometime."

Goddamn, she wanted to try *him* right that minute.

CHAPTER
12

After they'd made love, Teddie lay in Kell's arms, and although her needs were sated, her body remained taut, tension spilling over. They were squeezed together on the couch, wrapped in a blanket, the sounds of the generator muffling the storm somewhat.

Still, it was worsening, there was no doubt about it.

"It's going to be bad for a while, Teddie," Kell told her. "But we're going to get through it."

The storm was keeping her safe. In a brief moment of irony, she understood that. "I wasn't scared of storms like this until I got caught in one." The memory of those hours could terrorize her even now, with Kell's arms protecting her.

"How old were you?"

She didn't want to go back there, but talking it out

could only help. "I was seventeen. We were in Jakarta. We'd been preparing for the hurricane for days. Over the ocean, it was really strong, but it was supposed to come down to a Cat One by the time it made landfall."

They'd lived through a lot of storms, mudslides, earthquakes. She'd thought she'd seen everything. She'd actually been blithe about it, had planned on going outside with her camera and snapping photos.

It was the day she'd realized she wasn't going to live forever. That her life could be taken from her at any time. In many ways, that storm had forced her to move on with her life and stop doing the destructive partying path she'd been on.

She had reason to be grateful for that goddamned hurricane, but that night . . . "We got word that the hurricane had actually gained in strength and was about to hit us as a Cat Four. It became obvious that we wouldn't be able to stay at our house, which was about fifteen minutes from the embassy on a normal day. We were told to go to the embassy to wait with the other Americans. There were soldiers who came to the door and told us that the area we were living in might not survive the hurricane." She stared at Kell and thought about the men who'd risked their own lives to help get her and her family to safety.

"I know the area" was all he said, which meant he knew the terrain, the potential for mudslides and nearly complete destruction, which was what had happened that evening.

"The soldiers were from the local military—gave us

ten minutes to grab what we needed to take with us. I had a small bag I packed with some clothes and my camera, because there wasn't a lot of room in the truck for much else. When we left the house, it was already pouring—a horizontal rain—and there were mudslides and flooding and I got into the back of the truck and just prayed. We almost ran off the road countless times. I didn't want to look out the window but I couldn't stop myself. My parents sat there, so silently, but I knew they were scared too. They didn't want to freak me out any worse than I already was, I guess."

She hadn't realized her voice had been trembling until it cracked a little. But she swallowed hard and kept talking. "It took two hours to get to the embassy and it was so horrible and the storm had barely started. Just like this one."

"We're going to be okay," he told her, probably for the millionth time, and she wanted to believe him.

"I thought getting to the embassy meant we were all safe. They didn't tell me that being there gave us only a small chance of survival," she said softly.

"Small is better than none," he countered. "And you made it through."

"We did. And those soldiers were right. We barely survived . . . the roof of the embassy was torn off . . . so much damage and destruction. And it was a slow-moving storm—it took a full ten hours to pass. It just sat there, over us, like it would never move."

The sounds were the most awful part: the creaking of the roof tearing off, the screams of the women, the tears, the crash as the outer walls collapsed onto one another. "It didn't end after the storm passed. We were together for six days before any help could reach us." She paused. "There were American military there with us too. Marines, actually. They were nice."

He snorted. "Yeah, make sure you tell the next Marine you see that he's nice."

"You know what I mean."

"Yeah, I do." He glanced over at her when she jumped as the wind whistled. "What happened that night?"

"I already told you—the storm." When he continued to look at her, she averted her gaze and stared down at her hands, which were splayed on her knees. She'd moved off of him during the telling of the story and had created her own space, and he'd let her.

Now her knees were up to her chest, and without even realizing it, she'd curled herself into a tight ball, the way she'd done that night in the embassy, with her mother next to her.

God, she'd nearly forgotten that—or she'd probably pushed it to the back of her mind—because that was the night she'd learned the horrible news. "My mom told me she was dying," she whispered, her voice cracking. "She had breast cancer and it had spread before she was even diagnosed. She was supposed to go into the hospital for surgery the next morning."

God, how horrible that had been, learning that as they all prayed to get through the night and the next week, only to be told she'd lose her mother a short month later, right before she was scheduled to leave for college.

"I'm sorry, Teddie."

"You think it's that simple—that I hate storms so much because of what my mother told me during one?" she asked and he cocked his head.

"I think that could be part of it. But no, I don't think that's all of it. I'm not a shrink, I just know when people are holding something back."

"Even from themselves," she murmured. "A handy skill."

"Sometimes." He tugged her back to him and she let him.

Teddie had more to tell him. Kell knew it the way he knew this storm wouldn't let up for much longer than the weather service had reported. The pain behind her eyes was heartbreaking, letting him know she'd get there before the hurricane ended.

That would be worth it for him. If nothing else came out of this, that would be enough.

Bullshit.

"Reid told me you used to fish on the Bering Sea," she said. "You must've seen a lot worse weather than this."

They had. "When we were on the crab boat, we almost died nearly every other day. Seriously, the storms there are not for the faint of heart. I think it desensitized us to danger, and sometimes not for the better," Kell told her. "Someone was always in trouble—lots of man overboards, near misses. It wasn't an easy life and I knew I didn't want to do it forever. But some of those guys did. It made them happy."

"It didn't do that for you?"

"I never worried about being happy," he said. He'd had too many other things to concentrate on. Survival. Not losing himself to his parents' legacy.

Whether or not it was time to let some happiness in was something he'd honestly never considered.

Until now. Because, despite everything, when he was with Teddie, things were right again, so much so that he'd had trouble recognizing it.

Teddie burrowed against him and although she was toughing it out, he felt her trembling. And the storm had barely started.

It would give Dylan and Reid time to figure things out, and Kell time to keep Teddie safe.

For now, that was enough.

It sounded like the house was coming down. She heard glass shatter behind the shutters as the storm intensified and the generator slowed to a near stop as if it couldn't handle the brunt of the hurricane.

She understood how it felt.

She curled up, continued to mull over Kell's last admission, about not worrying about being happy.

"How do you do it?" she asked him finally. "How do you stay emotionless? Because I need to learn that if I'm going to survive."

"That's the last thing I would ever want to teach you." His voice was colder than it had been, but his eyes were fiery, snapping with anger.

She'd meant it as a compliment of sorts, but obviously he'd taken it far differently than she'd intended. But she didn't let it go. "Everything I've ever done from an emotional standpoint has gotten me into major trouble. If I could just learn to shut off my emotions . . ."

"Then what? You'd hold Chambers hostage and demand your answers? Because you had no problem holding a gun to him the first time—or shooting someone, it seems."

"That's not true."

"Glad to hear it. Once you shut off your feelings, there's always the risk that they'll never come back on. And that's a hell of a way to live."

Was he talking about himself? She didn't think his emotions were shut down completely—no, there were more than hints of that, most especially the fact that he'd actually agreed to help her, for no other reason than she'd asked.

"I get why you did it—he set your father up, might have even had him killed; he's not who you thought he was."

Through gritted teeth, she said, "He's exactly who I thought he was. I found that out right after the storm." In so many ways, the destruction from that night hadn't ended, even though her mother had died a month later.

"There's more I need to tell you . . . about Samuel," she said. "But I have a feeling you already knew that."

He didn't confirm or deny but she could see in his eyes that she was right. He'd seen through her from the start, and she wanted to confess it all to him—her dreams, her sins . . . everything in between.

"I know I told you I've known Samuel my whole life. He went to college with both my parents—they were great friends. Always really tight. Samuel was part of the family, although we didn't see him very much when he and my father were both active diplomats. And then he retired and he started coming around more often."

"Don't stop now," Kell told her when she hesitated, and then tried to pull away. "I know you want to, but you've got to tell me. It can only help in the long run."

"I went through a wild phase at one point," she admitted, because starting from there was easier. "I was fifteen, living in a strange country. I rebelled, snuck out . . . drinking, smoking, boys . . ."

He watched her, waited patiently for her to continue.

"I got caught a lot. My parents threatened to send me away to boarding school. I wish they had."

"Did you stop being a bad girl?"

She smiled at that as her naked body rubbed his. "Obviously not."

"That's a good thing, in my book."

"After the hurricane and my mother's announcement, my party days came to a crashing halt. We had to live in a hotel several cities away while everything was being rebuilt. I was on a separate floor from my parents—I had a suite. And Samuel came to check on us as soon as he could. He was worried sick, between the storm and my mom's cancer . . . he just wanted to be there to help."

She practically spat out the last word.

"Did Samuel . . . hurt you?"

"Yes." She raised her eyes to him, defiant, as if waiting for him to blame her, the way she'd blamed herself for so long, but the only thing she saw was his concern. "He tried, but he didn't succeed."

She saw relief in his eyes, still masked by the anger that rose when he'd first asked his question.

"He came up to my room in the hotel to talk to me. Wanted to see if I was playing by the rules. Wanted to talk about college—I was headed to the States in time to take summer classes. I'd wanted to get a jump on things—at least that's what I told my parents. What I really wanted to do was party and get out from under their reach. Typical teenage rebellion, I guess. Looking back, I realize I really had nothing to rebel from." She took a breath, because the words were coming fast and furious now, she couldn't have stopped them if she tried.

"He was drunk. He cornered me. Tore my shirt and kissed me." Even now, she wiped her mouth off on the back of her hand as if she could still feel him on her. "I pushed him off, but he grabbed me again, hard. I had bruises all over my arms the next day. He got me onto the floor and he said . . ." She paused. Swallowed. Shook her head. "He told me if he couldn't have my mother anymore, I was the next best thing."

Jesus. Kell didn't know what to say so he just listened.

"I mean, he was supposed to be my father's best friend. He thought so little of him that he could betray him like that? And my mother too. How could she do that to my father . . . to our family?" She fisted her hands. "All of that got me so angry. I kneed him in the balls and I ran to my bathroom and locked myself inside until he left. I told my parents that I was sick, because how could I face them?"

"I'm sorry, Teddie."

"I don't want you to be sorry. I want you to understand why I have to get to the bottom of this, no matter what. It's so personal. And that's why I'm all screwed up. I felt so guilty and angry at the same time."

"You have nothing to feel guilty about—this was his crime, not yours," Kell told her.

"I'm not going after him because of what he did to me—it's not revenge for that. It's for my family, so I can get proof of his guilt . . . and now my father's innocence. It was one thing for him to have an affair with my mother—she was complicit. But then to use my father like that . . . he was devastated. He discovered the affair the same time he found out that Samuel and my stepmom were involved. And I didn't have the heart to tell him that I'd known about it."

She pulled away before he could see the tears and wished she could leave, run through the night until her lungs were bursting and her body was exhausted, and even then she knew her mind wouldn't stop reliving the memories.

It hadn't since the murders. "I could've done more. Should have."

"What are you talking about?"

"I knew he wasn't to be trusted and if I'd just said something back then . . ."

"You were afraid they wouldn't believe you about his attack?"

"Maybe. Or maybe I was afraid that they would.

Either way, it would've been horrible, but my father might still be alive today."

She could barely face her mother or father after what had happened—but her mother's health had declined quickly—that month she was ill was still a blur. After the funeral, Teddie had taken off for college as quickly as she could and hadn't really looked back. She couldn't bear to spend time with Samuel and thankfully he hadn't been around when she did have to go home for a holiday here and there.

"You can't blame yourself."

"Just because you say it doesn't mean I'm going to believe it," she said, more harshly than she intended.

It was simple—when Kell touched her, the craziness in her mind just vanished.

He was close, but not close enough. She needed the contact so she could stop thinking about the past . . . and the unresolved present problems.

But he was making her deal with it, despite the fact that she didn't want to.

"If you tell the marshals this—" he started, but she shook her head.

"No. Bad enough I told you."

"Why?"

"Because saying it out loud makes it true."

He stroked her cheek. "Yeah, it does. But it happened. And you have to put your trust in someone."

"Who? You're the one telling me my own father couldn't be trusted."

"I thought you wanted my help."

"How do you trust anyone when your own family betrays you?" she asked.

"I'm still working on that," he told her, and then shut that part of the conversation down by saying, "Tell me exactly what happened in the restaurant with Chambers."

"I met him like he'd asked. He was waiting for me at a big table in the back—they obviously knew him there."

The look on Samuel's face when he saw her . . . there was still lust there, and satisfaction, as if he finally had her where he wanted her. He liked her vulnerable. And she'd played that card to the hilt on the phone and in person. "I didn't know what else to do but work him like that."

"You did what you needed to do," he told her fiercely.

She'd avoided Samuel's hug by sliding in next to him. Let him kiss her on the cheek as they sat toward the back of the crowded restaurant.

Even out in full view of the public, she still didn't feel safe. Had pretty much given up on the idea that she ever would.

But the gun tucked in her bag went a long way toward helping. "He asked me how I was holding up. Told me I looked really good."

"Bastard," Kell muttered.

"I said that I needed to stay with him for a while, that I couldn't go back into hiding," she said. "He told me he didn't think that was possible, but he'd see if he could find me a place. The look on his face . . . like he'd be setting me up to be his mistress or something."

And then she'd caught sight of the men and froze, but only for a moment. "I couldn't back down . . . I knew it was literally my last chance. If I was going to go down, I'd do it fighting."

"Sounds like you did."

"I got behind him, grabbed him around the throat and put the gun to his head. The men—to anyone else, they were just a group of men walking into a restaurant for a meal—but I knew. And then everyone started screaming, because of me. And I backed up and headed to the rear exit and the men followed. I shot Samuel to distract them—I pushed him forward and shot him in the arm and then I shot at the biggest man."

"You were firing in self-defense at a man you were hiding from in witness protection. You gave the marshals the pictures you took of the mercs, and you still have the one you kept. You can put them in Khartoum the day of the murders. You're an eye-witness."

"But I shot Samuel—I grabbed him," she said. "If I can't prove that he's guilty, I'm going to be sent to prison in Mexico. God, I can't do this."

Kell gathered her up before she lost it. "I won't let that happen."

"I shot people."

"Self-defense," he repeated. "We'll prove it." But they'd never have to if he and Reid got to Chambers first—and Reid was halfway to taking care of it. "Once Reid and I get through fixing things, no one will have any doubts that Chambers was in on the murder of your father and the kidnapping scheme from the beginning."

"I never thought this would happen. All those secrets . . ."

"Secrets are never good."

"I wish I'd been able to talk to my mother about this before she died. I just wanted to know why, but then she was sick and I just couldn't. I hope she didn't know what a bad man Samuel was. Because if she did . . ."

She regretted not telling her parents about Samuel's attack, regretted her refusal to burden her father after her mother died. And so she'd stayed away from her father for far too long and he'd stopped asking when she was coming to visit.

She'd gone home reluctantly that next summer, because he finally did ask, and she discovered her father had found someone new.

They were already married, her new stepmother already pregnant with twins and her father appeared happy again.

That was what mattered. She hadn't cared that she hadn't been asked to go to the wedding. She'd understood, because she probably wouldn't have been able to watch it happen anyway.

"What about your happiness?" Kell asked, and she wondered why she'd let the story spill so easily with him when she'd stuffed it down for so long.

"Mine?"

"When you were traveling, doing the photography, did you find what you needed?"

"I was happy. I thought I was." She paused to consider. "Maybe I was just still running."

She sagged under the weight of that realization, but Kell was there to catch her—he held her, stroked her hair, told her that it would be all right.

Despite the battering storm, she believed him.

Grier was most definitely interested in more than just getting intel, and Reid was as well, and way too much for a situation like this.

Of course he knew where Teddie was. But he could pass a lie detector test while lying, so no matter what, he was in the clear here. Now he just needed to get that address to Chambers, who would head there after the storm was over, right into Kell's trap.

The longneck beer was cool against his palm and he watched Grier shift nearly imperceptibly under his gaze. There was a slight flush on her chest where her shirt was unbuttoned, showing her tanned skin.

Before he could say anything else, his phone buzzed in his pocket. "'Scuse me—I've gotta take this."

She nodded and continued eating as he stood, pulled his phone out, noted the number was blocked and answered it, keeping her in view.

"Nice to finally chat with you, Reid." The voice was icy. In control.

Crystal. Had to be. His hand tightened on the phone, his anger shot through the roof but he bit it all back. He was going to reel this fish in. "Who is this?" he asked, kept his voice purposely sounding like he was bored as shit.

"Don't tell me Dylan doesn't talk about me. That'll hurt my feelings."

"Dude, I do not have time for games."

"Name's Crystal. But you knew that. What you don't know is that I'm going to kill you."

Well, that was direct. "Good luck with that. Any particular reason?"

"Because you like playing with fire." A pause and then, "That pretty little marshal . . . a shame she won't live to see the end of the week."

Reid could barely breathe but he held it together. "What did she do?"

"She got involved with you."

When the phone clicked off, Reid wanted to smash it to shit, but he knew he needed to try to get a trace.

If the guy had been trailing him all this time, he was good.

It was time for Reid to be better.

Because Reid had a feeling Crystal wasn't tailing him as much as he'd been tailing Grier. She'd gotten into Reid's mess but good. She was in trouble because of him. And although before this Reid's only goal had been to keep her off Kell's trail long enough for him and Teddie to get away, now he'd involved an innocent.

Reid couldn't stomach that. Even though he and Grier were working opposite sides of this mission, he'd have to find a way to keep her from harm's reach.

"I thought maybe we could trade a little intel," he said after he sat down and ordered a second beer.

"What happened during that phone call to make you suddenly want to trade intel?"

"I got a call from the man who I think's been feeding you information," he said. "If I'm right, he's the one who gave you the tip about me and Kell in the first place."

She didn't deny it. "There was someone who came into the office in Texas and offered up a lead on where Teddie was and who she was staying with. Why is he contacting you?"

"To let me know he plans to kill me." Reid bit into a soft taco like he hadn't just announced there was a death sentence attached to him.

He couldn't be that desensitized to violence, could he? "Why is that?"

"I'll let you know as soon as I figure it out." He wiped his mouth with a napkin and crumpled it in his fist. "Anything you can give me would be great."

"You need my help?"

"Not really. But I figured you'd be happy if you thought we could trade intel."

That grin again. In the space of a single second, she wanted to both kiss and strangle him. "You're really going to give me info on Teddie's location?"

"She's safe from Chambers for now. But he wants her dead."

"You're not going to tell me how you know this?"

"It's the truth, Grier. And I'll get you proof."

She paused and then pulled a picture out of her pocket, the one the security cameras had captured of the blond man who was her informant. "This is the guy who gave me the information on you and Teddie. You're positive it's the same man who called you just now?"

"If I can keep this, I'll send it to someone who'll know for sure," Reid said, studying the picture. From the way he appeared to commit the face to memory, she could tell it was the first time he'd seen the man. "What did he tell you?"

"He knew your name and Kell's. Said you were military. He knew the address of the house in Mexico. He also knew about the bomb and that you crossed the border."

Reid's face hardened. "He knew about the bomb because he put it there. Why hasn't Teddie's father's murder been investigated more thoroughly? Didn't anyone believe Teddie when she showed them the pictures of American mercenaries?"

Grier cocked her head and stared at him. "That's the reason she was taken into custody. Although the evidence collected indicates that Teddie's father was the mastermind behind the kidnapping-for-ransom schemes—the authorities found money transfers into several offshore accounts that corresponded with the release of the hostages over the years. The mercs are being pursued, but it's believed that they murdered Teddie's father because he screwed them out of money, and so Teddie was put into hiding because her life is in danger until they're caught. Samuel Chambers was investigated but we never had a connection between him and the kidnappings and murders. We still don't."

"Did Teddie tell the authorities—or the marshals—that she believed Chambers had something to do with it?"

"She never said that. She just insisted her father was innocent. No one could prove that. There's still an active investigation into the three men from the pictures she took the day of the killings." She paused. "Did Teddie tell you she believes Chambers's involved?"

"Yes."

"I'm sure that's what her father wanted her to believe." She took a sip of her beer and pointed to the pocket where Reid had put the picture. "Why didn't she tell us?"

"Why do you think?"

Because she was planning on doing the job herself.

Grier could understand the need for personal vengeance. She'd sat through the sentencing of the men who'd killed her sister and realized that no amount of time would be enough. She'd wanted justice—wanted them dead, the way her sister was. "She took a shot at Chambers for what seems like no reason. It wasn't a shot to kill—she wanted him alive."

"She wants him to confess. Otherwise, she'd have killed her only witness."

Grier couldn't deny the truth of that statement. "What's the guy's name who's been feeding me information?"

"John Crystal. Former military. Merc. Spy. Very dangerous and out for only himself."

"And he's after you and Kell—and you have Teddie. She's in danger."

"Teddie's safe. You'll have a chance to question her when this is all over."

"Reid, my job doesn't work like this."

"There's no way you have the resources to keep her safe."

"You don't get to make that decision."

"It's already been made. And I'm not jerking you around." No, he was trying to help a friend decide on his own goddamned feelings.

"I'm going to lock you up until you tell me where she is."

"That leaves you unprotected."

She looked at him incredulously. "You think you're protecting me?"

"I know I am." He paused. "You're tied to me through all this. Your life's in as much danger as mine is."

"Are you threatening me?"

"Stating a fact." He stared at her. "Crystal told me you'd be dead in the space of a week. This week. That doesn't leave more than two days' worth of time."

"So what are you saying? I should stop investigating and go hide?"

"Yes, that's exactly what I'm saying. You have no idea what this man is capable of. I know you've seen some tough men, dealt with them, but you've never seen anything like this one."

"I've never run from a fight."

"You should run from this one. Go back to Texas. I'll get Teddie to you."

"Nice try. You've been playing me for a fool."

"I'm not the one playing you for a fool, Grier. Crystal's been doing a hell of a job of it all on his own." He stood and threw some money on the table, enough to cover their tab. "I can protect you from Crystal, but you'll have to let me. You know where to find me if you change your mind."

Reid left before she could sputter out a curse or a question or both, and yeah, he'd left Grier abruptly, but he'd given her a lot of information as well. Probably more than he should have, but when someone's life is on the line, he felt they had a right to know.

It was a quiet walk to his motel, and Grier didn't come after him. About ten minutes before he got there, he got the call he'd been waiting for from Chambers.

"Reid here," he said when he picked up the phone, and Chambers wasted no time.

"You hurt one of my men badly."

"Wish I could say I was sorry, but he jumped me. Fair is fair."

"I called your references."

"I trust it all checked out."

"You've led an interesting life," Chambers commented. "It's about to get more so."

"That means you have a job for me?"

"I'll need your information first."

"Doesn't work like that. Job first, then I'll give you the intel."

Chambers was silent for so long, Reid thought he'd either hung up or the connection was lost. But finally, he heard the man sigh. Reid continued walking, keeping an eye out for anyone tailing him.

"Be at Mariano Escobedo Airport at nine tomorrow evening. You'll be looking for a couple—American—you'll be their chauffeur. Their last name is Moorehill."

"I didn't sign up to be a driver."

"You're not going to take them where they want to go, Mr. Cormier," Chambers said. "You'll get more information when you arrive. Now, I'm assuming you have some for me as well."

Yes, plenty. He rattled off the address of Riley's place in Florida and Chambers repeated it and then hung up. Reid stared at his phone, checked it to make sure the conversation had been recorded.

You're going down, Chambers, straight to hell, and I'm going to be the one driving.

He emailed Dylan to give him the pickup time. According to plan, the Moorehills would be intercepted and federal agent decoys would take their place, wrapping up Chambers's kidnapping business nicely. Then Dylan would contact Kell on Riley's satphone.

Satisfied, he shoved his phone in his pocket as he got to the motel parking lot . . . and that's where the assault began. Reid knew it was Crystal, that he'd been lying in wait for him, judging from the blow he took across his back—not so much the force of the hit, but the style was Special Forces all the way.

According to Dylan, Crystal was in his mid-forties, but for a well-trained man, age meant relatively little. It was a good shot and Reid mentally cursed himself for getting caught off guard, for being too wrapped up in Grier's safety to remember most of his own rules.

He opened his eyes and got up off the fucking pavement quickly, turned to see the man who'd promised to personally make all their lives miserable.

Crystal stood about five feet from him, his stance a fighting one. And then, in a move that surprised Reid, who thought he could never be surprised by much in combat, Crystal smiled.

Smiled. Asshole.

Reid took the moment to recoup, stared at Crystal and realized that he looked a lot like Reid himself would in fifteen years. Probably charmed his way into a hell of a lot of places, the way Reid had his whole life.

Fighting yourself. Excellent.

What the hell, he'd been doing it for years anyway.

"Hey, Reid." Crystal's voice was a loud boom and he didn't bother to lower it. Not that anyone was really around, and certainly no one likely to help either of them.

Crystal would be the one who needed medical attention—or the morgue—when Reid was done. Or maybe he'd just send the fucker to prison.

"Hell of a greeting," Reid growled.

"Wanted to see what you can handle." He spouted off Reid's PT scores, starting with goddamned boot camp and then detailed a few of his other accomplishments that were deemed classified, much like the rundown the men in the alley had given Kell. Crystal was impressive as hell and Reid could appreciate the merits of that despite the fact that he wanted to kill him for having fucked with Dylan.

Granted, Dylan had given as good as he'd got. It was something you risked when you worked jobs like this.

"You'll get a taste of what I can do."

"This won't end here, I promise you that," Crystal told him. "I just needed to see what you're made of. Then again, I know what drives you—not being able to save your family still eats at you."

Reid wanted to tell the man to fuck off, but he channeled the anger back inside, because it made a hell of a fuel, and instead stood calmly, staring at his would-be opponent.

"Am I boring you?" Crystal asked.

"Yes. I've got a lot more important things to do, so let's get this over with."

Crystal laughed, like Reid had just told him the best joke in the world, and then he pulled out a wicked-looking small knife. "Have at it."

Reid always preferred fighting one-on-one bare-handed. It was a more intimate way of fighting—and an easier way to get a feel for one's opponent. While he understood the need to bring a knife to a gun-fight—or any fight—he felt fighting with no weapons showed who the better warrior was.

It would be him this time, no question about it. Because this fight wasn't just for him—it was for Kell and Dylan and all the other men and women he called family. They were worth fighting for.

They circled each other and Reid thought about Dylan, about how his friend would never forgive himself if Reid didn't extricate himself from this situation.

It wouldn't be easy. Good thing he never thought anything would be.

Crystal jabbed the air with the knife, going for Reid's upper body, and Reid dodged it, jumping out of the way. He let Crystal pump his arm over and over, then swung into a half spin and kicked the knife out of the man's hand. At the same time, he grabbed Crystal's wrist and twisted until he heard a satisfying pop.

Crystal brought up his other arm and caught Reid with a stiff jab to the side of his neck and a kick to the side of his knee. Reid released and recircled his enemy, kicking the knife well out of reach, his neck aching. If Crystal had gotten him in the right spot, Reid would've been unconscious.

"Come closer and play," Crystal taunted, moved

forward a step and swung, but Reid ducked and got in a slam to the side of Crystal's head, hard enough to bring the man down to the pavement. But he didn't stay there, moved to chop the back of Reid's knees, which buckled them. He then grabbed Reid's calves while Reid was already unsteady and pulled his feet out from under him in one smooth motion.

Reid blocked his fall with his hands, rolled out of the way of Crystal's grasp and kicked him hard, the blows landing against Crystal's gut. Reid heard the groan and the sharp intake of breath and took the opportunity to leap to his feet.

But Crystal, still surprisingly limber, was up again with only a bit of a stagger. He came at Reid, and Reid propelled himself at his enemy, throwing them both into the plate-glass window of a storefront their fighting had moved them toward. An alarm began blaring before the men could disengage, a tangle of arms and legs and broken glass.

Reid was breathing hard, but Crystal's breath came harder. His nose was broken as well as his wrist, and maybe his arm.

"Well done," Crystal wheezed.

"Can't say the same for you."

Crystal smiled then, and it was so full of menace Reid felt the chill to his soul. "I'll be back for you, Reid. And I don't think I'm going to kill you . . . since you fight so well, I've got a real special place for you," Crystal sneered.

"Who says I'm letting you go?" Reid asked. "Won't take me long to break your neck."

Crystal held up a remote. "Bomb in Grier's car. She's not at her hotel yet . . . my tracker says she's got another three minutes. The timer's counting down from two minutes. It's killing me or saving Grier—which one will you choose?"

Grier. Fuck, he couldn't risk it. Let the bastard go for now, because he believed a man like that didn't come into a fight without backup in place.

Killing a merc was never easy—it's why they kept their nine lives.

Crystal tossed the remote in the air and took off. Reid raced to get the timer before it hit the ground and then moved around the corner so the police coming to investigate the broken window wouldn't bother him. He knelt on the pavement, taking apart the black plastic carefully, mouth dry, watching the clock count down too fast.

He took his knife out—it wasn't the best tool for this, but time wasn't on his side. He checked the wires and double-checked and, knowing this could all be a setup, cut through the yellow one and saw the timer finally stop and let out a breath when the GPS tracker showed that Grier's truck continued to move past the three-minute mark.

He sagged with relief, his body aching and his adrenaline waning. He took a quick look around the perimeter, studiously avoiding the police activity. Crystal could be anywhere by now—and unfortunately he'd already learned Reid's vulnerability, even before he'd put on his little show.

He headed to his motel room and checked it thoroughly for bugs—or bombs—before he took out his phone and made a quick call.

Vivi answered on the first ring. "Are you okay?"

He smiled a little at the true concern in her voice. For bringing his friend Caleb back to life, Reid felt like the men owed her everything—Vivi seemed to feel the reverse.

"I'm okay. I need a favor."

"Name it."

"Find out what records of mine have been pulled recently."

"Military? I did that already."

He paused. "No, go back sixteen years or more and look for ones through DHS and CPS."

"Will do."

"One more thing, Vivi."

"What?"

"This goes no further than us. It can't. This is personal." It was business too, but he didn't want Dylan or the others knowing anything about it just yet.

"I've got your back," she said quietly, and he knew she meant it.

If his gut was right, this would play out much differently than anyone thought. Crystal had never been focusing on Kell, but on Reid. He'd had a feeling about that from the start, which was part of the reason he'd wanted to separate himself from the others.

He'd suspected it from the second Dylan had mentioned how Crystal liked to investigate pasts. Because none of the men knew the full truth about Reid's—and that was something he'd rather be kept under wraps.

Even now, Reid could berate himself so easily for what had happened that night in his house. But what no one knew, not even Kell, was that the perfect family he couldn't save wasn't anywhere near so fucking perfect after all. But that was a place he wasn't going tonight. Or any night, if he could help it. Lying to himself about this had become part of his life, and giving up the fantasy would rip his guts out again.

CHAPTER
13

After Teddie told her story, they both lay there, letting the weight of her confession—and its possible repercussions—settle in.

In Kell's mind, it didn't change much at all.

After putting it off as he long as he could, he dragged on his jeans and shirt and went to look at what was happening outside through a garage-door window.

A fucking mess. Good. No one was out there right now and that was just how he wanted it.

When he came back inside, Teddie had pulled on her T-shirt but remained wrapped in the blanket. She was still tense because of the storm but she wasn't nearly as frantic as she'd been earlier. "Is it almost over?" she asked hopefully.

"It's going to take a little bit longer."

"You don't have to break it to me gently, you know."

"I'll need to keep you occupied for the next day or so."

"Shit."

"Ah, sweetheart, you had fun today, right?" She smiled and blushed and he joined her again on the floor. "Don't worry, okay? Can you give me that for the next couple of hours at least?"

"It's not so much worrying. And actually, I'm not sorry to be feeling all of it," she started to explain. "After my mom died, everything changed. My dad went right back to work. He had to and I . . ." She shook her head. "I went into robot mode too. It's like I consciously shut down, and I don't think I've gotten out of it since—and it only got worse after the murders. But when you got hurt, something changed . . ."

He looked at her.

"And then I woke up and came back to life . . ." She turned to him. "I liked it."

"I scared you."

"It was more than that." She reached out and took his hand. He didn't resist, although he wasn't used to outward shows of emotion and affection either. It was a learning curve experience for both of them, for sure. "I have friends—acquaintances—all over the place. But I never really stuck around to have permanent home. You get used to that, being nomadic. Now I don't think it's a good thing. You're the first person—you and Reid—I've had in my life who worried about me . . . at least as an adult. It's nice to know there are people who've got your back. I'm tired of running, Kell. It seems like you aren't. It doesn't bother you?"

"I've been running in one way or another my whole life. After a while, you realize it's not such a bad deal. At least I'm never bored."

"But you have a place to go when things get bad, right?"

"Yes." Now, more than ever, thanks to Dylan and his contingency plans.

"I don't."

"You do, with me." The words came out before he could stop them, but he doubted he would've. That meant what he said had to be true.

She blinked, hard. Her eyes got wet and her voice husky and she simply said, "Thanks. You have no idea what that means."

He did, even though he wasn't ready to talk about it. But her next words threatened to put an end to that, threatened to pull him someplace he didn't want to go.

"When we were at the house in Mexico, when I talked about my family . . ." She seemed not to know how to finish the sentence and settled on, "Are your parents around at all?"

"No."

"Oh. Are they dead?"

He wanted to say something sarcastic, but the way she'd lost her family . . . he just couldn't. "No."

"Did they do something bad to you?"

Again, he bit back a sarcastic answer and settled on the truth. "Very bad. I haven't seen them since I was sixteen. Have no desire to see them ever again. I'm better off without them."

"I'm sorry, Kell."

"I don't need your pity," he practically growled at her; he couldn't stop himself. "I survived and now I stop the bad guys. That's what I do. I save and I kill and sometimes innocents get hurt in the crossfire. But you shouldn't try to paint me as some kind of saint, Teddie. Your first assessment of me was probably closest to the truth."

"You want me to stay scared of you?" She paused. "Reid told me I was smart if I was . . . but that I shouldn't let that get in the way."

Fucking Reid—when did he turn into the fucking Buddha all of a sudden? The man had never had a single, serious relationship in his life either and suddenly he was Dear Abby wrapped in Dr. Phil. "My family wasn't like yours."

"What? Mine wasn't perfect—you know that now."

"Sounds like it was pretty damned good for a long while," he said. "Look, my parents were—are—grifters."

"Thieves?" she asked. He nodded, and she continued, "How long were they like that?"

"My whole life."

"So you knew that they stole things?"

"Mostly money. And yes, I knew. It was something they were proud of—they wanted me to be a part of the family business. I used to work with them," he admitted. "I didn't plan to, just grew up in it."

He closed his eyes and tried to picture his childhood. He'd mostly blocked it out, to the point where all he remembered were bits and pieces of the lessons his parents taught him over the years, each one a milestone in their eyes.

Certainly, there were no birthday parties or normal parent-child time for him. He hadn't really known that existed until he'd finally been allowed to hang out at friends' houses, and even then, he was only supposed to be there to scope things out and report his findings to his parents to see if his friends were worthy of a grift.

"They weren't into things like pickpocketing. They called that petty thieving and looked down on it, like what they did was so far above it." He recalled Reid's ability to turn his skill for petty thieving into a hell of a career, with a chest full of medals to prove it. "They went for bigger things. We were always moving. Couldn't stay in the same spot after you'd bilked people out of hundreds of thousands of dollars. The funny thing is, we never had enough goddamned money—they were always broke, so it never made sense to me. The one time I brought it up, my father split my lip and I learned to keep my mouth shut about it."

For a while anyway, until he grew broader and taller than his father and decided he wasn't afraid of him any longer.

"I can't imagine any of this."

"Then don't."

The house shook and, to his amazement, Teddie ignored it in favor of pulling the rest of the story from him. "You don't trust me."

"The story of my life has nothing to do with trust."

"It has everything to do with it," she said softly. "I want to know all about you—good, bad and ugly."

Maybe if she knew, he could actually be free—she'd find out that there was no hope of redemption for him and she'd leave.

Anyone who'd want to try to make a life with him was out of their mind. Teddie had too bright of a future once this was all over to tie herself to him for any length of time.

"You said you met Reid in foster care. Did your parents put you there?"

"I put myself there." He pulled on his clothes; he'd never felt so fucking stripped in his entire life. The wind howled and he was sure he wouldn't mind if the house blew down around their heads.

He'd take something smaller, though, any kind of distraction. But none came. He was trapped—literally, and it was a trap of his own making.

The picture came through Dylan's email, courtesy of Reid. Reid had taken a picture of the picture with his phone, and while the quality sucked, there was no mistaking that it showed Crystal walking through the Texas U.S. Marshals office.

"I thought all these places were supposed to have security," Cam muttered, looking over his shoulder. He'd been pretty much connected to Dylan's hip since Crystal had resurfaced. Riley had been too, although she'd finally relented to some sleep and had gone into the bedroom.

"People let him in anywhere. He always looks like he belongs. Between that and a wicked collection of IDs, he's got a pass to pretty much everywhere." Damned asshole could probably bribe his way into heaven too. "Reid thinks he's in Mexico."

"Why's that?"

Dylan scrolled the email, wondering why Reid hadn't just called him.

"Probably because you'll yell at him," Cam said, reading his mind again. He took the phone from Dylan and read the email out loud—the gist of it was that Crystal had called Reid, threatened both him and the U.S. marshal looking for Teddie.

"Shit." Dylan paced the room. "I want Reid out of there."

"He's not going anywhere until he helps Kell with the Teddie mess."

"You've heard from Kell?"

"No. Fucking too many people using satphones these days and jamming up the lines. Probably won't have comms until the hurricane passes through. But he's there. He's safe," Cam said.

"Crystal's going to let me know where he is," Dylan said. "That's his MO. He wants me to chase him."

"Are you going to kill him when you catch him this time? If not, at least let me," Cam said, and Dylan clenched his fist. "Go ahead if that makes you feel better."

It wouldn't. But the ringing phone did, made Dylan grab for his cell on the kitchen counter and look at the number.

"It's him." Dylan flipped the phone to speaker and answered, "Crystal, what's it this time?"

"Your friend—Reid, is it? He's quite good. I've got big plans for him." Crystal laughed. Cam was already dialing Reid on his phone, mouthing, "voice mail," and he walked away so Crystal wouldn't hear him leave a message.

"Did he kick your ass?" Dylan asked.

"He tried. But you know I give as good as I get."

Dylan bit back his anger, wouldn't let Crystal know he was causing an ulcer to form as Dylan stood there with his forehead pressed to the wall. Didn't want to look at Cam when he returned.

This is my fault—should've killed this bastard when I had the chance.

No mercy was a good credo to live by for many reasons, Crystal at the top of the list. "You too chicken to come after me directly? Guess you've gotten soft in your advanced age."

"Dylan, where would the fun be in coming after you first? And you know me—I live for fun."

"Yeah, you're a fucking barrel of laughs," Dylan muttered.

"I'm going to make you suffer," Crystal continued, his voice unchanged, as though he was making small talk at a cocktail party instead of threatening Dylan's life. "You can try to catch me, but if you find me, you still won't have the balls to kill me. You never did, and that's your fatal weakness."

When Crystal hung up, Dylan needed to hit something. Didn't worry about breaking his hand before he slammed it through the Sheetrocked wall.

The pain that flashed through his fist radiated through every nerve in his body. He cursed, hit the wall again despite the pain, maybe even tried to make a pact with the devil, before Cam got hold of him and attempted to calm him down.

When that didn't work, he tackled him, pushing his face into the carpet.

"This isn't helping anyone, Dylan."

"Making me feel better." But it wasn't. Anger and hate curled up in a tight little ball and Dylan didn't like that he was rethinking everything, including pulling Riley deeper into his life.

"No regrets, my friend. It's how you always told me to live," Cam reminded him.

"Maybe I was wrong."

"Fuck, where's a tape recorder when you need it."

Grier knocked softly and Reid grunted for her to come in. He'd left the door unlocked, because whoever was out to get him—whether Crystal or McMannus—wasn't going to be stopped by a motel room lock.

She walked over to where he sat at the small table, stood next to him.

"What happened to the other guy?"

"It was a fucking tie." His fist hit the table hard and he winced. "Goddamned bastard."

She ran a gentle thumb across his cheekbone. The bruise under his eye was already turning black. And then she took one of his hands in hers. "Looks that way. Was it someone from Chambers's crew?"

He snorted. "Not even close."

"Who did this?"

He glanced at her. "Crystal almost killed you tonight."

She started, but she didn't let go of his hand. He

didn't mind that all that much but he reluctantly pulled it from hers. "Stay here, I'll be right back."

He went out to her truck, got on the ground and slid himself underneath and found the bomb easily, the timer frozen, showing thirty-nine seconds left.

He started to sweat just thinking about it, pulled the device off the chassis and worked himself back out from underneath the truck. He cut a few more wires with his knife before he went back into the room and put the disabled bomb on the table next to where Grier was standing.

He sank down into the chair. "This was under your car."

"He got away because you stopped to save me," she said quietly and he nodded.

"You should put yourself into protective custody for a while, until we can catch this guy."

"Do you know why he's targeting you?"

"Yeah. He's researched me. Knows I won't let anyone die on my watch, even if it means letting his ass go." The words came out in a fierce growl—he didn't intend it, but even that didn't scare Grier away. "My family died in a fire when I was fourteen. I was rescued from the house in time, they weren't."

"I'm so sorry, Reid. I can't imagine—"

"No, you can't. It was my fault." He glanced at her, gauging her reaction, wondering why the hell he'd chosen to tell her, of all people, instead of Kell. "I was supposed to be watching my mother."

"She started the fire?"

He nodded. "She was bipolar. Off her meds. Refused to take them, and when she went into a manic phase, it was bad. You know, from the outside, we were this perfect family. I've kept up the act all these years because it was ingrained in me. *Don't air the family's secrets in public.*"

"I don't understand why you think the fire's your fault."

"I was supposed to be watching her that night. My father stayed up on the weekends with her, but during the week, it was my job. And I fell asleep when I wasn't supposed to." He'd woken up to thick, choking smoke and his first instinct had been to search for his mother. "The firemen dragged me out. It was too late to save the others. They said it was an accident, but I knew better. Her fires were never accidents. But I didn't tell anyone because there wasn't a point. And ever since then, that's what happens to people around me—they die, and for some reason, I don't. I'm used to people trying to kill me, Grier. Happens all the fucking time. I don't die, but the people around me do. Fucking guardian angel bullshit."

She looked so concerned, so sad. He sighed and glanced up at the ceiling for a long moment. "I'm all fucked-up, Grier. All fucked-up. You should run from me," he murmured when he finally looked at her again.

"I know." She rubbed his shoulder lightly. "But I won't."

Fuck it, then. She knew what she was getting. And he reached up, pulled her onto his lap and kissed her, not caring that almost any place she put her hand would hurt, because he was sore as hell.

Except for one place, and that was the only one that mattered now. With her mouth on his, her body doing that sweet little dance of surrender against his, the pain no longer mattered. Her mouth was demanding, as if she'd been waiting for this. His tongue dueled with hers, and her hands wound in his hair, pulling him closer. He ran his hands up and down her back, wanting to feel her skin on his, not satisfied with waiting any longer.

"Strip for me, Grier." He murmured the order against her mouth. "Do it, and let me watch."

"I don't want to move from this position."

"Nothing's going to happen until you're naked."

"And then what?"

"And then you strip me."

"So I'll be doing all the work, then?"

Reid's smile stretched lazily across his face but she wasn't deceived. She leaned back and unbuttoned her shirt, let it slip off and then unhooked her bra. She flushed when he let out a soft whistle of obvious approval.

She was in good shape—had to be. And if she looked at herself with a critical eye, she knew she looked good.

But seeing herself through Reid's eyes . . . well, that level of appreciation was enough to last her a very long time. She wanted more. And she was going to make sure she got it.

She stood and unbuttoned her pants, let them drop to the floor so that she was left in lacy, see-through boy shorts.

Reid sucked in a hard breath and pushed off the chair and fell to his knees in front of her as if in some kind of erotic prayer. His hands held her hips and angled her toward him, his face settling between her legs. He put his mouth to her sex, breathed out hot against the thin fabric and she shuddered at the contact.

If he could do this through underwear . . .

And then he moved the thin scrap to the side with a finger and his lips found her, his tongue rooting and discovering her core with an astonishing ease. The sound that welled up from her throat didn't sound like her at all. It was filled with primal need and everything smelled like lust and all her senses were keenly awake.

His tongue continued to seek her as his hands tore away the fabric completely so that she was free to him. Naked, and he was fully clothed.

It was the hottest thing ever, as if he was only there for her pleasure.

And yet, she knew that Reid, naked, would be a beautiful thing and very much worth savoring.

She realized she had nothing to hold on to, but that didn't seem to matter because Reid caught her hips in his hands and held her in place as he continued to lave and lick and drive her absolutely over-the-edge mad in the most delightful way possible.

She was aware that she was yelling—in a motel like this, it probably wouldn't register, and normally she wouldn't be caught dead here. But being on the edge of Reid's dangerous life was making every experience seem far more exciting.

When she came, it rocked her entire body, rolled through her like a tidal wave . . . like nothing she'd ever felt before. And he wasn't pulling back, continued to keep his face buried against her as the orgasm crested.

Her legs trembled. At some point, Reid stood and

carried her to the bed, laid her down against the soft, worn sheets, and the overhead fan felt good as it pushed air against her too warm body.

She opened her eyes to see Reid standing next to the bed, stripping off his shirt and pants without ceremony. His eyes never left hers, letting her know they were so not done here.

Good. Because while she couldn't move right now, pretty soon she was going to want a whole lot more of him.

The mattress dipped next to her as he climbed into bed. He tugged her close to him and she could barely catch her breath, pushed her hair from her face as she settled against his naked body. He was warm—his body hard in all the right places, and looking so good despite the many bruises and contusions.

He didn't seem to be in any pain and she wasn't in the mood to be gentle. Not after what he'd aroused in her. Her lips pressed to his chest, then moved down to capture a nipple in her mouth, plying it with her teeth until she felt him stiffen, heard him groan.

He pulled her back, his face serious. "Just so we're clear, I'm not giving you any more intel."

"What I'm looking for has nothing to do with intel." Her hand wrapped around his cock and it was warm and smooth and she loved hearing Reid's groan of surrender. His head went back against the thinly veneered headboard and his eyes closed as she stroked up and down, watching his hips falling in with her rhythm.

"Nice, Grier."

"Nice?" she practically growled, then brought her mouth down around him, her tongue swirling the head of his cock before she took half of him in her mouth.

"Fuck. Fuck yes."

That was a much better response. She continued to work him with her hand and her mouth, using lips and tongue and even a light drag of teeth, feeling his body shuddering under her control. One of his hands caressed the back of her neck, the other tightly fisted on the bed next to him, like he was struggling to keep some semblance of control.

She wanted him to lose it the way she had and so she doubled her efforts to bring him to climax. But he was tugging at her, telling her to stop, that he needed to be inside her now—and that turned her on too much to continue.

She wanted the same thing and she kissed her way up his body, savoring the tightly rippled abs and hard chest. He tasted good under her tongue, a heady mix of lust filling her senses.

When she began to nibble on his collarbone, he wrapped his arms around her, practically threw her back down to the mattress and spread her thighs with one of his. There was no asking—he was taking what he wanted and as he entered her it was her turn to clutch the sheets.

It had been a while—she was wet but tight. He penetrated her slowly as he watched the look on her face—the surprise and pleasure mingling together. The way her mouth opened and only small, incoherent moans emerged.

She was so goddamned hot, he couldn't help but press into her without pause, wanting to drive himself fully inside without any further wait. Her body accepted him, opening to his movements, and soon he was thrusting against her, the bed creaking under them, the fan doing nothing to stop a film of sweat from covering his body from the exertion.

He didn't want it to end too soon, and between her impromptu blow job and this, it would.

To make it last, he leaned back and held her hips, pulled her slowly back and forth against him, his cock massaging her clit, making her arch and clutch for him. She moaned for him to go faster and he went even slower, enjoying the hot drag on his cock. Everything else from the day—and the previous ones—melted away, and he watched Grier's body writhe, her nipples darkening with arousal, her body flushed a beautiful color, mixing with her tan.

She was enjoying herself and she had no problem letting him know it. He grit his teeth as his balls tightened, and knew he'd be unable to stop himself from coming. He leaned back over and took her, hard and fast, until her climax brought his forth and he willingly let himself go over the edge with her.

After a return to earth, Grier rolled onto her stomach, propped herself on her elbows to look at Reid. The man was like a lion, tousled, lazy-eyed and looking content after a somewhat marathon session of seemingly never-ending sex.

She certainly wasn't complaining, although her stomach did rumble. Loudly. "Any places that deliver around here?"

Reid grinned. "Yeah, there are some menus in the night-table drawer, right next to the Bible."

She snorted. "I'll call the front desk to see if they've got a recommendation."

They did, to a place around the corner. Reid told her he'd have whatever she was having and she placed the order, was told twenty minutes, and she checked her messages, text and otherwise, to make sure no one from her team was looking for her.

She'd told Jack earlier she'd be available for anything that came up—and in the meantime, he'd been running scans for Kell and Teddie's credit cards, both of which were coming up a big empty.

"Have you heard from Kell?" she asked.

"My phone's been on the table the whole time— I haven't heard it ring once," he said. "I told you, I won't hear from him."

"So he can keep you innocent."

"No one's attempted that for years."

"I've got a tail on Chambers; you know that, right? So if I take him in and you're caught working for him, you're going to jail."

"Thanks for the warning. We both know if you had anything on me, I'd already be there." He lay on his back staring at the ceiling and she went to the bathroom to shower before the food got there. When she came out, dressed in only her shirt, her hair damp, she found Reid unpacking their takeout on the small table in the corner.

She pulled up one of the chairs and began to dig in almost immediately. Reid did the same.

"Aren't you worried about getting yourself in trouble by being with me?" Reid asked.

"Does it look like I'm worried?"

"Marshals don't worry?"

She didn't answer that question, chose to continue eating.

"Why did you choose the marshals?" he asked finally.

"Why do you do what you do?"

"I'm good at it. I like danger."

He made it sound so simple, and it probably was in a way, but it was also complicated by what had happened to his family. The guilt in his voice when he'd told her had been palpable, and she understood—she carried around a hefty dose of guilt herself. "I was a debutante from a wealthy family. According to them, especially on paper, I didn't fit into this world at all. I fought with everything I had to get here. I fight every day to stay here."

Grier admitted to her vulnerabilities in a way Reid had never been able to. She accepted them, even if they pissed her off.

Reid tried to process that. Hell, it was obviously working for her.

"I'm a woman doing a man's job. I took a lot of flack on the way up but I didn't let it get to me. At least I never showed in public that it did." Grier smiled. "Sometimes, I'm too tough and it affects the personal side of my life."

"You felt pretty damned soft to me," he told her. "The job's hard. You've got to be tough to survive."

"At first . . . at first, it was all for me. It felt right. The job fits me. And then my older sister was killed. She was in a convenience store during a robbery and she was shot. They were holding people hostage and they wouldn't send her out for medical attention. She died on a linoleum floor." Her voice caught and Reid gently tugged her to his shoulder, like he knew she was going to cry and wanted to pretend she wasn't. She fought the sobs for a few seconds but in the end, she was unsuccessful in remaining stoic.

Goddammit, now she remembered why she hated the aftermath of sex. Way too many emotional minefields, brought on by hormones.

Men had it so much easier.

"It just makes me so angry. She did charity work . . . God, it sounds so cliché to say that it should've been me."

"I've lost people," he said finally. "My best friend . . . I know he feels like that, that it should've been him in certain situations. I know I do, all the fucking time."

"But we lived for a reason."

"Is this one of those everything-happens-for-a-reason speeches?"

"No. But my job is important, I honor her memory by doing it to the fullest."

Something fell away when she said that. For Reid, it was like a brick wall crumbled inside of him, lightening his load immeasurably. It was like a renewal, and for that moment he and Grier understood each other better than anyone in the entire world. They clicked, and while not everything made sense, Reid felt better.

Actually, he just felt, and for the first time in a long time, that was all right.

"Wasn't it Shakespeare who said, what's past is prologue?" she asked.

"I don't know—*Macbeth* is my favorite."

"Ah, the dangers of too much power." But she

smiled as she said it and maybe she tugged at him first, or perhaps it was he who pulled her close, but their bodies meshed together, tangled, mouths hungry for each other.

"Grier."

"Yes."

"Yes, what?"

"Yes, to everything you want to do to me now," she told him, and he didn't hesitate to bring her back to bed.

CHAPTER
14

Kell had walked away from her after their discussion of his parents. Teddie could tell he needed a little space, heard him in the kitchen, and she stayed under the blanket and tried not to let the sounds from outside upset her.

Still, her head pounded, the stress of the day—the past months—catching up to her. She rolled her neck and brought her hands up to rub some of the tension away.

Before she knew it, Kell was behind her and his hands were moving to the back of her neck. They were cool and strong and they massaged the hurt away in a way no one else had ever been able to.

She moaned softly as his hands moved under her shirt to her shoulders.

How hands that did such violent work could make her melt, she had no idea, but she was grateful for it.

"Sorry about before. It's a subject I don't like talking about," he said finally.

"I can understand that. For a long time, I just concentrated on trying to forgive my mother."

"Did you?"

"I've come to terms with what she did," she said. "I had to. She was gone, and that was hard enough. I couldn't hate her. You know, I think she did the best she could. Sometimes, it's nowhere good enough."

Kell gave himself credit for not rolling his eyes at her attempt to be Zen, because she was serious as a heart attack. And when you were trying to reconcile why your parents had screwed up and fucked you over, you clung to anything you could.

For a while, at least.

Eventually, you gave up and realized that sometimes certain people were just completely for shit and didn't deserve a second chance.

"You don't believe a word I just said."

"It's not something I need to believe. If you do, that's okay."

She snorted, leaned her head back against the couch. "What happens for you when this is all over?"

It was a question he wasn't sure how to answer. "I figure out what I want to do."

"You won't be working with Reid and your other friends anymore?"

"I don't know. I didn't know if I wanted to work for them this time, but I decided to try. I didn't want Reid to go it alone."

"Does Reid know how you feel?" she asked. "I think it's high time you two hashed some things out."

"Reid knows." Reid, who was scared to death that

he'd lose Kell, and Kell had nearly made his worst fear come true. He was a fucking bastard who didn't deserve a friend like Reid, didn't deserve any of them. "It'll be better that way. At least that's how I feel now."

"But things can change," she murmured, falling asleep against him. "Things can always change."

It was early morning when the light woke Grier. She shifted with Reid's heavy weight still on top of her. There was no getting away easily, and she suspected he wanted it that way.

He wasn't asleep, probably hadn't been for quite a while. She, on the other hand, had been in a dead, multiple-orgasm-induced sleep after a long, hot shower together. Now she attempted to extricate herself with a small smile, because there was no graceful way to do this after a one-night stand.

Although it didn't feel like one—not last night, and not now. But she didn't have time to ponder that.

He wasn't moving. "Um, Reid . . ." She pushed her hands against his pecs to send the *get off me* message, but it didn't work.

Instead, he murmured, "Leaving so soon?" and let his hand wander between her legs. She parted her thighs without a second thought, because he was that talented.

"Maybe I could wait a little longer." She moved her hands from his chest to his shoulders to allow him better access to all of her.

"Good." His fingers stroked her gently, which was good, because she was sore and achy—in a nice way.

And his touch was soothing, made her sex wet quickly, especially when his mouth fastened on a nipple, catching it lightly between his teeth and making her gasp.

She dug her fingers into his shoulders and let him lead. And that was wonderful—she didn't need to worry about being in charge or Reid going all alpha on her.

Well, he was, but that was okay because she liked alpha, very much so. Especially because he respected her alpha status as well.

She buried her face in his hair as she began to pump her hips and grind against his hand, riding the sharp edge of her arousal toward release. When she exploded, she swore she saw stars, let the orgasm take her far away from everything—and when she started to come back down to earth, her ears were still ringing.

Unless . . . wait, that was a phone. *Her phone.* "Reid, I need to get that."

Work, he understood. He shifted immediately, grabbed her cell from the side table and handed it to her.

It was her supervisor and she tried not to wince outwardly at the tone of his voice, as it certainly ruined her afterglow. He never sounded happy, but this was decidedly pissed and she would bear the brunt of his wrath.

"Yes, sir, I'm gathering intel as we speak."

"She went running around Mexico shooting people. Now she's been kidnapped by a mercenary—and that happened while a marshal under your command watched. It doesn't sound to me like you're keeping your people in line. Maybe you're not up for this job."

"You know I am, sir."

"I don't know shit beyond the fact that your witness remains at large. You have seventy-two hours to make this right, or you're off the case." He paused. "You know there's a line ten deep behind you, right? And they're all chomping at the bit to get your job. Don't give me a reason to give it to one of them."

She knew how many competitors were waiting for her to fail. It kept her up nights knowing that, as a woman, she'd be given far fewer chances and very little leeway for screwups, even ones that weren't directly hers. "I'll have her back in custody within seventy-two hours."

"No excuses."

She'd never been one to give them in the first place. "No, sir."

She closed the phone, all too aware of Reid's eyes on her. Although he'd only been able to hear her side of the conversation, she was sure he could read her expression.

She didn't bother to try to hide it. "My boss."

"I've been on the receiving end of a few of those."

"I have seventy-two hours to find Teddie."

He nodded, but didn't offer any further insight. Arresting and interrogating him wouldn't work worth a damn—she knew that. The man could be thrown in jail for aiding and abetting, except he couldn't be placed at the scene of the alleged kidnapping in the first place.

He'd let himself be interrogated for days—weeks, months—and he'd never break. Not on principle, and certainly not where his best friend was concerned. And then the military would get involved and take him out of her jurisdiction anyway. It would be like trying to move a mountain. She needed to go around it—and him—instead.

"We both know I just want to protect Teddie," she tried again.

"I don't know that for sure."

She sighed at the losing battle. "Look—"

"You guys lost her once already. How does that happen?"

She'd already heard it from her boss—would no doubt hear it again until Teddie was safely in custody and able to explain her actions in the restaurant.

"I've got to go," she muttered, rooted around on the floor for her clothes and began to pull them on without looking at him.

Reid got out of bed, still naked, and took her chin in his hand, forcing her to look at him. "Your sister—you would've done anything for her, right? Anything to see her happy?"

"Of course."

"Kell's my brother. For all intents and purposes, he's my family." Reid said it so fiercely that she started.

"Point taken."

"Why are you refusing to tell your supervisor that your life's in danger?"

"I never received any threat."

"The bomb in your car wasn't enough for you?"

"How do I know this isn't part of some giant scheme to keep me off the scent?"

"It began like that," he admitted, and she was surprised that he'd told the truth.

"And now?"

"Things have changed. Look, if you took Teddie into custody now, you'd have to deal with the Mexican authorities. She's facing charges. She'll come back to you cleared."

"Because you're Superman."

"Because I know what I need to do to make it happen."

"I've known you for less than a day and I'm supposed to believe you can do this?"

"I never said it would be easy to trust me. Sometimes, you've got to put yourself on the line for what you believe in. I believe in this."

"And I need to believe in myself more." She yanked her face away and finished dressing. She left Reid's room without glancing back at him as her phone rang again. She didn't recognize the number, but when she said hello, the voice that greeted her unmistakably belonged to her informant. Who, according to Reid, wanted her dead.

"I trust you found the woman you were looking for?"

She leaned against her truck, glanced around surreptitiously. It was crowded on the streets, and this man could be anywhere. "Were you waiting for a thank-you card?"

A short laugh with absolutely no humor followed and it left her chilled. More so when he said, "I hear you let her escape."

She didn't answer him, but he continued, "I can give you her new location."

"Why would you do that?"

"In the name of justice."

"You're serious."

"The man you've been spending time with is not a Boy Scout, Grier."

"And I should be mistaking you for one? I saw the damage you inflicted."

"I'm not the one hiding a fugitive from you."

Well, he had her there. Reid's warning and the scolding from her supervisor were ringing simultaneously in her ears; the pressure to do her job overrode Reid's concerns.

So far, she also had no real reason to trust Reid, beyond a gut feeling. And with her job on the line right now, that wasn't enough to outweigh the prospect of finding Teddie.

"Give me the location."

"Not on the phone. In person." He rattled off an address as her stomach lurched. It was near an abandoned lot, well off the grid.

She put her hand on her holster for reassurance. "I'll be there in half an hour."

"Come alone."

"I'll be armed. You?"

He just gave the same eerie laugh and hung up.

She immediately dialed Jack and told him to go meet this Crystal guy—and to bring backup. She'd join them there and they'd bring him into custody for questioning. Because while she didn't want to believe Reid, she also wasn't stupid. Crystal had a lot of information, more than he should.

For a second, she felt a chill run down her back. She rubbed her arms and looked around again.

It was time to put this case to bed. First, she would take care of Crystal, and then Chambers.

"What the hell are you about to do?"

She whirled around and found Reid, half-dressed and leaning against her truck, blocking the driver's-side door with his body.

G et out of my way," Grier demanded.

Reid didn't move a muscle. Her face was pale and she'd been trembling since before he spoke to her. Now Reid was more concerned than ever, because she was ignoring her gut. "You're not okay."

"I have to be—I've got a job to do."

She was flustered and pissed and trying to hide it as best she could. She'd just gotten a major ass-chewing, and yeah, he'd been there. But with guys, it was different. Feelings, in his estimation, always got in the way of work.

Add to that a phone call he had no doubt was from Crystal, and he was ready to stop her from leaving, by any means necessary. "You're not going to meet Crystal."

His hand was on her biceps and she jerked free, pushing at him hard, and the only reason he let go was so he didn't hurt her.

"Whatever happened in your room last night doesn't give you the right to play protector or bodyguard or jealous lover," she spat. "My job's on the line."

"Your life's on the line."

"Why do you care so much? I'm the person trying to have your friend arrested—and I will do it. And when I find out you were involved, I'll arrest you too, without a second thought."

"After you tell everyone you slept with me?"

She slapped him, right across the face, and yes, he probably deserved that—and worse—but he wouldn't stop trying to convince her.

"I won't let you get hurt by him."

"I'm not meeting him alone. I have Jack, my partner, waiting. He'll bring backup." She shrugged away from him.

And still, something didn't sit right in his gut. "Let me come with you."

"I don't need a bodyguard. And if I'm seen with you, they'll want to know why I haven't taken you into custody."

"Why haven't you?" he challenged, and she stared at him, her eyes bright but her expression grim.

"I wish I knew. You'd better be as good as I think you are, Reid. And I'm not talking about your bedroom skills." She touched his chest over his heart with a gentle fist, tapped it a few times. "You promised we'd get Teddie back."

"Give it another forty-eight hours. On my honor. And that's all I've got, Grier. If you don't have Teddie, I'll turn myself in to you instead."

She believed him—he could tell by the way she nodded.

"Give me the address, Grier. It's the only way I'm letting you go."

She pushed the small pad she always carried with her into his face. "There. Satisfied?"

"This isn't about satisfaction."

"If you go, don't you dare let anyone see you or I'll have you arrested for obstruction."

Reluctantly, he moved away from the truck and watched her get in, start it up and drive out of the parking lot.

He didn't like the way she left. Didn't like her doing her job when she was in such a vulnerable state. She shouldn't be going to meet Crystal—not even with a shitload of backup. Dylan said Crystal didn't leave loose ends. And Grier was rapidly becoming one of those.

Because she's involved with you.

The weight of that responsibility hung heavily on his shoulders and he went inside the motel room to grab his shirt and gun and headed off to run down those twenty blocks between her and the meeting place.

CHAPTER

15

Grier left her truck so she could move more stealthily to the meeting place, when a man stopped her to ask for directions. She was wearing her U.S. Marshals jacket and her gun and badge were in plain sight, and she pointed him along his way. He smiled and thanked her and she was about to resume walking when she felt the pinprick in her neck.

She reached back to see if she'd been stung and saw that the man was still standing there, laughing. Looking at someone over her shoulder.

She whirled around in time to see a second man, but before she could grab for her gun, the first man had her arms pinned and was carrying her behind a building to a deserted lot.

"No one's going to find you once we're through with you," a third one said, and she went to punch the one in front of her before they multiplied further.

She missed, which made no sense. Her head felt heavy and her limbs oddly light. "I know you," she slurred. She furrowed her brow and tried to figure out from where . . . and then, "You. Teddie. Her father."

The man from the picture in Teddie's file laughed and threw a punch of his own.

It didn't hurt when she was knocked to the ground, but she knew it was supposed to. Knew she should be fighting back, punching and kicking, but none of that happened.

One of the men laughed and the sound seemed to echo in her ears—she covered them to stop it. Her shirt ripped and she wondered if they were going to rape her. She brought her knees up and tried to get into a fetal position, but they tugged at her and her limbs flattened like jelly.

One of them kicked her—hard enough to suck the breath out of her, but she couldn't move away any longer, could only lie there and take whatever they were dishing out, and that's when the realization hit.

They were going to kill her. They might rape her along the way, but that wasn't their main goal.

Those thoughts rolled through her fuzzed brain with a sickening clarity she wished she could obliterate along with her muscle control. Her stomach lurched, her ears were ringing and she still couldn't breathe well. She heard herself gasping for air and the men's faces were beginning to blur.

You're a failure, just like they all said. And she hated that that would be her final thought.

Everything was a blur—time was rewinding and then playing forward at a sickeningly fast pace. Everything felt heavy.

She looked up and thought she saw the face of an angel. An angry, beautiful angel . . . She tried to reach up and touch him but then he was gone.

Should've listened.

The ability to control her body was lost—her mind drifted, became as numb as her body, and she actually felt her breathing slow. Was she having an out-of-body experience . . . or was she simply dying? It felt oddly peaceful, more so than she thought death should be.

Should've listened.

She could do nothing more than close her eyes and accept the loss of control.

Reid made it within two blocks of the meet-up in record time. He didn't see any telltale black suburbans around, but he knew the marshals were hiding, waiting for Grier to show.

She wasn't there.

That meant . . .

Fuck. That meant this *was* a setup, courtesy of Crystal.

He called out, "Jack? I need to talk to you about Grier. She's in trouble."

After a minute, a tall, dark-haired guy stepped out of the alley, gun drawn. Reid put his hands in the air. "Grier's in trouble—come with me to find her."

"Are you Cormier?" Jack asked, his eyes narrowed like a big, protective older brother, and Reid didn't have time for this shit.

"You in or out?" he asked, and Jack motioned toward

one of the trucks. Once inside and moving, Jack said,
"What are you thinking?"

"I told Grier that she can't trust the guy who's feeding her information."

"You think he took her?"

He knew it, but he stopped talking, was too busy
scanning the area. When they got to a place where
alleys dotted the main street, they left the truck and
began to patrol on foot.

After ten minutes, nothing.

He forced himself to calm the fuck down, because
panic slowed things in the long run. He and Jack ex-
changed numbers and split up to cover more ground.

Finally, Reid spotted her truck parked in a small
restaurant lot and called Jack with the locale as he
continued searching the immediate area. It was still
early morning, and there was only one other car next
to hers. It would've been a longer walk to the as-
signed meeting place, but obviously Grier had been
looking for a back door, wanted the element of surprise in case something went wrong.

He was afraid she'd stumbled on her own surprise
instead. He checked her car, just in case—no sign of
her. He circled around and paused, listened and heard
a hard thump and his pulse raced.

It was the sound of someone being kicked. A small
moan punctuated the air as if to tell him he was correct, and he took off at a dead run in its direction,
following an alley to a half wall.

When he jumped it, landing hard on the other side,
he saw four figures—three men, and Grier on the
ground, attempting to curl up in a fetal position.

None of the men was Crystal. It didn't surprise

Reid that Crystal wouldn't do his own dirty work. What did was seeing McMannus and another man from Teddie's picture—the third he didn't recognize.

What the hell?

Crystal had set up the meet and he wasn't at the appointed spot . . . the only way these men would've known to be on the lookout for Grier was if he'd told them.

So when did Crystal and Chambers get together? But he couldn't take the time to wonder about that, because they'd sent in three animals to take out a woman. The anger that rose in him—for Grier, for Teddie—was indescribable.

Grier's shirt was torn open, her pants halfway down and McMannus leered at him when he got close. "You want in?"

Reid didn't think, slammed his way into the fight and took them on with the fury he'd been holding for Crystal. It would go to far better use here. He unleashed his agony with a force that would've frightened him—should have—but he didn't worry. Let that dark, ugly place work for him as he went for McMannus first, took him down the way he should have in the alley the night before, slamming him first against the building, letting momentum and gravity help.

"Bastard," he hissed at McMannus, even as one of the other men attempted to grab him off McMannus. He brought an elbow back into the man's throat, offing him temporarily. And then he heard yelling and saw that Jack was there, taking on the third man.

McMannus put up a good fight, used a knife to try

to get Reid in between the ribs and nearly succeeded. But Reid shifted, let the knife slash at air before turning McMannus's arm. McMannus grunted with surprise as he saw his knife sticking into his own chest. Reid yanked it out and pushed it back in, hard, with a twist, finishing the job.

And then he heard the shot and turned, saw Jack had taken out one of the other men. The third, the one Reid had thrown off, was attempting to stagger up.

Reid lunged for him, grabbed him around the neck, held him in place and put a knife to his throat. "Where's Chambers?" he demanded.

"I don't know."

"What about Crystal?" Reid asked.

"Don't know anyone by that name."

"Bullshit."

"I work for Chambers. I do what he asks. I'm for hire, just like you," the man spat at him.

"You are nothing like me," Reid told him.

"Reid, there are airline tickets here," Jack called. He was next to Grier, trying to comfort her. "I found them in this guy's pocket. Florida."

Reid's blood ran cold. He knocked out the man in front of him, because he couldn't kill him in front of Jack and expect the man to look the other way. He'd have to be content knowing two of the three had gotten what they deserved and this one would spend serious time in jail, with Teddie's testimony.

He let the body drop to the ground heavily.

Crystal had known Grier was coming to him, and now Chambers and his men were involved too. Where was Crystal? Was he taking Chambers to Florida? How would he even know where Kell was?

Because he's damned good at his job. And maybe Reid was overreacting, but better safe than sorry.

Florida. Crystal had found a way around Reid that none of them had considered.

He looked over at Grier, who was watching him as Jack held her hand, a glazed look in her eyes. He saw the syringe lying on the ground near her.

They could've given her anything—she looked half-paralyzed, and maybe it was GHB or another drug meant to disable her.

It appeared Crystal had wanted her beaten to death, wanted her helpless while it was happening.

The man was as good as his word. He must've followed Grier—and by default, Reid—to Chambers and figured out a way to align himself with him. Crystal wouldn't give a shit about the outcome of what happened to Teddie or Chambers himself. This was simply a way in to harm Dylan, and all the rest of them by association.

"Help's coming, Grier—you hang on," Jack told her.

She didn't say anything but her mouth opened and closed, like she wanted to. Reid moved closer to her and Jack said, "I'm going out to the street so they can find us more quickly. Stay with her."

Reid nodded. With Grier at hand, he dialed his phone quickly. Dylan picked up on the first ring with an expectant hello and Reid jumped right in.

"Dylan, you've got to get in touch with Kell for me, however you can. I think Chambers's met up with Crystal . . . I found his men with tickets to Florida. To Miami. Fuck, Chambers could've been calling me from Miami—he might've had the address long before I gave it to him, from Crystal. That's intel Crystal could've gotten."

"A storm's not going to stop Crystal." Dylan cursed, but Reid hung up before he could say anything else. As soon as he found out Grier's status, he'd be on the next flight that would get him as close to Florida as possible. Probably have to land two states away and drive because of the storm, but he'd do it. For now, he cradled Grier and said, "Don't you dare leave me now," heard the urgency in his own voice.

"Don't feel . . . pain," she told him in an attempt to reassure him.

"They drugged you, honey. You're not dying, you're just numb. Keep breathing, dammit." He shook her, hard enough to make her gasp in a breath. "That's it, more of that. I need to see some color in your cheeks."

He heard a siren in the distance. "Can you hear that? Someone's coming to help you—we'll get you to a hospital and you'll be good as new."

She looked up at him, slurred, "You knew this would happen. You think I'm terrible at my job."

"No, sugar. Not even close," he said softly. Stroked her hair and fought the urge to pick her up and run with her to the closest hospital. "Just try to stay with me."

"Stay with you . . . I couldn't keep up with you."

"You're fighting a losing battle, no one's ever been able to—part genes, part training." He watched her eyes, which were glazed. "Besides, you got me to come to you."

"Pity," she shot at him groggily.

"You wish. Listen, I don't come back for people I pity."

"Angel . . . saved me."

Angels. Motherfucking guardian angels.

He guessed he'd owe them another one if they got Grier to a hospital safely.

Kell started to make them something to eat and Teddie went to shower. She stood under the hot spray, feeling sore and stiff but somehow far lighter than a week ago.

She was more alive, if that was possible, even living under the constant threats. Wanted to get out, do things, wanted to take her life back, immediately.

Would Kell be included in that? She would let him . . . but would he let himself?

He was still angry—mainly at himself for revealing too much, and she understood that. It was not easy to let others see the demons of the past, and the storm around them seemed to mimic one that was just beginning for both of them.

It was far from over—both their personal storms and the one battering the coastline. What they were experiencing now was the eye of the storm. When she'd been in the embassy, she'd had a false sense of calm when this had happened, hadn't realized that the worst was yet to come.

Now she recognized that was entirely possible, but she also realized that good things might actually come after the storm finally passed.

Kell had said he needed to discuss the next stage of their plans with her. There was a state of emergency in Florida at the moment, which meant they were still in this safe little bubble for a while.

But the next steps . . . she had no idea what they might be.

She was restless, wanted to make love with Kell again, but approaching him now seemed akin to standing naked in a storm. And so she walked around Riley's house—it was quite modern, without a lot of personal photographs at all, like a beautiful shell, and Teddie could see why Riley no longer spent time there.

Kell mentioned that she and Dylan lived together in upstate New York, that this had been her place when they'd been separated. Teddie wondered if their road had been tough. She'd learned enough about the tight-knit group of friends Kell and Reid shared to realize that the women who stayed with these men had to be extraordinary.

Did she have that inside of her? If Kell decided not to bail on them all, she hoped she'd be given the chance to find out.

She let her hand brush along the objects decorating the shelves in the living room. Riley collected many things from all over the world—Teddie used to do the same.

All of those things were in boxes in storage, because when she was working, she never had a home base. She'd never been in any one place long enough to call it home. The nomadic lifestyle had worked for her.

Once the protection had started, there had been no going back for her belongings. She didn't know what had happened to them and hadn't wanted to ask.

Possessions had never defined her, but the thought

of losing them all did make her a little sad, thinking about what she'd given up over the years.

When she picked up a photo of a woman and a young girl, she found something she couldn't resist. Behind the large frame, pushed into a corner was a camera case. Tentatively, she pulled it forward and took it in hand, careful to replace the frame where she'd found it.

For a few minutes, she didn't open the case. A fear ran through her—maybe she'd lost her touch and wouldn't be able to take the kind of photos she used to . . . or maybe she'd love it as much as she always had and it would be too hard to give it up a second time.

In the end, the camera won. She held it in her hands, feeling its weight. It wasn't digital, and had nearly a full roll of film in it.

She'd owe Riley for this. But taking photos in here wouldn't be satisfying unless she could take some shots of Kell, and he was certainly in no mood for that.

She went to one of the French doors that led to the deck and unhooked the hurricane shutter and moved it away to stare outside, saw the sun and could almost feel its warmth. The urge to leave the house was strong, but she resisted, because this was far from the aftermath of the storm.

It was ridiculous to think that making love to Kell and spilling her secrets had set her free from her storm phobia. Her heart pounded as she touched the handle on the door and opened it. She could see the palm trees still swaying and the wind whistled, but it wasn't as fierce or furious as before.

She'd survive this storm . . . and she'd come out stronger for it.

Even though the brunt of the storm would hit them soon, they were still safe. She let that comfort her for a long moment as she basked in the salty air and began clicking on the beautiful destruction that lay all around the house—life and death, all wrapped together, clinging to the last moments of the brilliant rain. She snapped the pictures with a vengeance.

It was so nice to hold a camera again. She stared into the viewfinder and felt like she was finally standing upright again.

There was a man walking along the beach—slowly, watching at the water like he didn't have a care in the world. She took a few shots of him, because the background of the setting sun and the debris on the beach, coupled with his lanky frame caught her eye. Maybe he was a surfer or a local or a stranded tourist. It didn't matter.

For the moment, she felt as free as he was.

CHAPTER
16

Grier lay in the hospital bed feeling vulnerable as hell and hating herself for it. She shifted and winced and tried her best not to be more annoyed with the nurses, doctors and even her own team for forcing her to stay in this place for a twenty-four hour observation.

All for a stupid concussion. She'd had them before. Once they'd flushed the drugs out of her system, she felt much better. Well, semi-better, except for the bruised ribs, which hurt when she moved, or breathed. Those men had had a time with her, for sure. The only thing that had saved her from breaks was actually the drugs—they'd relaxed her body to a point that she didn't resist the punches.

She'd looked in the mirror once, when the nurse had helped her into the bathroom—her face was a mess on the right side, purple bruises that would soon turn ugly green and yellow, and her eye was swollen, as was her bottom lip.

Her body had fared equally badly in terms of being Technicolor right now, but she'd been lucky.

If she hadn't trusted Reid . . .

You did.

He'd been with her when the ambulance came, but he'd deferred to Jack riding with her.

"Don't want to get you in trouble, sugar," he'd drawled softly, had extricated his hand from hers, and it was only then she realized she'd been literally clinging to him.

The ride in the ambulance had been hellish, the drugs beginning to make her jumpy instead of calm and the EMTs wouldn't give her anything to counteract their effects until a doctor examined her. And even though they had the attackers' syringe, they still couldn't be sure exactly what was in it, so after the flush, she couldn't take anything stronger than Motrin and Tylenol until they were sure she'd been fully detoxed.

The doctors promised her more painkillers within the next few hours. So for now, she remained as still as possible, even though her body continued to feel restless. She clicked through the TV channels, flipped through a pile of magazines aimlessly . . . knew all the while that nothing would satisfy her until she left this place.

"They're gonna have to tie you down by nightfall."

His drawl was slow and sweet like honey and she could almost taste him. Reid stood in the doorway, holding flowers.

"Any way you can sneak me out of here? They're talking about keeping me for twenty-four hours at the minimum."

Reid looked like he was considering it. "I hate hospitals too, but I think you're right where you need to be."

"You've had a couple of rough days too, you know."

He walked into the room then, set the flowers on the rolling tray in front of her.

She tried to think of the last time a man gave her flowers and came to the conclusion that it had been never. "They're beautiful—thanks."

"Would've brought ammo but I didn't want to cause a scene."

He was serious and she wanted nothing more than to pull him into the bed with her.

Now, that would certainly pass the time a lot faster.

"I wish I'd gotten there sooner," he said quietly as he stared at her face.

"It's not as bad as it looks," she lied, and he gave her a small half-smile.

"You've got to be careful, Grier. Crystal sent Chambers's men to get you. He's serious as hell, and he's not stopping."

Reid hadn't moved and she was about to snap back some kind of *You think I can't do my job* retort, but she didn't. Because he was right. And he was telling her so out of concern, not disdain.

Crystal wasn't an ordinary street criminal. He was as highly trained as Reid, and she'd seen what he could accomplish. "How did Crystal and Chambers start working together?"

Reid hesitated for a long moment and then said, "Crystal followed you, and you followed me. It wouldn't have been hard for him to discover Chambers's connection to Teddie's case."

"Shit."

"Has he contacted you again?"

God, she didn't want to tell him—hadn't wanted to tell anyone, but Jack had been monitoring her phone and he'd been the one to listen to the message. "Yeah, he called. He threatened me. He said, 'Job's not done.'" She couldn't bear to see the pained look on Reid's face. He turned away for a few moments, and she heard him muttering something to himself.

"What kind of protection are they looking to give you?"

"I turned it down."

He whipped around to face her. "You are fucking crazy."

"He's after you too," she reminded him. "Does that not worry you? Or are you going to tell me you can handle yourself?"

To his credit, he didn't say that, although she was one hundred percent sure it's what he thought. Instead he told her, "Crystal doesn't like loose ends of any kind, no matter how small. He won't stop until either you or he is dead."

"Then I'll make sure it's him."

"You'd better." Reid looked as though he wanted to say something else but he remained silent. Instead, he touched her knee through the blankets, a comforting rub with a big hand. And then he finished with,

"Rest up," and he walked out with a quick glance over his shoulder.

She stared at the flowers, saw the card attached. Pulled it out and found a note and phone number on the inside.

We can protect you.

She didn't doubt it, even though she wasn't sure who the *we* entailed, beyond Reid.

When she turned the card over, she saw a series of numbers—four of them, listed one under the other. They looked like they might be bank accounts. And they were written by the same hand as the flip side.

A swift rap on the door made her start, pull in a too fast breath. She winced before she said, "Come in," thinking it was Reid again.

But it wasn't—it was her supervisor, with a man she'd never seen before. She tucked Reid's card under the covers with her and said, "Sir."

She tried to sit up straighter but her boss held up a hand.

"Please, Grier. Stay where you are." He came to the bed. "We have some serious business to discuss."

The satphone hadn't been working well during the hurricane—the signals were congested, no doubt because satphones were pretty much the only comms during a natural disaster.

Instead of dwelling on it, Kell had watched Teddie open the back door leading to the pool—hadn't wanted to bother her because she'd seemed so intent on what she was doing. Now she was outside, holding the door open with her foot. The sound of the wind was pretty deafening, coupled with the ocean roaring.

He couldn't bring himself to call her in, lecture her . . . because she was taking photos for the first time in a year.

Right now, she was free. In the moment. To call her back inside would mean taking all that away . . . and she deserved this. He knew as well as anyone that life was full of risks, and she'd simply have to find her own balance.

Besides, he'd wanted to give this back to her, and now that she had a taste of it again, she wouldn't be letting it go. He was sure of it.

Whatever happened now, he'd make it so she wouldn't have to live in secret. Chambers wouldn't take any more of her life away than he already had.

Kell moved back into the kitchen, wanted her to think she'd gotten away with something by being out here. Because that always made things more fun.

The next sounds he heard were all too familiar—to an untrained ear, they would have sounded like bombs, but they were flash-bang grenades, similar to those that had gone off with the actual bombs, which caused far more damage, at the house outside of Juarez.

Which was too big of a coincidence for his taste.

Although the grenades were loud as shit, over the wind and the surf, Teddie wouldn't hear them or be affected by them, since she was outside. And he had to warn her—save her.

But as he tried to make his way out, he felt the pinprick in the side of his neck and clamped a hand there, pulled out the syringe. Tried to read the words on it but his eyes were already blurring from the flash-bangs and the drugs.

He thought of Teddie blithely shooting photos, being happy, and he didn't want things to end this way. He hoped whoever was doing this would just take him and leave her.

He managed to pull his phone out of his pocket, was in the process of dialing when he realized there was someone standing in front of him.

He had no doubt it was Crystal.

"Want me to pose?" Crystal said to him and then laughed. Kell snapped a picture of him and shoved the phone away from him, knowing Crystal wanted Dylan or Reid or Cam to find it there and know he had Kell.

It was the best he could do before he blacked out.

Someone was watching her. She had a feeling it was Kell—she'd been outside for so long that she'd lost track of time, and he'd no doubt missed her long ago.

She hadn't meant to stay at the door for so long, and she'd been selective in her photography because she hadn't wanted to fly through the film too soon. When she had enough at her disposal, she usually took the shots in rapid succession, always afraid she'd miss something.

She realized now she'd been missing out that way as well.

Now that it was starting to get dark, the uneasy

feeling from earlier returned—and she wanted to move inside to the safety of the house, and Kell.

The wind was picking up—a sign that the storm was coming back strong. The skies darkened further and the door pushed against her—and she fought the panic rising up in her throat.

Calmly, she backed inside and shut and locked the French doors. Stood there and watched the storm pick up for about ten minutes and then locked the shutter into place.

She was surprised Kell hadn't come out to her in that time. She rested the camera on the table, was just about to open it and pocket the film when a shadow moved across the doorway.

She lifted her eyes and prepared to smile, but it quickly disappeared and she dropped the camera to the floor, fell to her knees beside it because her legs could no longer hold her up.

Samuel. His gun pointed at her.

"Nice to see you again, Teddie. We didn't really have much time to catch up at the restaurant."

Because you wanted to kill me.

She couldn't get the words out and he motioned for her to stand. She struggled but couldn't get on her feet.

God, Kell . . . where was he?

"I'm not going anywhere with you," she managed, put her hand down behind her to grope for the heavy camera.

"You have no choice, Teddie." Samuel walked toward her, put the gun to his side and half dragged her to her feet. Once on that semi-level playing field, she swung her arm up and hit him in the side of his face with the camera, heard him yelp with pain as it crashed against him.

She backed up, knowing she couldn't go far, but hoping she could find Kell. Ran into the kitchen and saw no sign of him. Samuel was on her tail, his cheek bloody and the anger in his tone unmistakable.

"You always were a little bitch—time to teach you a lesson."

"Maybe you're the one who needs the lesson," she spat. "I know what you did to my father . . . you'd been trying to break up my family for a long time before you finally killed him."

"Looks like I succeeded," he said with a wicked smile, wiping away the blood that trickled close to his mouth. "You've got no one to help you now—your friend is dead."

She hung on to the kitchen counter as she tried to absorb that sudden blow.

Dead. Kell was dead. She swirled those words around in her mind and realized they didn't sit right with her.

There was no way. She didn't believe Samuel for a second. She would've felt it somehow, like a blow to her gut.

She'd connected with Kell, on a level she hadn't experienced with anyone else. Ever.

If he were gone, her soul would have been ripped out. "You're lying."

Samuel told her, "You shouldn't have trusted him with all your deep, dark secrets. A man like that is too dangerous. He has too many enemies and he can't be expected to do anything good."

"Neither can you," she said quietly, but Samuel was through talking. He grabbed her arm instead, held the gun to her back.

"Let's go."

The storm . . . he was taking her out of the house and into the storm. Her body began to shake violently. "I can't go out there."

"You no longer have a choice."

CHAPTER
17

Kell woke, found himself bound with chains to the floor in some kind of basement and immediately lunged for Crystal.

The man didn't move a muscle, just sat there, staring at Kell for a long moment.

"Are you thirsty?"

"Are you going to drug me again?"

"No."

"Where's Teddie?" he asked.

"With Chambers. They'll be here shortly, I'd imagine, if they're not here already." Crystal passed him some water and a sandwich and Kell got over his *what the fuck?* quickly, because he needed his strength.

As he began to eat, the chains clanking, he noticed that Crystal was studying him again, and so Kell did the same to him, noting that the man looked as though he'd been beaten up recently. "Who fucked with your face?"

"Reid."

Kell put the sandwich down as his gut tightened.

"Don't worry, your friend's fine. More than fine," Crystal told him.

"Teddie better be fine too," he growled.

"If you had a choice—stay with her and die, or leave her behind and live—which would you choose?" Crystal asked him and Kell knew it was a test, knew which answer Crystal would want to hear.

Even that wouldn't guarantee that Kell would make it out of here alive, and so he told the truth. "Kill me and let her go."

"Ah, that wasn't a choice. But props to you for being creative. Thinking outside the box. How very . . . Delta Force of you."

"I'm not Delta," he said through gritted teeth.

"You love her."

Crystal said it as though it was a completely foreign concept to him—and it no doubt was.

"Yes."

"Have you told her so?"

"No." Fucking psychological bullshit. "But I'd appreciate any time I could get with her."

"You'll get twenty-four hours once she arrives, but I can't put you in the same room—too dangerous, and I'm not that stupid. She'll be right next to you, though. I'm sure you can find a way to communicate. After that, Chambers's got plans for her. Keeping her alive won't keep him out of jail, so . . ." Crystal looked bored as anything and Kell thought that he could probably rip the chains out of the walls with his bare hands right now with the amount of adrenaline pumping through his body.

But in order to understand Crystal's game, he needed to remain as calm as the merc in front of him. "I thought you liked working alone."

"I like bringing people together. Think of me as a facilitator." Crystal smiled.

The man was so fucking unhinged. "What's your game?"

"Making you feel helpless." Crystal looked around the barren room. "Sure is nicer than the prison you sent your team into."

Calm it down, Kell . . . do not engage.

Figuring out how to save Teddie was far more important than rehashing the past, and she was right next door. Or would be soon.

"You can't believe Dylan's letting you get away with this."

"Dylan letting me? That's rich." Crystal paused. "Dylan's lost his edge. It's sad, really. But I've got someone else in mind anyway for the job."

Kell wanted to keep him talking but the sound of a door opening above them distracted him. Crystal left Kell alone to wonder who the new player was, and how bad that development was for him.

He bucked against the bonds, his muscles straining even though he knew the chains wouldn't break. But never surrendering was a part of his DNA and so he rattled them, if no other reason than to prove he was alive.

The pain helped with that as well. He hated being separated from Teddie.

He checked the room out to see if there was anything

he could do to escape. But it was concrete and win-
dowless. He could use the chains to strangle Crystal,
if the man got close enough.

Goddammit, he wanted him to get close enough.

Chambers is going to kill her and you're helpless.

The thought made him so ill he nearly lost what
little he had in his stomach. He tried to stand. He had
to get the hell out of his cell and get to Teddie.

He pounded against the wall, and called her name
until his throat was raw. "Teddie, answer me."

He heard nothing in response. He imagined this
was very much like what happened to Reid and the
others in their underground prison cells in Africa and
shook that thought off immediately. Looked around
and saw nothing he could use that was within reach
of the chains. They were fastened into the cement
floor, not the wall. He rolled over and knocked on
this wall—it sounded hollow, like drywall, and he
began to poke at the loose molding along the floor.

He didn't see any cameras in the room. That was
helpful. And the floor was half dirt under the wall.
First, he would dig through until he could see and
hear what was in the next room. Then he'd figure out
a way to get these goddamned chains off.

He'd be ready when Crystal walked back into the
room.

The car ride was truly terrifying—they shouldn't
have been on the road, and Teddie prayed they'd be
pulled over, but since they were in a stolen van from
the local electric company, no one stopped them.

The wind blew the van all over the road and she

huddled in the back in a ball, feeling the sway, the splash of water under the tires, the hard lash of rain bands as they threatened to unleash their fury at any moment. Samuel was behind the wheel, holding it tightly and cursing. His gun was tucked into his jacket and there was no way to grab it without killing both of them.

She'd have to find another way out of this, cursed herself for freezing up and letting herself be taken from Riley's house.

She realized she should be looking out the window, trying to figure out where Samuel was taking her, but she was barely breathing. Tried to think of Kell, how he would tell her to be strong.

But someone had gotten to him.

He hasn't let you down yet. So now it was her turn to make good.

She would fight with everything she had.

When the van came to a stop inside a garage, she waited until the door closed out most of the sounds of the storm. They'd driven for maybe an hour, but in this weather, they might only be fifteen miles from Riley's house.

Samuel had the gun out again, told her to "hurry the hell up," and she climbed out of the van.

It was dark in the garage, save for the penlight Samuel held to guide them, a heavy hand around her biceps, which felt like a lead cuff sucking the energy from her.

"Why are you doing this?" she asked when he dragged her inside the house. It was dark, just a lantern on the floor, highlighting that the house was empty.

She didn't see anyone else, but she did notice wet footprints leading across the floor.

"You got in touch with me, sweetheart, remember? Good old Uncle Samuel will save the day." His smile was mirthless.

"You haven't been good old uncle anything to me for a long time. You owe me an explanation."

"So much like your father. So righteous. Everything so black and white."

"You were never his friend. He was always smarter, better, kinder than you, and you leeched onto him in hopes you could be a quarter of the man he was." The words were meant to seek the truth—judging by the way Samuel's eyes flashed anger, she'd hit on it.

"I could kill you, Teddie. But I don't think that's what I'm going to do." Samuel stroked a hand over his beard, a familiar gesture from her childhood, when she'd thought everything was idyllic.

"How long were you with my mother?" she asked finally, not sure if she wanted the answer.

"Forever," he answered shortly. "We were always in love."

"So why didn't she marry you instead of my father?"

"I never wanted children. She did."

Teddie's head ached. Could she have been the reason her mother hadn't married a man she loved, the reason Samuel had tried to ruin her father, or was this just another of his lies?

Did it really matter? Teddie needed to stop blaming herself for everything, needed to stay alive, no matter what it took.

She knew both her parents would've wanted that.

"I can't believe it took your father so long to figure it all out. I took his women right from under his nose—he was too wrapped up in being a good little diplomat to notice. He was wonderful at his job. At love, not so good."

Bastard. She went to lunge at him, but he grabbed her hard and pushed her to the ground.

"Fighting won't help you this time."

"What are you going to do with me?" she asked.

"You'll find out soon enough, Teddie. And this time, I'll make sure there's no one to stop me.

"I'm going to stop you, you bastard."

Samuel ignored her, grabbed her arm again and pushed her down a dark staircase into a large basement with several closed doors. He opened the first one and shoved her inside—it was damp and she was cold and shivering. Samuel threw a towel at her and closed the door. She heard a lock turn even as she lunged for it, turning the handle frantically. She slammed at it with her palms until her hands ached and then she turned away and cursed. Fought the tears—her anger helped with that.

She'd have to stave off panic attacks as the basement of the house began to take on water, and she heard the house's shutters rip off with the wind through the small windows above.

This place was nowhere near as secure as Riley's house . . . but for the first time in years, something scared her more than the storm.

And then she heard it—the scratching at one of the walls, turned to see if it was some kind of creature . . . or something else. Still holding the towel, she walked over to where the sound was loudest, had to get down on her knees to see the small hole that had been dug into her room.

"Kell?" she whispered, held her breath and spoke his name again.

"Teddie? Thank fucking God."

At the sound of his voice, she breathed a deep sigh of relief. "He told me you were dead. I knew he was lying."

"Are you okay? Did Crystal hurt you?"

"I'm okay. It was Samuel who took me."

A pause, and then, "Well, Crystal's here too. Is there anything around you that you can use as a weapon?"

"I don't think so . . . it's pretty bare in here. Just a plastic water bottle."

"Are you chained?"

"No." She swallowed hard, rubbed her face with the towel and then wrapped it around herself to try to get warm. "What does Crystal want?"

Kell didn't answer her, instead slipped a thin piece of metal that looked like it had been ripped off a doorjamb through the hole. "Take this. Don't let anyone see it. Use it if you need to." He paused, then said, "Go for the carotid on the side of the neck. If you can't, go for the eyes. The throat. Anyplace soft. Can you do that?"

"Yes," she whispered, then she said it louder. "I'll do whatever it takes to get me back to you."

"Good girl."

Crystal already knew we were with Teddie. It wouldn't be a stretch for him to track me through

Grier in order to hook up with Chambers and his men—and in doing so, he knew he'd cause enough chaos to keep us rattled." Reid had spent the better part of the morning rolling that around in his brain and was damned pissed about it.

Now, on the phone with Dylan and Cam, the men were putting it all together.

"Check your phone," Cam told him.

"We've been using throwaways since Crystal came on the scene," Reid confirmed. "I checked my phone—nothing's been planted."

"Vivi checked your number too. Seems to be fine," Dylan confirmed. "You weren't tracked going in or out of Mexico."

"Definitely not by border patrol." Reid ran a hand through his hair, looked around the dingy motel room and thought about going back to the hospital to spend more time with Grier. "We were never sure who planted the bomb in Mexico, not until Grier confirmed Crystal knew the address."

"He was there when it went off, the fucker," Dylan muttered.

"He bugged the truck, followed us out of Mexico, found our address in Texas and watched us take off in separate directions." Reid drummed his fingers on the small table he sat at, with a view of the street through the partially opened blinds. "He was able to follow me back here with no problem, and he was able to track me through Grier.

"And if he didn't know exactly where Kell was before, Chambers did," Reid said grimly, and dammit, he'd handed that intel off. "If Crystal grabbed a private plane with Chambers right after he fought with me, he could've landed close by and driven the rest of the way in. If The Weather Channel can move around during a hurricane, Crystal certainly can too. We've got to get in there."

"We're on it, Reid."

"I'm getting on a plane tonight," he said. "And I'm going in no matter what."

He had a ticket booked out of a Texas airport for later that day—he'd fly as close to the hurricane zone as he could, and walk the rest of the way if he had to.

Grier was getting sprung that afternoon, later than she'd first been told, according to Jack. So far, she hadn't used the number he gave her, and he was planning on forcing the issue, putting her on a plane and helping her to disappear.

It was the least he could do.

He had no doubt she'd already used the other information he'd given her regarding Chambers's overseas bank accounts, which Vivi had emailed to him after an exhaustive search of Chambers's assets. That plus the pictures and Teddie's testimony should put to rest any doubt that Samuel Chambers had been behind the kidnapping scheme.

When Reid stopped by the hospital, they told him she'd already been released, which he found odd.

"If you hurry, you can probably catch her," one of the nurses told him. "She was just being taken down on the north elevator."

He took the steps two at a time, went around the front of the building and spotted her. She was getting out of the wheelchair that hospitals always made their patients ride out in, for liability issues. Jack was at her side, looking around for any trouble.

Without warning, a black truck sped around the corner, taking it almost on two wheels, the screech of tires making everyone jump back and Reid jump forward, because the car was racing close to where Grier was standing.

Too close.

He yelled her name, but he wasn't close enough. She'd turned to look at the truck too and he wanted her to run the hell away.

Instead, she stood there as if paralyzed, rooted to the spot.

The shots rang out as he raced to get to her but the truck blocked his view for a long moment that seemed to spiral on forever. His own gun was drawn, and as the truck pulled away, he took a few shots at the tires and windows to try to stop it, losing interest quickly when he spotted Grier on the ground.

Grier. God, no. Just fucking no.

Jack was kneeling next to her, talking into his cell phone, presumably calling the police.

When he saw Reid, he got up and tried to hold him back as the emergency staff came out with a stretcher.

Reid pushed Jack away, knelt as near to her as he could get without interfering with the doctors and nurses swarming around her, or maybe his knees buckled and he fell, but it didn't matter. Her eyes were glassy, breathing shallow, and the blood . . . my God, so much blood.

Jack was still trying to remove him, and he fought to get closer, vaguely heard, "Let them do their job, Reid. They've got to get her inside."

"We're losing her!" one of the doctors called. "I'm starting compressions."

Reid was half off the ground now, met Jack's eyes and saw a fear he knew was reflected in his own.

"She'll be okay," Jack told him, like he had to say it out loud in order to believe it. "She's so strong."

Reid opened his mouth but nothing came out. His throat was tight and this was all too goddamned familiar.

And he was so goddamned responsible in the first place.

The doctor and nurses were working frantically now—CPR continued as Grier was lifted onto a stretcher and wheeled inside.

Instead of trying to keep him away, Jack tugged him inside the hospital, following the triage to the ER, even though Reid didn't want to go. They followed the maze of hallways until they got to the double doors the stretcher had just been pushed through. A nurse pulled the curtain around her and he and Jack stood there until another nurse came up to them and asked if they could please wait outside the working area.

"No," Jack told her, and she started. Reid's body was barely functioning. All he could do was stand there, propped against the wall, staring as if he could will Grier's heart to keep beating.

The shots had gone right into her chest—he'd seen the dark holes through the white buttoned-down shirt she'd been wearing. Two of them.

Dark holes. Not skin. Bullet-fucking-proof vest.

Fuck.

He glanced at Jack again, and this time his numbness was for a different reason. He pushed off from the wall and made his way out of the hospital to where the police were mulling around the spot Grier had gone down. Got close enough to see the blood. To smell it.

Instead of going back inside, he made it his mission to put as much distance between himself and this hospital as possible.

It was all a blur and this time Grier didn't have any drugs to take away the pain. She was being wheeled somewhere, totally covered, and she felt tears slide down her cheeks.

But her arms were strapped down, so she couldn't do anything but let them run freely.

After what seemed like an eternity, the stretcher she was on was being collapsed and she was being lifted into the back of a van, just like she'd been told she'd be.

It was only when the van began to move that the bag she'd been in was unzipped. It was unsettling enough to have to play dead, but zipped inside a body bag . . . well, the ultimate irony of that wasn't lost on her.

"We're clear," the man she'd first met yesterday in her hospital room told her. He was a marshal like her . . . like she had been, she supposed, and didn't dwell on that, because right now the thought would kill her faster than any bullet.

The straps around her arms and legs were unfastened and she sat up, too fast for the broken ribs and the new pain where the bullets had hit her.

They'd been real, because they needed to leave casings.

God, Reid's face . . . she hadn't wanted him to be there, but she'd known he would be. That was part of the plan—they'd even waited for him. She supposed it would help him to move on . . . she just hoped she could too.

And still, the card with the message and the phone number he'd left her was tucked inside her shoe.

"Come on, I'll help you get this stuff off."

She was still wearing the bloody clothing—some of it, at least, because the doctors had cut through it to get to her. But they'd left enough on so that the bulletproof vest was still covered.

The doctors and nurses had been mostly FBI agents. And they'd had to do this before, many times, and in hospitals all over the world.

She gratefully stripped off the bulletproof vest, because it was hurting her ribs, which were already sore from the shots. The fake blood looked a little too real and for as long as she lived, she'd never be able to forget the look on Reid's face when he thought she was dying.

"He thinks you're gone. It had to be that way," her boss had argued when he'd come in her room after Reid left, but deep inside her heart, in a place she hadn't realized existed, she disagreed.

She took the clothing that the man named Dave handed her. Changed without modesty because there was no time for it. A pair of jeans, a white T-shirt, hair pulled back in a ponytail until she could dye it or cut it or whatever she needed to do.

She didn't even know where Dave was taking her.

"This was the only way, you know that," her supervisor had told her.

She was one of them now—one of the nameless, faceless WITSEC victims who walked around with fake names and fake documents, looking over their shoulders every second of every day, no matter what their handlers told them.

"This is temporary," she'd said and her boss had nodded, but she could tell he didn't really think so.

They had no leads on this man Crystal. Only a death threat so serious that the head of the marshals had decided that it was not only a danger to Grier if Crystal thought she was still alive, but to every other marshal she worked with or had come into contact with.

She'd hated the plan, railed against it for hours in the hospital room with the door shut and her supervisor—and his—waiting her out calmly, knowing she'd come to the only conclusion possible.

They'd laid it out for her, step-by-step. They'd used the hospital before—had a doctor and some nurses who would help by getting her down to the morgue, where she could be taken out without anyone seeing her.

When she'd finally consented, and then requested to be left alone until morning, they relented. Still, she was sure they'd posted some kind of guard to make sure she didn't sneak out on her own, which for the first half of the night she'd seriously thought about doing.

The next few hours she'd spent holding her phone, staring between the keypad and the card with Reid's number on it.

He hadn't been back to visit her, but she supposed

he was busy hunting down Chambers and Crystal. He'd been telling her the complete truth, she knew that now.

You can call him . . . tell him you need to disappear for a while.

But she'd be going against all the tenets of witness protection—and possibly putting him further in harm's way.

He would feel guilty, but she supposed that was all there was to it. They'd known each other for a matter of days, and no matter how much they'd bonded, it was still too soon to know if there was anything close to real between them.

She was getting proficient at lying to herself. Hopefully, she'd be just as good when she got her new identity.

CHAPTER
18

Dylan prided himself on his ability to get into places others deemed impossible—and he'd made a career out of it. Anywhere, anyplace, any-fucking-time . . . and this trip would be no exception.

He and Riley and Cam flew into Florida, hitching a ride on a Coast Guard plane that would be flying into the hurricane to study its center. He'd called in more than a few favors to get on that flight, which ultimately dropped them several hours from their destination.

It was either that or take the trip into the hurricane with the crew. Once they'd landed and procured a truck, they got on the road, the two-hour ride to Riley's house taking four.

Cam dropped them as close to Riley's house as he could get—the area was a fucking mess, and Dylan and Riley needed to make their way through an obstacle course of downed trees and power lines. It took them two hours to get near the place.

There were roadblocks stopping people from entering the affected areas without reason. Riley thankfully had her Florida driver's license, claimed she was picking up her mother from the house. The police let them through and they approached the house hesitantly . . . as though neither of them really wanted to see what was inside.

There were no outward signs of struggle—everything was locked up tightly, hurricane shutters in place, and there was lots of storm damage to the plants and trees but thankfully not the roof. The garage door was closed and the generator was running.

They stood outside the front door, Dylan calling Kell's phone . . . and hearing it ring and ring inside.

Shit.

Dylan motioned for Riley to use the key—she did, then backed up to let Dylan go in first, gun drawn. She was right behind him, with the same weapon stance.

Riley's camera lay broken, smashed to pieces on the floor. There were a few blood splatters, but they were small, like from a split lip.

A few streaks were on the hallway floor, as if someone had been dragged against their will.

Kell's phone was on the floor of the kitchen. The only thing that had been disturbed was a bowl that had crashed beside it. There was also a syringe—empty—that had rolled under the table. Dylan picked it up with a paper towel.

"At least one of them was drugged," he said.

Riley's expression looked pained. "Crystal has both of them, then."

"Chambers could easily be with him," Dylan muttered. They'd heard from Reid earlier that there was no sign of Chambers at his house or any of his usual haunts. "Where the hell would he have taken them?"

"You're going to hear from him soon—the whole point of this is to make you suffer," Riley said grimly.

Dylan picked up Kell's phone. The camera was open and he clicked on the last photo.

Crystal—standing in Riley's kitchen, posing for the fucking shot.

There was also a new number in there, entered about twelve hours earlier, the same time the picture had been taken. He dialed it and put the phone on speaker as Riley came in after having checked the other rooms, shaking her head as if to say, *no go.*

Crystal picked up on the second ring. "Dylan, I'm disappointed it's taken you this long."

"Blame mother nature."

Crystal chuckled, the bastard. "Better late than never, I guess."

"I want Kell and Teddie back—safe and sound, in the condition you found them," Dylan told him through gritted teeth.

Crystal laughed. "You really have lost your edge, haven't you? The Dylan I knew would've protected his friend a little better."

Dylan winced at the characterization. "Are they safe?"

"They're fine—for now. You want them back, you do a job for me. Otherwise, no deal. I'll give you twenty-four hours to decide, and then I can't be responsible for what happens to Kell. But just so you know, I'm not responsible for Teddie at all." Crystal hung up and Dylan stared at the phone as Riley touched his shoulder.

"You can't let him hold you hostage like this, Dylan," she said fiercely.

"What choice do I have?"

"You have plenty. We'll come up with them together."

Dylan acquiesced for the moment, although he knew that Riley didn't really see any way out of it, just like he didn't.

He'd started this by partnering with Crystal early on. The only way to end it was to put himself back under the man's thumb, and then kill him.

Kell felt better now that he knew Teddie was all right—and that he'd passed her the old rectangular piece of metal he'd found in the dirt under the crumbled portion of the floor. It was as good as anything he'd used for wet work because it had a sharp edge, but Teddie using it effectively would be a far different story. He'd never thought he'd be grateful that she'd seen him use a pen to kill someone, but at least she knew the correct spot to try to land the metal into Chambers's neck.

He had twenty-four hours to make sure she could do it properly.

What would you tell someone you loved if you knew you only had a day left with them? It seemed like a bad movie, but right now it was his life.

One day was more than enough for him to come up

with a way out. The storm was on their side. Now that the eye had passed, it had picked up in intensity again, which locked them inside with Crystal and Chambers. This house was nowhere near secure—if he was lucky, the roof would blow off and take Crystal and Chambers with it. If not, he'd just have to figure out a way to kill them, while keeping Teddie safe.

"You still with me?" he asked Teddie now, since she'd been quiet for a few minutes.

"Yes. I'm just practicing what you told me."

Practicing how she would attack Chambers if he came near her. Reid's gut clenched. "Good. I know you can defend yourself, Teddie. Right now, that's what you need to concentrate on."

"Right now, I'm really glad you're dangerous."

"You're as dangerous as I am, you just don't realize it."

She blinked. Thought about every death-defying stunt she'd pulled since she'd had her outing with Samuel the week before, including pulling a gun on both him and Kell. . . . and discovered that maybe Kell was right about her. "That's what attracted you to me?"

"Part of it."

"It's that simple," she mused.

"That's what Reid told me," he said. "I'm finally beginning to believe it."

"Maybe this isn't the time, Kell—or maybe it's the best time—but we never finished our conversation back at Riley's house. About your parents."

"That's the last thing I want to waste my breath on."

"Something must've happened, something really bad, Kell. Because when you talked about your parents earlier, you got this look in your eyes . . . I haven't known you that long, but I'd never seen you come so close to looking . . ."

Hollow. That's what she wanted to say—he was sure of it. He'd seen the look in his own eyes in the mirror often enough throughout childhood to recognize when someone was upset by it. Social workers, judges, his foster mom, they all tried their best to rid him of it.

He knew it never went away—he'd simply learned to hide it, to push it down and forget about his past. The jobs he did as an adult made it easy. Concentrating on staying alive took up a hell of a lot of his concentration. "They pushed me too far. I pretended I was like them for a really long time. That I had no conscience. That I enjoyed pulling the scams. And then, on that last one, I knew it was over for me."

"Tell me," she urged, and yes, she'd already spilled her deepest, darkest secret to him, so it was only fair.

But while she'd had no control over her situation, he didn't have any excuse for what he'd done in those spring months right before he turned fifteen.

"When I was a freshman in high school, we moved to Connecticut. I was enrolled in an expensive private boarding school, because it was easier for me to get information for my parents about the wealthy families of my classmates than it was for my parents to seek it out. And they'd use it to run cons, but it was never tied back to me. The perfect crimes. I was far away from them, and for the first time, I felt . . . normal. I had a real friend, my roommate, which doesn't

seem like a big deal, but at that point it was everything to me. He was really wealthy. I hid that from
my folks for months, because I knew what they'd do.
And I just wanted to be a regular kid who went to
class and played sports and had parents who gave a
shit. And Brandon's parents . . . they visited him all
the time. They'd take me along to dinner with them.
In those months, they were more like parents to me
than my own had been in fourteen years."

He paused, didn't want to bare his belly like this,
expose his soul to her . . . but he'd come too far to
stop now. She deserved to know.

She seemed to already, because she said, "Oh, no,"
very quietly, could see the setup a mile away.

"My parents found out about my roommate. Or
maybe they'd known all along. Maybe they allowed
me to get close to him to teach me, once again, that I
couldn't trust anyone or anything, that I should never
let myself get close to anyone, because the world was
out to get me. And then they told me I had to help
them run a con on Brandon's family. If I did it, he
wouldn't know it was me who robbed them. If I refused to help, they'd make sure Brandon thought I
alone had stolen from him. Either way, I would lose
my new friend and his family. I didn't want him to
ever know I was involved. And so I distanced myself
from him, so it wouldn't hurt when I screwed him
over, the way I'd always done . . . And it wasn't that
hard at all."

"They lied about not letting Brandon know, didn't
they?"

He nodded. "It was an object lesson for me. One of
their many, and I learned it."

God, the look on Brandon's . . . It would haunt him forever, or so it seemed. "My parents moved us to Alaska to escape the heat, because Brandon's parents were intent on hunting us down. After we got settled and my parents thought I was over it and stopped watching me like a hawk, I called the police and social services and turned them in."

The police came, because he'd called them. He'd thought about it before, had stood, receiver in hand. One time, he'd even waited outside a police station for a few hours, but had ultimately gone home.

Apple doesn't fall far from the tree . . . No one's going to want you anyway.

Beyond his parents, he didn't have anyone. They never talked about their families, and he never found any pictures or letters or any kind of connection to relatives. And he'd begun to hate being in his parents' company, had only taken the job of attending the out-of-state fancy boarding school so he could escape them. Although it turned out it had probably been the worst—and best—mistake of his life. It was the last time he'd seen either parent, although they'd attempted to contact him since.

He'd spoken to them exactly five times since he turned fifteen. He didn't know how they'd gotten all the information they had about him, although really, it shouldn't have surprised him. If they'd been normal, they would've been great covert operatives. But having no soul did not make for a good op, or even a good merc.

"I was put in a temporary juvie place for a few weeks before I went into my foster mom's home. She was nice, but I didn't make any friends after Brandon, because I never again wanted anyone to hurt that badly because of me. If I was cold and calculating, like my parents said, no one could touch me. And for a time, no one did."

He stared down at his knuckles, still raw from where he'd punched Reid. "Reid gave me back a humanity I'd thought I'd lost."

"He's a good friend," she said softly. "He understands a lot more than you think."

"I don't deserve good friends like that," he said, his voice hollow, thinking about how they'd sent him in to collect his things and face Brandon alone, telling him not to screw up getting out of the building or they'd leave him behind for the police to deal with. "I'll never forget the look on Brandon's face after he learned how I'd screwed him. I will never forget that."

"That's what worried you most of all."

He didn't answer and she continued. "You've been trying to make up for past mistakes . . . and for the sins of your parents. But you don't have to repent for their mistakes."

"I've made plenty of my own," he said.

"Please, Kell, you can't do this to yourself. It's no way to live."

"I guess you'd know about living with guilt."

"Yes."

"Reid doesn't know my whole story. No one does."

"Kell—"

"Don't, okay? It's part of my past, I know."

"I think you've done enough. I also think you had nothing to repent for. You were doing what you were told, what you were taught, listening to the people you were supposed to trust. They should've protected you, not hurt you like that."

"I have that inside of me, somewhere," he whispered, barely able to get the words out. And he was glad he couldn't look at Teddie as he spoke.

"No, you don't." Her voice was urgent and he wanted to tell her that she was being too nice or naive or a combination of both, but he didn't want to talk about it any longer. "Please, Kell, don't shut down on me."

"Forget I said anything."

"I can't. You can't let yourself believe you're anything like them."

"I already told you, I got my team made and captured last year. Because I was working alone, looking for vengeance. I let it get too personal."

"How could you not?" she asked as the storm raged—both outside, and inside Kell.

"I'm not supposed to."

"Not supposed to what? Be human?"

"Pretty much."

She paused. "It was hard for you to tell me these things. Hard for me, too."

"To tell me things, or to hear them from me?"

"Both, I guess," she admitted, and for the first time since he'd been shoved in this basement, his face held a trace of a smile.

Reid hadn't stopped moving since he'd left the hospital—and Grier behind the curtain—because if he stopped, he was pretty sure he wouldn't be moving ever again. The weight on him was just too heavy and he'd do whatever he had to in order to get closer to Kell.

Finally, he made contact with Dylan, because he needed to know where they'd set up base in Florida.

"Where are you?" were the first words out of Dylan's mouth.

"Just tell me where you are," Reid said, in no mood for anyone's questions. When Dylan gave him the address, Reid told him he'd be there in half an hour, hung up and turned off his phone.

When he got to the house, it was obvious that Dylan had been pacing the floors, waiting for him. Cam looked equally pissed, although he was slightly better at hiding it.

Riley was sitting quietly by the back window, her gun at her side.

"What the hell happened to you?" Dylan demanded when Reid walked in and dropped his bag by the front door of the small rental house three hours away from where the worst of the hurricane had hit. "I've been calling you for the past ten hours, and when you finally get in touch, you hang up on me?"

Reid ignored most of the question. "I drove part of the way."

"Must've driven like a bat out of hell," Cam commented.

"I grabbed a private plane outside of El Paso." He'd paid a pretty penny for it too, especially since they'd had to land in some godforsaken place because no airport near Riley's house would take them. And he'd walked for a few miles until he got cell reception. "And then I called you."

"What. Happened," Dylan repeated, but Reid shook

off the question again, was so tired of replaying it in his head.

"Where's Kell?" he asked instead of answering. "Something's happened—I know it. Chambers and Crystal are both MIA."

No one argued with him, and finally, Dylan said, "I've been in contact with Crystal. He's got Kell and Teddie."

"What does he want?"

"I don't care—but I know what he's getting. Me."

Reid stared at him, saw the impossible decision there, the struggle in Dylan's eyes. The man could give himself over easily, and would too, but there was no reassurance that Crystal wouldn't keep picking them off, one by one. "I can't believe how fucked-up this got," Reid said. "Kell waited six months to come back, until he felt he was ready to handle this shit, and now he's been captured."

"You can't blame yourself. Blame me." Dylan put a cup of coffee in front of Reid, and Reid heard Cam talking about making him something to eat.

"Don't bother," he told him, not willing to blame Dylan for any of this. "I want to go see the house."

"We've combed over it," Dylan told him. "I've got Kell's phone—with Crystal's picture and his number. There's nothing in there to give us a clue about where he's taken them. They could be anywhere. With the curfews in the city, it's going to make finding Kell that much harder."

"No one's heard from Chambers?" Reid asked, and Dylan paused for half a second before shaking his head no. "Fucking tell me everything, D."

"Crystal said that Teddie's not his responsibility."

"Meaning that even if you turn yourself in, she won't be spared?" Reid asked, not expecting any answer but yes.

Teddie was the one for Kell—Reid had never been so sure of anything in his entire life. If he could do something to save them both—anything—he would.

"Reid, we'll take care of this, we'll find them. Kell will find a way out too. He's damned good," Cam reminded him.

Reid knew that—Kell would fight like hell to save Teddie. But in this case, he was for certain going to need a guardian angel. "I need to take a walk, clear my head, think," he told the group finally. "I won't go far."

He didn't give them any room to argue, strode out of house and down the walk. The wind hit his face, the smell of sand and beach, and he ambled on for about two blocks. As soon as he got to a place he could hide, he dialed the number he'd taken off Grier's phone. He figured he had about twenty minutes before someone noticed he'd been gone too long.

When Crystal picked up, Reid went ahead and allowed himself to become the sacrificial lamb, because it made the most sense to him. "Take me instead of Dylan, and leave the others alone."

"So Kell's the real love of your life."

"Don't be an asshole. Kell has someone to live for. You and I don't. We'll make a damned good team."

"I like the way you think. And the way you fight." There was a long pause, and then, "I'll consider it."

"I'll work off Dylan's debt—the money you had to pay the Albanians."

"And kill me in the process?"

"I've got everything to lose. I fuck up, I could get court-marshaled," Reid pointed out. "I'll work for you, you leave them alone."

"Why should I do this?"

"Because you and I are a lot alike . . . but you knew that already. I'll come over right now—if you'll let both of them go."

"Like I told Dylan, Teddie's no longer my responsibility."

Fuck. Reid rubbed the back of his neck and waited, until Crystal asked, "Why now?"

"Safer for everyone involved. Except maybe you."

Crystal laughed. "Start walking toward the park. I'll give you directions from there. And if you don't come alone . . ."

"I'll be alone. One thing," Reid said. "You don't tell Dylan any of this."

"And where will they think you've gone? You know they'll suspect me."

"Let them suspect. Don't confirm. That's my condition."

"Before you get any ideas about screwing with me, just know your marshal's been very busy, running from motel to motel," he said, and Reid's gut clenched. "I think we'll work just fine together, Reid."

Reid had a sneaking suspicion they would as well.

Jack hadn't left her side for more than a few hours at a time. Grier told him he'd have to go back to catching fugitives soon, but he systematically ignored her.

Instead, they'd already moved around to several

different places, until Jack figured they'd lost Crystal's tail.

For the moment anyway.

But when Grier's phone started ringing, she jumped in spite of herself. Jack stared down at it. "It's Reid."

"Answer it."

Jack did, started talking and then stopped to listen. His expression paled and he handed the phone to her. She tried to wave him off because, hello, she was supposed to be dead.

"He knows" was all Jack said.

Her hand was shaking as she took the phone. "Reid?" she asked softly, and there was a long pause, enough to make her wonder if the connection had been lost.

Finally, Reid spoke, his voice gruffer than she'd ever heard it. Colder too. "Grier, you need to get out of there. Find someplace safe and don't tell anyone you've moved. And don't use the car you've been driving, it's probably bugged."

"Reid, how did you—"

"Crystal knows where you are." Reid gave her the address—and the room number—where she was staying, and she felt like throwing up. "Do you understand? Get out."

"I will." She paused because he didn't hang up. "I'm sorry."

"Don't, Grier."

"I couldn't tell you."

"Yeah, you could've. You didn't. Now just get the hell out of there or else the blood will be real this time."

Teddie wasn't keeping track of the time. Although the storm was ebbing and excess water was still seeping into parts of the basement, she ignored that in favor of listening to Kell. He was telling her stories—of him and Reid, in the foster home, on the Bering Sea—and for part of it, she closed her eyes and pretended they were back at Riley's before they'd been taken captive.

"You and Reid have really lived," she said after she'd stopped laughing at one story. Laughing, in the middle of all of this.

"No regrets," he told her.

"No regrets," she whispered back, her cheek against the wall. She imagined that he was lying in a similar position on the other side.

"Did you get some good photos today?"

She thought back to the abandoned film and realized that it didn't matter it got left behind—the act itself was the most important thing. "I did."

"It made you happy."

It had. "Before that, it was easier for me to pretend my photography didn't exist. Giving it up . . . well, it wasn't just a job to me."

"I saw your work. It's beautiful."

"I thought it was all I had. All I was. It felt so good to have the camera back in my hands, but it made me realize that everything up until now has been . . . a warm-up. A practice. But meeting you has been like a true beginning. Because it was so real and stripped down. No pretense. No lies."

"No more lies," Kell said, but there was no rancor, only truth in that statement.

"I never lied about the way I feel about you. But it

came on so quickly. We've gotten down to brass tacks a lot faster than most." And it had been fast and furious and totally unexpected, given the circumstances. "What if I'd never met you?" she whispered. "The night I ran away from Samuel . . . things could've gone so many ways, and so many of them for the worst."

Just the thought of her running so close to Juarez, at night, alone . . . the men who'd killed her family would've grabbed her for sure if not for Reid and Kell.

They were mercs themselves, and yet they were unlike any men she'd ever met.

And Kell . . . the way he'd gotten her to open up . . . the way he'd opened up to her.

"The past doesn't matter," she said, finally believing that. "We've done the best we can—and we can't let the past eat us alive, Kell. That's what I've realized, especially now, with time boiled down like this."

She heard the doorknob squeak behind her. "Kell, someone's coming in."

She turned toward the door, saw Samuel, gun tucked into his jacket.

"Remember what I told you," Kell said.

She tucked the metal piece into her sleeve, held the edge in her palm. She'd been practicing pulling it out the entire time she'd been talking to Kell. "I will."

She swiveled toward the wall for a second. "I just want you to know, for the record, the good in you far outweighs any bad. I may not know much, but that I know. You need to know it too."

She faced Samuel. "What do you want?"

"Your time is up," he told her.

She turned back to the wall. "I love you, Kell."

She was met with silence and Samuel laughed. "I told you that you couldn't trust him. Now get up."

She did, sliding up the wall, careful to keep her palm semi-closed so she didn't drop the thin piece of metal Kell had passed to her. But she didn't walk in Samuel's direction at all, stayed where she was, as if being next to the wall, as near to Kell as possible, would give her the strength she needed.

Samuel began to walk toward her and she fought the urge to move, to try to outrun him in some way.

You're going to have to let him get close.

The thought made the bile rise in her throat. She steeled herself, waited until he'd closed the distance between them. Allowed him to reach out to grab her, pull her close—and then she struck.

She let the metal piece slide into her palm completely and went for it, jabbed him in the neck with its sharp point, but he was too quick for her, blocked her and yanked the metal out. She hadn't hit hard enough, not in the right spot—she'd ruined her chance.

"Bitch," he spat. Threw the makeshift weapon to the ground and bared his teeth as he circled her. She kept moving but the room wasn't big enough.

He was coming at her and she felt helpless.

She thought about Kell in the next room, handcuffed and chained to the wall like an animal. He didn't think he was helpless.

She would fight with everything she had—and pray for a miracle. When Samuel finally managed to grab her as she went for the door, he pulled her to the floor. She was screaming—clawing—running on pure fear and adrenaline, but Samuel was far bigger, stronger, his thigh shoving hers apart, his hot breath on her neck . . .

She almost vomited when he unzipped his pants.

The total destruction of her family—and now this, the final desecration. How could one man hate so much?

"Don't bother to fight, Teddie. You'll like it. Your mother did. So did your stepmother. I know how to take care of women."

She struggled harder but he simply smiled.

"Maybe I will keep you for myself. Given a little time, I'm sure you'll be up to performing under me. You'll have no choice, of course."

There was always a choice. She finally understood that. And she did the only thing she could—she screamed as she attempted to gouge out his eyes.

CHAPTER
19

Kell had his ear to the floor, was listening to muffled sounds from Teddie's room, and pulled at the chains around his wrists, frustrated. The sounds got louder, he heard a scuffle—and then something that chilled his soul.

Teddie started screaming at the top of her lungs, long and loud, close to a howl, and it burned in his gut, made him jump off his feet and jerk at the chains in the wall as hard as he could, not caring if Crystal heard it.

He turned, put his feet up on the wall and used his legs' strength to pull, didn't care if he broke his wrists—he had other ways he could be deadly.

All he knew was that he had to get to Teddie.

Slowly, the chains began to pull from the old floor. The water that had been leaking in, wetting the already damp concrete, helped a hell of a lot. He strained and pulled, had no doubt the adrenaline boiling his blood made it possible.

Finally, they pulled free. He gathered up the chains, wound one around his hand for a weapon and the other around his arm so he had one hand free. He went to the door—it was locked, as he'd suspected, but it kicked open easily. Crystal hadn't had time to reinforce this house at all.

Kell ran to the doorway of Teddie's prison, where the yells were now muffled, and Kell knew what was happening. He only prayed he'd get there before it was too late.

The door was locked, and there was no window for him to see through. He kicked the door a few times, then resorted to picking the lock—slower, but he'd get there.

He burst in, was halfway to Teddie when Crystal came through the opposite door into Teddie's room, which must run along a back staircase, stopping all of them in their tracks with his drawn gun.

Kell stopped, not wanting Crystal to start shooting anywhere near Teddie.

Teddie, who looked angry and scared. She'd raked her nails down Chambers's cheek. Seeing her pinned under him made Kell crazy—his hands fisted and it was the hardest thing he'd ever done not to lunge at Chambers, rip him off Teddie, smash him against the concrete wall and then beat him to a pulp.

A quick death was too good for him.

"Don't move." Crystal's words were directed at Kell, but his eyes were surveying the entire scene before him, Teddie pressed to the floor . . . Chambers on top of her, his intent obvious even though they were both fully clothed.

Kell stilled at the look in Crystal's eyes when they met his, and saw something reflected in them that scared him . . . and gave him a thin spark of hope.

Crystal wasn't seeing Teddie on the floor—the only thing Kell could think was that maybe he was flashing back to his sister, the way she'd been brutally raped and murdered. Dylan had said Crystal came unhinged after that and Kell could see it plain as day in the man's eyes.

"Let me have him," Kell said, speaking to Crystal, letting him see that he'd gotten his hands free.

Crystal shook his head, but something was different. His gun came up, pointed at Kell, but it switched quickly over to Chambers.

"What the hell are you doing?" Chambers demanded.

"Both of you—up," Crystal ordered, and both Chambers and Teddie complied, Kell waiting for the opening to make his move. "What are you going to do to her?"

"Why? Do you want a turn before I'm done with her?" Chambers asked, completely misjudging Crystal's tone, not seeing that the menace in the man's eyes was pointed directly at him.

Something snapped inside of Crystal—or maybe it had done so long before this and was only rearing its ugly head now.

Either way, it could really work in their favor.

"Why should I let you go? What's your defense?" Crystal asked Teddie, ignoring Chambers's sputtering that it wasn't his choice. It was like Crystal was judge and jury, holding the scales of justice in his hands.

She jutted her chin at him. "He betrayed and killed my father. I can't let him get away with that. I'll die trying." She was so strong—that really shouldn't surprise Kell. She was stronger than him any day of the week; she'd proven that over the past days.

"Raping women is how you get off?" Crystal asked Chambers.

"I'm supposed to believe you have a conscience?"

"No, not me," Crystal said quietly, and Kell tensed so hard his bones ached. But he needed to let this play out—and be ready to strike at a moment's notice. "You need to move away from her."

"I don't take orders from you—we're partners in this."

"You are not my partner."

"We talked about this, the woman is mine," Chambers growled to the other man.

Something in Chambers's words was triggering Crystal—the man seemed far away, even though his gun never wavered from Chambers.

As Teddie backed up slowly, Chambers turned to her. "Don't move."

He grabbed her by the upper arm and held her tight. It was only then that Kell saw Teddie's palm, curled toward the sleeve of her shirt. She must've gotten the metal piece back when they'd been rolling on the floor, had been ready to use it when he and Crystal burst in.

Jesus Christ.

"Let her go," Crystal said again, his voice agitated,

the calm, easygoing man Kell had met earlier completely gone, replaced with the killer Kell knew he was.

Chambers held Teddie more tightly, and Crystal leveled the gun at his head. Teddie remained still, even when Crystal fired off a shot that purposely sailed by Chambers's head and hit the wall to the left of Kell.

Teddie used that to her advantage—this time, she didn't miss when she plunged the metal piece into Chambers's neck. He howled, dropped his gun and staggered to the side. Teddie ran to Kell and he shoved her behind him, because Crystal was still holding a gun.

Chambers crashed to the floor, clutching at his neck.

"Are you okay?" Kell asked her, but she buried her head against his back, the enormity of what she'd done obviously hitting her hard.

Crystal set his gun down, stared at them, then turned and walked out, not locking the door behind him. Teddie slumped into a dead faint behind Kell. He turned to catch her before she hit the floor, and then slung her over his shoulder, not giving a shit about the storm or anything else but getting the hell out of this hovel and taking her to safety.

Crystal was gone—where, Kell had no clue, since it would be tough walking among the debris left by the storm.

Driving would be equally difficult, because of all the downed trees and wires, but when Kell found the van in the garage, he knew there was no way he'd hang around here. He put Teddie inside gently—she was still out of it, and maybe it was better that she not see what they were driving into.

He hotwired the van easily and only then did he get out and push the garage door open, tire iron in hand in case Crystal waited on the other side of it.

The only thing that greeted him was debris and wind. He got into the van, slammed out of the garage. Both hands on the wheel, he drove as fast as the storm would let him, looking for a safe shelter, where he could get in touch with Dylan or Reid.

No one was following him because no one was crazy enough to be on the freakin' road but him. Did pay phones even exist anymore? Because he needed one ASAP.

Teddie, wake up—you stayed out too late again but you're not missing school.

Her mother, nudging her. And although she wasn't very comfortable, she was *sleepy. Didn't want to open her eyes.*

"Teddie, come on, wake up."

She heard the words, but it wasn't her mother's voice any longer. It was Kell's.

"Kell." She opened her eyes—saw him looking tired, but relieved. "Where are we?"

"Some parking garage."

"How? I mean . . ."

"Crystal left. I don't know why, but I didn't stick around to question it." He paused. "You did great, Teddie. Whatever was going on in there, you played it right with Crystal."

"Are we safe?"

"I'm not saying a word on that front." She noted he had a tire iron in his hand and a grim look on his face. "As soon as this lets up a little more, I'm going to drive around and find a pay phone . . . or a cop. I'll get in touch with Dylan and get us the hell to real safety."

"Why do you think Crystal did that—turned on Samuel?"

"I don't know why a man like that does anything," he admitted.

She stared at her hands—they should still have blood on them, but they were clean. She glanced up at him.

"I wiped it off," he told her.

"Thanks." She paused. "I thought I'd feel different after having to do that. Guilt. But when it came down to saving us, I realize that doing what you need to in order to survive is most important."

"Good, because you have nothing to feel guilty about. That was self-defense, pure and simple. And if Reid and the rest did what I know they're capable of doing, they've uncovered evidence that the marshals will use to prove what Samuel did, beyond the fact that he kidnapped you. They already know about the mercs—it's not going to take much to convince a judge it was self-defense."

"And then I'll be free."

"Yes."

"And you'll stay with me?"

"You'll have me while we get this all cleaned up."

"What does that mean, *I'll have you*. Does that mean for protection?"

"Yes."

"I can hire someone for that."

"I don't know what you want me to say."

"I don't either." But that was a lie—a big one. She wanted to hear that he loved her, that despite the fact that they'd only known each other for a very short period of life-and-death time, he was falling in love with her too.

Because she could feel it from him. Could see it in his eyes, feel it in the way he touched her . . . reveled in it when he came and murmured her name like she was the only person in his world.

"Maybe the only reason you're with me is because you have nowhere else to go. I'm not interested in being someone's default."

"That's not what you are to me," she protested. Even in the beginning, when she'd had very little choice, she'd been drawn to him. It seemed ridiculous, was inexplicable, and her feelings had only intensified over the past week. "Can we call it fate?"

He snorted. "I was in the military. The day you start believing that mumbo-jumbo shit is the day you've lost your nerve."

"You're not in the military anymore."

"A technicality."

"You did the most important thing. You put everything on the line for me—your job, your friends . . . and you brought me back to life. There's no way I can ever thank you enough for that . . . but I'd like to spend a long time trying."

"Has there ever been anyone special in your life, someone you've loved?" Kell asked with a sudden fierceness that made her smile.

"No, there hasn't. I always said it was because there

wasn't time, but that's not true. If there had been someone special, I would've made the time."

True that, Reid would've agreed, because both Kell and his friend lived the same way.

"I wouldn't want to drag anyone into the kind of life I lead," he told her. "And I still don't know if I plan on quitting anytime soon. Even if I try to get out, there's always going to be something to pull me back into the danger. And it would pull you too."

"Does that mean you don't want me in your life, or are you trying to get me to leave you because that's easier?" she asked, her words a punch to the gut.

He stared at her, taking in the way her hair tumbled loosely over her shoulders and her skin glowed and he said, "I want you in my life," before he could stop himself.

She smiled a little. "I'm not going anywhere."

"It's the truth. You've seen a small part of my life, and you think it's over, but it's not. For me, it's never going to be over." He ran his hands through his hair as the rain battered the outside of parking garage.

"I didn't say I wanted to follow you around. I want to return to my old life. I want to start traveling, taking photos again."

"I have enemies."

"And they'll all be hunting for me?"

"Because of you, I'll be vulnerable. Because of you, I am vulnerable. And I hate it as much as I love you."

She moved into his arms, molded herself to him, her face pressed to his shoulder before she spoke.

"Say that last part again," she said quietly, less of a demand, more of a request, and still there was no denying her anything.

"Jesus, Teddie, you're killing me. You've been killing me since the night I met you," he muttered.

"I know."

He tilted her face to his with a finger under her chin. "I love you, Teddie. Simple as that, and trust me, that's the only thing that's simple about our relationship."

"I love you, Kell Roberts. Let's worry about everything else once the storm has passed."

For once, the choice was easy.

CHAPTER
20

Kell was hesitant about driving the stolen electric company van around after the storm, for many reasons, the least of which was being stopped by random people asking for help restoring their power. So he borrowed another car from the lot and drove them to the nearest hotel he could find with vacancies. Left the car abandoned in the garage and called Dylan with his location.

He'd never heard the man sound so relieved. "We're coming for you guys, don't move," he admonished Kell.

"Not a problem."

He turned to find Teddie pacing nervously, and he understood—she still had hoops to go through before she'd be fully free. But he'd be with her the entire time—just let anyone try to stop him.

"Come here," he told her. "Try to relax."

"Yeah, okay." She allowed him to pull her to him, stayed next to him until there was a sharp rap on the door, maybe twenty minutes later, and Kell didn't bother to ask Dylan—or Riley and Cam, who trailed in after him—how he'd gotten there so fast in the aftermath of the storm.

After introducing Teddie to them, Kell set about explaining what had happened. He ended by asking if they'd heard from Crystal. "I can't imagine he'd just walk away like that, he must have a plan."

"Reid left with him."

Kell felt his breath come harshly. "You are fucking kidding me."

"Wish I was." Dylan stopped. "Crystal told me he was okay with the trade. Said Reid is trainable."

Kell went cold. "What the hell did you do? Why the hell?"

"Crystal wanted me back to do a job for him. Reid went instead," Dylan said. "We would've stopped him if we'd known that's what he planned on doing."

"You wouldn't have been able to. Once Reid makes up his mind about something . . ." Kell trailed off. Dylan handed Kell his phone, and Kell stared blankly at him for a second, then turned it on. He found a couple of texts there, from Reid . . . recent texts. And his heart nearly stopped. Teddie came up next to him, as if she knew he suddenly felt weak. He thumbed through the messages.

Sometimes, you've got to make a choice.

That night fourteen years ago, when Kell had dragged Reid out of the car, the young blond kid unconscious and bruised as hell, he'd had a decision to make. Now Reid was telling him that he'd always understood Kell's choices, even when Kell hadn't.

He was also giving him an out on the guilt, as evidenced by the second message.

You deserve to be happy. Be fucking happy.

The final one though made Kell smile. *This state sucks.*

"I need your truck," he told Dylan. "Right now."

"Crystal could've coerced those texts out of him," Dylan said, but Kell shook his head.

"He didn't. Reid's got a plan."

Crystal drove along the storm-battered roads in a stolen truck. The police lining the area could give two shits about that now, and neither did Reid. He was just waiting until Crystal hit the open road along the coastline, near the private airstrips.

"What's the job?" Reid asked finally, like it didn't matter to him one way or the other. He'd gotten word on his phone earlier that Grier was safe and sound in a new place, counted on that since as he drove Crystal was holding in his palm the remote start to a bomb in Grier's hotel room.

He'd shown it to Reid as soon as he'd picked him up in the park.

"I'm working with the Albanians," Crystal said.

Crystal would never be out of their debt, thanks to Dylan. But Reid would make sure Crystal was out of the team's lives, no matter what it took.

Reid had no doubt Crystal had more safeguards in place, in case of his untimely demise, but Reid couldn't worry about his friends any more than he already was right now. They'd cut the head off this monster and fight the remaining fallout when and if it came.

Could be that Crystal was just a damned good illusionist.

"Do you feel guilty you couldn't save your family?" Crystal asked.

"Do you feel guilty you couldn't save your sister?" Reid asked, watched the man's hands tighten on the wheel.

"It's a secret you keep all to yourself," Crystal continued. "Your mother's mental illness."

"Yes."

"Why?"

"My father asked me to." Reid paused. "Your sister's killers were never brought to justice."

"No."

"I thought you were supposed to be the best."

Crystal was getting more agitated by the second. He'd expected to be able to do that to Reid, but spilling his guts to Grier had helped Reid in ways he couldn't have imagined. Saving her from Crystal had helped too, despite the fact that her betrayal stung like a hard slap.

"I mean, how hard could those men have been to find?" Reid continued. "If that was me, I'd hunt them down to the ends of the earth."

"Your friend forced me underground for years," Crystal roared before calming down. He'd been off since he'd picked Reid up, so whatever happened with Kell and Teddie helped to throw him more easily than Reid had anticipated.

Time to make his move, because no way was he getting on a plane with Crystal.

Reid had learned a lot about cars over the years—what made them crash and burn, what could cause a roll that could kill . . . or a rollover that could save your life.

He'd never wanted to crash again without being able to save himself. Now that's exactly what he was going to do.

Of course, he'd still need Kell. And he had no doubt his friend would be there for him.

"You put yourself in that prison," Reid told him, and then he grabbed the wheel and jerked it hard toward him, leaving Crystal cursing and trying to right it, ultimately jerking it too far to the left, and that's when the heavy truck lost its center of gravity.

Reid braced himself by willing his body to relax—too taut and every fucking bone would break. But no matter what, the impact would still be a bitch and a half.

"You wanted this," he said, wasn't sure if Crystal registered his words or not. Either way, Reid's ghosts were dying tonight in this truck.

He'd do everything necessary to make sure he didn't go down with them. Now he just had to close his eyes and pray that the motherfucking guardian angel would show when he needed her again.

He wasn't sure how long it was before his eyes opened. He felt the concrete under his back and realized he was half inside the now-flipped truck. He smelled the gasoline and smoke and knew that wasn't a good combo, even in his groggy state. Tried to pull himself out, looked inside and saw Crystal, slumped and unmoving.

They were both out of their misery now.

Strong arms grabbed and pulled him from the downed vehicle.

"Going to kill you one of these goddamned days," Kell was muttering.

"Did you even stop to ask if I could move everything?" Reid shot back and Kell smiled, and Teddie was there too, and so was Dylan, cursing, and yeah, things were right back to the way they should be. Finally.

EPILOGUE

Three months later

All the bruises had finally healed. Kell had barely left Reid's side in the hospital—neither had Teddie— not until Reid sat up and insisted that they *get the fuck out of here and clear up Teddie's shit*.

And they'd listened. Up until that point, Dylan had kept the marshals and the FBI at bay—the FBI had the evidence about Chambers's bank accounts that Reid had given to Grier. But Teddie still had to face some music, because she had been part of witness protection and therefore subject to all their rules and regs.

The marshals hadn't been happy with her—and even less so with Kell and the fact that he refused to leave her side through any of the proceedings. Neither had the lawyer Dylan utilized, an ex-JAG who was effective as hell at cutting through bullshit.

It had taken a month to untangle everything, but the murder she'd committed was obviously self-defense, so she wasn't charged. Teddie was then cleared of jail time for possessing an illegal firearm and shooting in a public restaurant, instead pleading to lesser charges in exchange for a year of probation. The judge had okayed her checking in with a parole officer in upstate New York, where she'd be staying put—with Kell—until the year was up.

All in all, it had been a relief to bring Teddie here, to Mace's.

Today, a week after Kell had brought her in to meet the other members of the team he'd only told her about, they were all gathered in the newly renovated bar, which boasted two additional floors—enough room for all of them—plus a war room with banks of computers. And an underground bunker.

Yeah, they were prepared for anything.

Kell surveyed the scene playing out in front of him as Teddie leaned against him, his arm draped around her waist. Paige and Mace were dancing, married ten minutes earlier in a no-nonsense ceremony that still brought tears to everyone's eyes. And then Caleb and Vivi joined them on the dance floor, followed by Dylan and Riley.

Cam and Sky were too busy making out in the corner, like teenagers, which made Kell snort when he caught sight of it. Then he looked down at Teddie and wondered if he could pull her into the back room.

She glanced up at him and wagged a finger, because what he was thinking must be written all over his face. And for the first time in forever, he didn't care that no poker face in the world would work on her any longer.

"Fine, I'll be good. For now," he muttered, and she snuggled against him.

"When are we going to look at the property?" she asked, referring to the piece of land two hours away he'd purchased years earlier, and now planned on building a home on for the two of them.

"We can go tomorrow," he told her. It wouldn't be their last solo trip. He'd already made plans to go with her on an extended photography tour of Jakarta at the end of the month.

Translation—she wasn't going anywhere like that without him. But he was damned glad he'd get to see her doing a job she loved. After that, he'd alternate between her work, and his with this group.

And he could think of nothing better.

Reid had cut in and was dancing with Vivi now and Caleb was grumbling good-naturedly.

"Does he know?" Teddie asked, and Kell shook his head. Because he'd known Reid would've refused to contact the marshal so Kell had done so himself.

And even though Reid might kill him for it . . . Grier knew where to find him.

The rest would be up to them. For the first time, Kell realized that it really was that simple. And when he pulled Teddie in for a kiss, murmured, "I love you" and heard her say it back to him, he knew Reid had been right all along.